HAUNTING
RACHEL

HAUNTING

RACHEL

KAY HOOPER

BANTAM BOOKS

New York Toronto London Sydney Auckland

Hoo

HAUNTING RACHEL

A Bantam Book / December 1998

All rights reserved.
Copyright © 1998 by Kay Hooper.

Book design by Dana Leigh Treglia

No part of this book may be reproduced or transmitted in any form
or by any means, electronic or mechanical, including photocopying,
recording, or by any information storage and retrieval system,
without permission in writing from the publisher.
For information address: Bantam Books.

Library of Congress Cataloging-in-Publication Data
Hooper, Kay.
Haunting Rachel / by Kay Hooper.
p.   cm.
ISBN 0-553-09950-7
I. Title.
PS3558.0587H38   1998
813'.54—dc21   98-607160
CIP

Published simultaneously in the United States and Canada

Bantam Books are published by Bantam Books, a division of Bantam
Doubleday Dell Publishing Group, Inc. Its trademark, consisting of the
words "Bantam Books" and the portrayal of a rooster, is Registered in
U.S. Patent and Trademark Office and in other countries. Marca Regis-
trada. Bantam Books, 1540 Broadway, New York, New York 10036.

PRINTED IN THE UNITED STATES OF AMERICA

BVG   10   9   8   7   6   5   4   3   2   1

HAUNTING
RACHEL

PROLOGUE

"It won't take long," Thomas said reassuringly. "A week, maybe a bit more. Then I'll be back."

"But where are you going? And why does it have to be now?" Rachel's demand held all the natural impatience and indignation of a nineteen-year-old who was about to be deprived of the company of her fiancé at a somewhat inconvenient time. "Tom, you know Mercy's giving that shower for me on Thursday, and—"

"Honey, men are never welcome at those things. I'd just be in the way." He was still soothing, but also a little amused, and he smiled at her with the complete understanding of a man who had known her since her auburn hair had been worn in pigtails and at least two front teeth had been missing. He

1

was ten years her senior, and at that moment every year showed.

Rachel didn't exactly pout, but when she sat down in a chair by the window, it was with a definite flounce, and her expressive face was alive with frustration and disappointment. "You promised. You said there wouldn't be any more of these mysterious trips of yours—"

"There's nothing mysterious about them, Rachel. I'm a pilot, and I deliver cargo. It's my job. You know that. All right, I know I said there wouldn't be any more trips out of the country, but Jake asked me to do him a favor, and he *is* my boss. So—just a quick run down to South America."

"You promised," Rachel repeated, not much interested in reasons.

Thomas put his hands on the arms of her chair and bent down, smiling at her with all the charm in his definitely charming nature. "Would it make you happier if I said that Jake's giving me an extra week off if I take this run? That's another week in Hawaii, honey. Think about it. Lazing around in the sun on Waikiki, breakfast on a balcony with a magnificent view—and shopping. Lots more time for shopping."

She couldn't help but smile. "You know that isn't my thing."

He chuckled. "Yeah, but you're no slouch at it. Come on now, say you're not mad anymore. I'll have a miserable few days if I fly off knowing you're mad at me."

It was virtually impossible for Rachel to resist his blandishments, a fact both were well aware of, and her sigh held resignation as well as a touch of resentment. "Oh, all right. But you'd better not hang around down in South America. Just remember what'll be waiting for you back home." She wreathed her arms around his neck and kissed him.

The passion between them had been nearly impossible for them to handle since the night of her sixteenth birthday and their first real kiss; familiarity had not bred anything except a better under-standing of just how powerful desire could be, especially when it went unsatisfied. Though Rachel's willpower was shaky where he was concerned, Thomas, very conscious of the years between them and of her youth, had decided for both of them that sex would wait until marriage.

It wasn't a decision Rachel was happy with, and this wasn't the first time she had made an attempt to force his hand.

His voice was a little ragged when he pulled back slightly and muttered, "Stop that. I've got to go."

Rachel didn't want to let go of him. "You'll miss me. Say you'll miss me."

"Of course I'll miss you. I love you." He gave her a brief kiss and then firmly unlocked her arms from his neck and straight-ened. "Make my excuses to your parents about tonight, all right, honey?"

She sighed again. "Right. And I get to spend a boring Saturday night all by myself. Again."

"Just three more weeks, and that will no longer be a problem," Thomas reminded her with a grin. "I promise, honey, no more lonely nights for either one of us."

"I'll hold you to that."

Rachel walked with him to the front door of her parents' house, received another quick kiss, and stood there watching him stride down the walkway to his fast little car. He loved speed, Thomas Sheridan did, whether on the ground or in the air, and often teased her that she was the only love in his life that characteristically moved at a lazy pace.

He turned and waved before opening his car door, and Rachel admired the way the sunlight glinted off his pale silvery hair. He was a rare blond Sheridan on a mostly dark family tree, so different from his raven-haired sister Mercy that both had frequently maddened their mother by speculating humorously about blond-haired strangers in her past despite Thomas's undeniable resemblance to his dark father.

"See you in a week or so, honey," Thomas called out.

He slammed the car door before Rachel could respond in kind, so she merely waved with a smile. She watched the car until it vanished from her sight, then went back into the house to tell her parents that her fiancé would not be joining them for dinner that night.

Rachel woke with a start and sat up in her bed before she even knew what had awakened her. The room was filled with the somber light of dawn, and she was astonished to see him standing near the foot of the bed.

"Thomas? What're you doing back so soon? I—" Her voice broke off as though it had been cut by something sharp. It wasn't right, she realized. *He* wasn't right. Because she could almost see the curtains through him. A coldness more gray than the dawn seeped into her body, into her very bones, and she heard herself make an anguished little sound when Thomas seemed to reach out toward her, his handsome face tormented.

4

"No," Rachel whispered. "Oh, no . . ." She stretched her hand out toward him, but even as she did so, he was gone. And she was alone in the stark dawn.

Thomas Sheridan's plane never reached its destination, and no trace of it was ever found.

O N E

April 21, 1998

It was no more than a glimpse of movement on a street corner that caught Rachel's attention. She turned her head more or less automatically, drawn as always by the glint of sunlight off silvery blond hair. She expected to see, as she always had, a stranger. Just one more blond man who would, of course, not be who she wanted him to be.

Except that it was Thomas.

She stood frozen, with four lanes of cars filling the space between her corner and his, and when their eyes met, she almost cried out. Then the light changed, and traffic began moving briskly, and a noisy semi blocked her view of the corner. When the truck had passed, Thomas was gone.

Rachel stood there until the light changed again, but when she rushed across the street, there was no sign of him.

No. No, of course there wasn't.

Because it hadn't been him.

Realizing that her legs were actually shaking, she found a table at a nearby sidewalk café where she could keep an eye on that corner, and ordered a cup of hot tea.

It hadn't been him, of course.

It was never him.

"Are you all right, miss?" the waitress asked when she returned with the steaming cup. "You look sort of upset."

"I'm fine." Rachel managed a smile she doubted was very reassuring, but it was enough to satisfy the young waitress. Left alone again, she dumped sugar into the tea and fixed her gaze once more on the corner.

Of course it hadn't been Thomas. Her mind knew that. It had been only a stranger with a chance resemblance that had seemed stronger because distance had helped it seem that way. And perhaps a trick of the light had helped, as well as her own wishful thinking. But it couldn't have been Thomas. Thomas had been dead nearly ten years. No, they had never found a body, or even the wreckage of the plane, but Thomas's life had certainly ended somewhere in the impenetrable depths of a South American jungle.

Even though he had promised to come back to her.

Her knees were steady once more when Rachel finally got up nearly an hour later and left the café. And she didn't let herself stop or even pause when she passed the corner where a memory had so fleetingly stood. Knowing that she was late helped her to walk briskly, and common sense pushed the memory back into its quiet room in her heart.

It was after three o'clock on this warm and sunny Tuesday when she went into a building in downtown Richmond. She went up to the fourth floor, entered the law offices of Meredith and Becket, and was immediately shown in to see Graham Becket.

"Sorry I'm late," she said at once.

"Rachel, you didn't have to come down here at all," Graham reminded her as he moved around the desk to take her hand and kiss her lightly on the cheek. "I told you I'd come to the house."

"I needed to get out." She shrugged, then gently reclaimed her hand and sat down in his visitor's chair.

He stood looking down at her for a moment, a somewhat rueful expression on his face, then went back around the desk to his own chair. A tall, dark, good-looking man of thirty-eight, and a highly successful attorney, he was accustomed to female interest.

Except from Rachel. He knew Rachel fairly well. He had been her father's attorney for nearly ten years and one of the executors of the estate after Duncan Grant and his wife had been killed eight months ago. But knowledge didn't stop Graham from hoping that one day she would notice he was a man who was closer to being one of her contemporaries than her father's.

And a man, moreover, who had been half in love with her for years.

Today, she hadn't noticed.

"More papers to sign?" she asked, her slight smile transforming her serene and merely pretty face into something haunting.

Graham had tried to figure out what it was about that smile that made Rachel instantly unforgettable, but to date had been unable to. Her features, taken one by one, were agreeable but not spectacular. Her pale gray eyes were certainly lovely, but the dark lashes surrounding them were more adequate than dramatic, and her nose might have been a trifle large for her heart-shaped face.

Gleaming auburn hair framed that face nicely, but it was unlikely that fashion mavens would copy the simple shoulder-length style. Her mouth was well-shaped and her teeth even and white, but there was nothing especially memorable about either.

Despite all that, Rachel had only to smile that slow smile of hers to become a stunningly beautiful woman. It wasn't only Graham who saw the transformation; he had heard more than one man and a number of women comment on it over the years.

And even then, her smile was only a shadow of what it had once been. Before Thomas Sheridan's death. Until the loss of her fiancé had changed Rachel so fundamentally, she had smiled often, her face so alive that strangers had stared at her on the streets. Afterward . . .

"Graham?"

He recalled his wandering thoughts and opened a file folder on his desk. "Yes, more papers to sign. Sorry, Rachel. But I did warn you that Duncan's estate was complex."

"It's all right. I'm just wondering when it'll all be over."

He looked at her across the desk. "If you intend to keep a hand in the business, it'll never be over. But if you mean to accept Nicholas Ross's offer to buy you out . . ."

"I'm still thinking about that. Do you think Dad would have wanted me to sell out, Graham?"

"I think he expected you to. The past few years, your life hasn't been in Richmond except for holiday and vacation visits home, and those were brief. Ever since you moved to New York, I think he realized it wasn't likely you'd come back here to live."

"Yes—but I don't have to live here to keep the business. I could hire a manager to run my half, you know that. Between you, Nicholas, and a manager taking care of things day to day, I'd have to show up only periodically for board meetings."

He nodded. "True enough."

"I don't know beans about investment banking, so I could hardly be a hands-on boss anyway. And all those investments Dad had personally, they're so diverse, there's no way I could keep track of them on my own." She seemed to be arguing with herself, frowning a little. "At the same time, several of the companies Dad invested in aren't in a position to buy out his interest right now, so I'd have to find other investors if I wanted out—that, or take a loss. Either way, it means time and trouble."

Graham looked at her searchingly. "In a hurry to get back to New York? I thought you said you'd taken a leave of absence and didn't mean to go back until summer."

"That's what I said, and what I meant. But . . . I don't know, I'm getting restless, I guess." She shrugged. "I'm not used to being idle, Graham."

After a moment, he said, "But it's more than that, isn't it? It's memories. The house is getting to you."

Rachel got up and went to stand before a window that offered a view of the busy street below. Graham remained in his chair, but turned it to keep watching her, and when she remained silent, he went on quietly.

"After Thomas was killed, you couldn't wait to get out of that house. Went back to college first and then to New York. And your visits home even then were always brief, because you were always busy."

"Trying to make me feel guilty for neglecting my parents?" Her voice was a little tight.

"No. They didn't feel neglected, if that's been worrying you. They understood, Rachel."

"Understood what?"

"How much of your past was bound up in Thomas. How old were you when you first knew you loved him? Twelve? Thirteen?"

Rachel drew a breath. "Ten, actually. He came to pick up Mercy from my birthday party, and he kissed me on the cheek. I knew then."

It required an effort, but Graham kept his voice dispassionate. "And since his sister was your best friend, you saw a lot of him. I imagine he was at the house quite often even before you two began dating. You were sixteen then, weren't you?"

She didn't seem surprised by his knowledge, probably attributing it to her father and casual conversation rather than any extraordinary interest in her. "Yes."

"So Thomas spent a lot of time at the house. Years, really. All the time you were growing up. Eating meals in the dining room, sitting with you in the den, listening to music in your bedroom, walking by the river. That place is filled with him, isn't it?"

She turned and leaned back against the window casing. She was smiling just a little, wistful, and it made her beautiful again. "Yes, the house is filled with him. And even now, after all these years, it hurts to remember him."

"Of course it does. You never really let him go, Rachel. You couldn't. There was no funeral where you could say good-bye, just a memorial service months later when his parents had finally given up hope. And, by then, you'd bolted off to college, where there weren't any memories of Thomas. For you, there was never any . . . closure."

She looked at him almost curiously. "You knew him, went to school with him. Was it so easy for you to accept his death?"

"Easier than for you, because I was never close to him. I wasn't . . . emotionally involved. His death was a tragedy and I was sorry, but no memories haunted me."

She hesitated, then let out an unsteady laugh. "Haunted. That's a good word. I thought I saw him today."

"What?"

"On a street corner while I was waiting for the light to change. I looked across—and there he was. I could have sworn it was Thomas."

"What happened?"

"A truck went past, and when I could see the corner again, he was gone. I ran across and looked, but . . . My imagination, I guess."

"You guess?"

"Well. My imagination of course."

"Or just a man with blond hair," Graham said steadily.

"Yes. I know."

"But this isn't the first time you thought you saw him."

Lightly, she said, "I'm going nuts, is that what you're saying?"

"What I'm saying is, don't let memories and wishful thinking become an obsession, Rachel. Thomas is dead. Don't you believe that if he were alive, he would have somehow gotten word to you, that he would have managed to come back to you?"

"Yes. Yes, I do believe that. Because he promised he'd come

back to me." *And because he came back to me once, came back from death to say good-bye to me.*

But she didn't say that, of course. She had never told anyone about that, not even on that horrible dawn when she had awakened both her parents insisting her father try to get in touch with Thomas's boss because she was certain something terrible had happened.

"Then you know that what you saw was simply someone who looked a bit like Thomas." Graham's voice was still matter-of-fact.

Rachel felt a faint flicker of amusement as she left the window and returned to her chair. "I think you really are worried about my sanity, Graham. Well, don't be. I was shaken at first, but my common sense asserted itself pretty quickly. I know I didn't really see Thomas on a street corner."

Except for that first instant, when she had been *sure* . . .

"I'm glad. But, Rachel, if you need someone to talk to—"

"Thanks." She was grateful for his concern and the offer, and it showed in her affectionate smile. "But I think it's just as you said. I never got the chance to say good-bye to Thomas, and I've never faced up to all the memories at home. He's just very . . . alive to me right now. It's something I'll have to work my way through, that's all." She smiled at him. "Now—didn't you say something about papers to sign?"

The house where Rachel had grown up was an elegant Georgian mansion built on extensive acreage on the James River. The house was more than two hundred and fifty years old, and had been in the Grant family for much of that time. Remodeled from time to time by various Grants, it now contained such luxuries and conveniences as carpet, closets, and bathrooms, as well as modern wiring, central heating, and air-conditioning. Yet it had maintained its graceful air despite those changes, and was considered one of the most beautiful houses in Richmond.

Rachel got out of her mother's sedan at the front drive and stood for a moment, studying the house. Not for the first time she wondered if she was being hasty in even considering selling the place. Yes, the house was far too large for one young woman who didn't care for entertaining and didn't have to in her work—the only real excuse for a single person to own such a place. And, yes, there were too many memories here, many of them painful. And her uncle Cameron wanted it, would enjoy it, and would keep it in the family at least a while longer.

But . . . it was her home. She had actually been born in this house, with a doctor in attendance, since her parents had been determined to uphold that tradition. Until she had gone away to college and then moved to New York, Rachel had always lived here, just as her father and grandfather before her. Her roots were here.

Did she really want to give it up? And if she did, were her reasons the right ones? Or was she just being cowardly in wanting to run away once more to New York without facing the pain of loss?

Not questions that were easily or simply answered, she knew. Shrugging them off for the moment, Rachel went into the house. She was greeted just inside the door by the housekeeper, Fiona, who was as dour as usual. A part of the Grant family for more than twenty years, Fiona moved more slowly these days in late middle age, and her superstitious nature could be a trial at times, but she loved this house and took excellent care of it.

Which was why she resented any intrusion into her routine.

"That Darby Lloyd has been sending things down from the main attic all day. How'm I supposed to do my work with those men of hers tramping up and down the stairs, Miss Rachel?"

Rachel had known Fiona too long to be disturbed by the forbidding stare or acid complaint. Laying her purse on a side table in the large entrance hall, she shrugged and said, "You know it has to be done, Fiona. We have to have a complete inventory and appraisal of everything in the house—and that includes all three of the attics. Just be glad it's only Darby doing the appraisal. You'd really hate it if a bunch of strangers were constantly underfoot for the next few weeks. Wouldn't you?"

The housekeeper ignored the question. "But she has the second floor hallway filled wall to wall, and I can't even vacuum—"

"Fiona, you can vacuum later. I'm sure Darby's just moving the stuff out temporarily while everything's getting tagged, otherwise she wouldn't have room to work. Just be a little patient, all right? I'll go speak to her about blocking the hallway."

"If you can get through," Fiona sniffed.

Rachel was able to get through the upstairs hallway, though it required a bit of maneuvering. A family could fill large attics with an astonishing variety of furniture, especially over generations and many shifts in style and taste; items partially blocking the hall ranged from Revolutionary chests and Regency tables to—of all things—a sixties-style beanbag.

"My God," Rachel said when she finally managed to make her

way up the fairly narrow staircase to the main attic. "Has this family kept every blessed stick of furniture ever to cross the threshold?"

"That would be my guess." Strands of her coppery hair escaping from the casual ponytail she wore and a smudge of what looked like soot on her otherwise creamy nose, Darby Lloyd came around a huge wardrobe with a clipboard in her hand. "Sorry for the stuff in the hall, but there was no other way to sort through everything."

Rachel waved a dismissive hand. "Don't worry about it."

"Well, I know Fiona's upset." Darby grimaced. "One of my guys swore she put a hex on him when he asked if he could leave a Chippendale desk at the top of the stairs."

"She doesn't really hex people," Rachel said.

"Never underestimate the power of suggestion. Ten minutes later, Steve developed a migraine. Sam had to take him home. Which is why I'm up here alone and at my wit's end. Do you know, I think there's a fairly spectacular Queen Anne desk in that far corner, and I can't get to it. That's very frustrating, Rachel."

Rachel had to smile at Darby's intensity. A friend since elementary school, Darby had remained in Richmond after college, starting her own interior design company with a generous investment from Duncan Grant's bank. She was also an antiques dealer, which was why she was nearly drooling at what she was finding in the attic of this old house.

"You'll get to it eventually," Rachel reassured her soothingly. "Have you started the list of things you want to buy for your business and things you think you can sell for me?"

Darby rolled her eyes. "Have I ever. In case you don't know, there's a fortune in this attic alone. That first appraisal after your parents were killed was conservative, Rachel. Very conservative. I don't think that tax guy knew what he was doing, seriously. But you should send him flowers, because I'm willing to bet he saved you hundreds of thousands in inheritance taxes."

"I don't think he did more than open the door and glance in here," Rachel agreed. "All the antiques downstairs sort of dazzled him."

"They dazzled me too. But I've learned to roll up my sleeves and crawl into corners. And aside from all this glorious furniture—most of which is in fabulous condition, by the way—I've found three trunks so far, all filled to the brim with the kind of stuff to make an interior designer's mouth water. Vases, candle holders, figurines, picture frames. Jeez, Rachel, it's going to cost me a fortune to buy what I want just from in here."

"I told you we'd work something out. A consignment deal, maybe. I'm in no hurry for the money, you know that."

Darby's blue eyes brightened, but she shook her head even so. "You're being too damned trusting and way too generous."

Rachel laughed. "I don't think so. Look, Darby, financially, Dad left me in great shape. What I really want is for all these beautiful things to be seen and enjoyed by people. They've been locked away up here for far too long. And why shouldn't you benefit from that? You've worked your tail off to get your business established, and you've already developed a reputation for finding exquisite furniture for people who appreciate it. Clearly, you're the best woman for the job."

"Thanks, Rachel."

"Don't mention it. Now, why don't you knock off for the day? It's after four and, besides, you need your guys to move these big pieces for you. You can get a fresh start tomorrow." She smiled. "And I'll be sure and tell Fiona not to hex Steve again."

"I would appreciate that."

The two women left the attic together, and when they reached the second floor hallway, Darby said immediately, "I hadn't realized we'd moved so much out of the attic. God, Rachel, I'm sorry—"

"I told you not to worry about it."

Darby bit her lip, then said, "Tell you what. I'll make a list tonight of a few things I know I can sell quickly, and tomorrow I'll have the guys haul the pieces to my shop. They'll be out of your way and mine, and we'll get the ball rolling. Okay?"

"That's fine."

"I'll check with you first, of course, before taking anything away. There might be a few things you want to keep for yourself, maybe transport to your apartment in New York."

Like most of the people around her, Darby assumed Rachel would be selling out and leaving Richmond, an assumption encouraged by Rachel's attitude and decisions so far. It wasn't something Rachel disputed, even though she was still uncertain about what she meant to do.

So she merely nodded in response and said, "Sounds good."

"Great. Then I'll see you tomorrow." Darby rushed down the stairs with an energy that belied her rather fragile appearance, and a moment later the front door closed behind her.

Rachel went to her second-floor bedroom in the east wing and stood at the doorway, looking down the hall toward her parents' bedrooms. Though she had gone through her father's desk here at the house as a business necessity, she hadn't yet been able to sort through his and her mother's personal belongings. It was something she knew she had to do, not a chore she could assign to anyone else. It would take time and require decisions as to what to do with clothing and so on, and so far Rachel had simply not been up to the task.

And still was not. She shied away from opening those doors just as she had shied away from any other chore that threatened her control. She wasn't ready yet. Not yet.

She went into her bedroom, a room she had been allowed to furnish for herself when she was sixteen. Since Rachel had inherited her mother's elegant taste in antiques, even as a teenager she had not been fond of the fads and often peculiar color combinations in vogue with her friends; her room was decorated in quiet tones of blue and gold, virtually all the furniture Louis XV pieces, delicate and lovely.

Rachel was comfortable in the room, and after so many years took the stunning antiques for granted. She went into the adjoining bathroom and turned on the faucets to fill the big oval tub, deciding that a hot bath might ease her tension and soothe the restlessness she couldn't seem to get rid of. It only half worked, but half was an improvement, and by the time she climbed from the tub thirty minutes later, Rachel definitely felt better.

She wandered back out into her bedroom wearing a silk robe, and went to stand at a window that looked out over the front drive and lawns. Plans for the evening were simple; dinner, probably with her uncle Cameron, who was currently staying in the house, and then television or a book. It had become her routine since she had come home two weeks ago.

"Jet-setting heiress, that's me," she murmured to herself wryly.

The irony, of course, was that she could have jetted off to wherever she wanted—and simply had no interest in doing so. Money was not one of the things Rachel had ever had to strive for, and so it was not something that represented success or achievement. Not to her.

Achievement, to Rachel, was bound up in whether the designs she had created would successfully adorn the fashion runways when next year's spring collections made their debut. She had apprenticed herself to one of the best New York designers, and after years of hard work had the satisfaction of knowing that her designs would be shown under her own name.

But that was months and months away, and in the meantime she had to decide just how much of her past she wanted to abandon.

Rachel sighed and began to turn away from the window, when a flicker of movement down by the front gate caught her attention. There was considerable distance between the house and the gate, but what Rachel saw was clear enough.

And definitely real.

A man with silvery blond hair was standing at the gate, looking up toward the house. He was very still for a moment, and then, with a hunching movement of his broad shoulders that might have been a shrug or some gesture of indecision, he turned and walked away, hidden immediately by the high brick wall and numerous tall trees.

Rachel lifted a hand as though to stop him, but her flesh touched nothing except the cold glass of her window.

T W O

I'm sorry, Rachel. I should have done this months ago." Mercy Sheridan, Duncan Grant's former assistant, had come to the house to bring Rachel a box of personal articles she had cleared from Duncan's office at the bank. She was still with the company at least through the process of settling the estate; she hadn't announced her decision about what to do beyond that time.

She grimaced slightly. "But it was hard enough to go through his files when I had to, never mind his personal things. I think this is everything not directly related to the business, though—unless I come across something misfiled."

Rachel had meant only to thank her, but heard herself say a bit dryly, "Does Nicholas want to move into Dad's office?"

Obviously surprised, Mercy replied, "Not that I know of." Her violet eyes softened, and she said gently, "He isn't trying to take your dad's place, if that's what you think. In fact, he's been pretty adamant about keeping Duncan's memory alive at the bank. He wants his office left just as it was, wants that portrait to hang in the lobby with a brass plaque saying that Duncan founded the company. And he doesn't mean to change the name after you sell out to him, Rache. It'll go on being known as Duncan and Ross Investments, Ltd."

Rachel hadn't known that, and it made her feel she had done Nicholas Ross an injustice. But all she said was "I'm glad. Dad would have liked that." He had chosen to use the name Duncan in his business because it was his mother's family name and because he'd liked the sound of it—especially once Nicholas Ross's name had been added to the letterhead.

The two women were in the den, a comfortable room where Rachel spent much of her time. Mercy left the box she had brought on a side table, then joined Rachel on the Victorian settee near the fireplace.

"You are going to sell the business to Nicholas?"

"Probably. It makes sense to, after all." Rachel shrugged. "I guess I just have to get used to the idea first."

Mercy leaned back and crossed one long, elegant leg over the other. A beautiful, raven-haired woman with a voluptuous figure, she was still single at thirty despite the attentions of half the bachelors—and more than one married man—in Richmond. Rachel suspected she was involved with someone at the moment, but Mercy seldom offered details even to her best friend, and Rachel had been too preoccupied these last months to ask for them.

"Rache, are you thinking of staying in Richmond? I thought going back to New York was the plan."

"I'm just having second thoughts. Natural enough, I suppose."

"Sure. You've got a lot of history in this house." She paused a beat, then added quietly, "And a lot of memories."

"Yes." Rachel started to tell Mercy about the blond man she had seen twice, but bit back the words. Mercy had adored her brother, and Rachel couldn't bring herself to open up those old wounds. There was nothing to be gained by having Mercy as upset as she was herself, she thought.

"And maybe it's time you dealt with those memories," Mercy went on steadily. "You didn't go on with your life after Thomas was killed, you just started a whole new one."

"What's wrong with that?" Rachel frowned. "You know I'd always wanted to be a designer, and the best place to learn was in New York—"

"Yes, I know that. But, Rachel, you didn't *move* to New York, you *bolted* there. Virtually cut yourself off from everybody back here, including your parents and me. Put your emotions in a deep freeze—all of them, as far as I can see. And though you haven't brought up the subject, I'm willing to bet you haven't dated at all."

"I have dated," Rachel objected.

Unmoved, Mercy said, "Then you haven't gone out more than once or twice with the same guy. True?"

Instead of trying to deny that shrewd guess, Rachel said, "The fashion business is demanding and competitive, Mercy—I've been trying to build a career. That hasn't left me much time for a personal life."

"Which is just the way you wanted it."

"And I don't see anything wrong with that."

"I didn't say there was anything wrong with it." Mercy's voice was patient. "The problem is that you never came to terms with what you left behind."

Rachel wanted to dispute that but couldn't. "So?"

"So maybe it's time you did that. Maybe it's past time. Rachel, Thomas wouldn't have wanted you to bury your heart with him. And I think we both know you aren't the kind of woman who'll be happy to spend the rest of your life alone—in New York or here." Mercy smiled slightly. "Maybe your doubts about selling out and moving away for good are trying to tell you something. Maybe you need to face the past before you can decide whether to abandon it."

"Maybe." Although, Rachel could have added, not feeling very much had its benefits.

Mercy hesitated, then said, "You changed so much after Thomas was killed. Part of you died—or else got buried so deeply under grief that you lost it. Your laughter and enthusiasm. Your spirit. What Thomas loved most in you."

Shaken, Rachel murmured, "I just grew up, Mercy, that's all. I stopped being a child."

"You stopped being the Rachel we all knew and loved."

Rachel was silent.

In a gentler tone, Mercy said, "It's the first time you've been home long enough for us to really talk, so forgive me if I blurt out what I've been thinking all these years. But it's true, Rache. When you smile, there's just a shadow of what you used to be. Even your voice is quieter. And though you've always moved as if you had all the time in the world, there's a stillness in you that wasn't there ten years ago."

"I can't help how I've changed," Rachel said, uncomfortable under this dissection of her character.

"You can start living again. Let yourself feel again."

"I feel."

"Do you?" Mercy got to her feet, then added deliberately, "You haven't let yourself grieve for your parents any more than you let yourself grieve for Thomas. But sooner or later you'll have to. And if it all hits you at once . . . it'll be like a mountain falling on you."

It was an image that stayed in Rachel's mind throughout the afternoon, while she went over furniture lists with Darby and found other chores to keep herself occupied. She knew that she had indeed run away ten years ago, run away from pain and loss, and she knew she had not allowed herself to grieve as she should have. And when her parents had been killed, the same urge to flee had sent her running back to New York immediately after the funeral, where work had beckoned and there was no time to think. Or feel.

But now she was home. Surrounded by memories, and by people who would not let her keep running away from them. Feelings she didn't want were lurking too close now, just around the next corner, and it was a corner she knew she would have to turn. This time. That was probably why she felt so on edge, so restless.

And why she had twice seen the image of Thomas—nearby but out of reach.

The offices of Duncan and Ross Investments, Ltd., occupying a single building on a tree-lined side street near downtown Richmond, were elegant and rather formal, as financial institutions tended to be. Strictly speaking, this place was not a bank, or at least not the usual sort; clients of Duncan and Ross offered their deposits to be invested in whatever business ventures the firm saw fit to back. The rewards could be enormous.

So could the losses.

Duncan and Ross, however, had a solid reputation for backing winners, and their clients were, for the most part, happy. If they thought it odd that Duncan Grant had chosen to put his first name on the letterhead, and if they wondered why he had suddenly taken on a rather unusual and rather mysterious partner around five years before, both circumstances were, by now, accepted and hardly worth comment.

Mercy Sheridan strode briskly across the marble-floored lobby on this Wednesday afternoon, headed for her office. She wasn't sure just how much longer it would *be* her office, but for now she still had work to do. The paperwork involved when a partner died suddenly was incredible, and between that and the work she had been doing for Nicholas as a favor—he had never used a personal assistant, but found the need for one now that Duncan was gone— she had managed to keep herself busy.

Once Duncan's affairs were settled, however, she would have to start sending out her résumé.

"Mercy?" Leigh Williams came suddenly out of her side office, frowning. "Now that you're back, I need those balance sheets for the auditor. I hadn't realized you'd be gone so long. You *could* give me the combination to Duncan's safe, you know." A tall and so-phisticated blonde, the office manager always made Mercy feel both underdressed and overly cautious, to say nothing of tardy and inefficient.

"Not without Rachel's permission," she said lightly, resisting an impulse to remind Leigh that she knew this fact of Duncan's will very well. "I'll get the papers and bring them to your office, Leigh."

"Thanks. Oh—and congratulations, by the way."

Mercy frowned. "For what?"

"For trading up. Or, at least, not losing ground."

"Leigh, what're you talking about?"

"Why, I'm talking about you becoming Mr. Ross's personal assistant." Leigh's pale blue eyes were coolly amused and not a little speculative. "That seems to be on the agenda."

Mercy shook her head. "You've been misinformed."

"Then so has Mr. Ross. He's been telling everyone you're going to stay on and work for him. I need those papers as soon as possible, Mercy." Smiling, Leigh turned and went back into her office.

Mercy stood there for only an instant, gazing thoughtfully at nothing, then went on through the quiet lobby. But instead of going to her own office or the one that had belonged to Duncan Grant, she went directly to the big corner office occupied by Nicholas Ross.

His door was open, but he was on the phone. Mercy closed the door behind her, then sat on the arm of one of his visitor's chairs. And while she waited, she studied him.

Even sitting as he was, and behind a huge mahogany desk, he was obviously an unusually large man, and unusually powerful. His dark suit was expensive and well made, his shoulders could fill doorways, and his presence was nothing less than massive and overpowering. One glance, and anyone would want Nicholas on his or her side no matter what the fight was about.

No one would ever call Mercy a small woman, yet Nicholas made her feel absurdly delicate. He also made her feel incredibly feminine, especially when her quiet voice was contrasted by his harsh growl.

She supposed some people would be afraid of him.

Maybe most people.

Because he was so big, because he sounded so rough and angry—even when he wasn't. And because he was ugly.

With the best will in the world, she could describe him only as ugly.

He was barely forty, but looked older. He looked, as the saying went, like ten miles of bad road. Maybe twenty. His face, tanned years ago almost to the color and consistency of old leather, was marked by several small scars he had gotten God only knew where or how, making him look even more thuggish. His cheekbones were high but flat, his brow high and wide, and his nose had most certainly been broken at least twice. There was a ludicrous dimple in his strong chin, his mouth was a straight, thin slash without any particular shape and definitely without softness or charm, and his deep-set eyes were such a light shade of brown that they were almost eerily hypnotic.

Like the eyes of a cat. Or a snake.

Mercy knew almost nothing of his background, except that it had been hard and that he had seen parts of the world tourists were warned away from. He didn't talk about himself, so what little she knew or had guessed came from observation, and from the occasional snippets of information he let slip while talking of something else. Such as when he had once said absently that the summer heat of Richmond was worse than the Kalahari. And when he had recommended to a Europe-bound client all the best places to eat in Florence.

And when he had startled her on various occasions by being fluent in French, German, Italian, and Japanese.

Wherever he had been, and whatever he had done, Nicholas

Ross had turned up in Richmond about five years previously, his ugly face already worn by time and experiences and his unsettling gaze cynical. He had been obviously wealthy, though the source of his wealth remained a mystery, and he had wanted to get into investment banking.

For reasons he had never explained to anyone, Duncan Grant—who had never needed and seemingly never wanted a partner—had invited him to join the firm.

Mercy had signed on as Duncan's assistant not long after that, and even that early Nicholas was already becoming known for his uncanny instincts for seemingly risky business ventures that would prove to be wildly profitable.

He was smart and he was lucky. Or maybe he was smart enough to make his own luck. In any case, Nicholas Ross was a success.

"You're looking very serious," he said to her as he hung up the phone, his voice harsh and deep.

"I have a serious problem," she told him. "Someone keeps telling people around here that I'm going to be your personal assistant."

Heavy lids veiled his eyes as Nicholas glanced down at his immaculate blotter, and continued to half hide his gaze even after he looked at her once again. "That doesn't have to be a problem."

"Nick, we've had this discussion before."

"I know." He grimaced slightly, producing a face likely to frighten small children. "But I hate losing. You know I hate losing."

Mercy sighed. "I'll say it one more time. I will work for you, or I will sleep with you. But I will not do both. You choose."

His eyelids lifted and those pale eyes flickered. "I want both."

"No." It was said very simply, very quietly.

It was his turn to sigh. "Have I ever told you what a stubborn woman you are? Dammit, Mercy, what would be the harm? I need an assistant and you're the best I've ever seen at the job. So what if we're sleeping together? We've managed to be discreet for nearly a year. The sky hasn't fallen in, and our clients haven't turned up at the door foaming at the mouth because you spend an occasional night at my place or I sleep over at yours. Nobody could even imagine you might be promoted or get a raise for any reason other than solid good work. So why the hell not?"

"I'm not going to sleep with my boss. Period. Full stop. End of statement. How much plainer do I have to be?"

"That's plain enough," he growled, clearly annoyed.

Mercy shrugged. She was actually getting quite good at pretending to be indifferent. "Hey, if a personal assistant is more vital to you, just say the word. I'll pack up the stuff I've left at your place and tear up my résumé."

He grunted. "You would too."

"Well, of course I would. Good lovers may be scarce, but good jobs are almost impossible to come by—and the latter pays the rent. Look, stop giving me a hard time about this, will you? You think I'm looking forward to being on the job market again?" Her family background held wealth, but Mercy always had and always would make her own way in the world.

Instead of replying to her hypothetical question, Nicholas rose from his chair and came around the desk to her.

"There's no lock on that door," she warned, but made no further protest when he pulled her to her feet and then into his arms.

He was always careful with her, always consciously gentle—or so it seemed to Mercy. It was the trait of a physically powerful man who knew only too well his strength could hurt and damage, and it never failed to move her in some way she couldn't explain even to herself.

He kissed her with astonishing skill, his hard mouth so sensual that her knees instantly went weak. Her arms slid up around his neck and held on. Even after a year and countless hours spent mindless in his bed, the hunger he roused in her was sharp-edged and intense, demanding satisfaction. It was not something she could fight, not even something she could manage, but, rather, an elemental force that overwhelmed her.

And it irritated Mercy no end that she was never the one to pull back, never the one to regain control easily and swiftly.

He was always able to.

Always—damn him.

Raising his head and smiling very faintly as he looked down at her, Nicholas unlocked her arms from around his neck and eased her down on the arm of the chair behind her. "So sure you could turn your back on my bed, love?"

He had always called her that when they were alone like this, ever since the stormy spring evening nearly a year before when he had offered her a ride home, and they had somehow—to this day, Mercy wasn't sure just how it had happened—wound up naked on the rug in front of her fireplace.

He called her love, but she didn't deceive herself into thinking it meant anything. Nicholas Ross was a hard, abrupt, and rather secretive man with very strong physical appetites, and a "relation-ship" was clearly not something he wanted in his life. Just a woman in his bed three or four nights a week, with no ties or promises.

Mercy had learned to play the game just the way he liked.

So, when she caught her breath, she made herself say dryly, "It would naturally be a severe blow, but I think I could manage."

He let out a bark of a laugh and stepped back to half sit on the edge of his desk. Crossing his arms over his broad chest, he stared at her. "You're not going to back down on this, are you?"

"Afraid not."

"So once Duncan's estate is settled and the bank back to normal, you'll resign?"

"That is the plan." She shrugged. "Look, you know I'm not doing this just to make things harder for you or the bank. There are some lines I won't cross, and sleeping with my boss is one of them."

"I'm your boss *now*," he reminded her.

"No, you're my boss's partner. Until Duncan's estate is settled and the future of the bank decided, I still work for him. It may be splitting hairs, but that's the way I see it."

Nicholas frowned. "Suppose Rachel decides to keep her interest. You could stay on here as her representative. Then she'd be your boss, not me."

Mercy was a little surprised. "I hadn't thought of that. But, anyway, it isn't likely, is it? You've always seemed so determined to buy her out. Aren't you?"

His frown deepened. "Yes, I'm still determined. But if she's anything like Duncan, she has a mind of her own. Is she like him? I haven't spent enough time with her to know."

"She's like him in some ways." Mercy considered the matter. "Smart, intuitive, creative. Like Duncan, she's capable of flashes of inspiration. Problem is, Rachel's carting around a lot of baggage right now, most of it painful. Until she sorts through that, there's really no telling what her decision about the bank will be."

"Your brother's death?"

Mercy nodded. "She's coping with that as well as the loss of her parents—or will be whenever that frozen shell of hers shatters. She needs time, Nick."

"I don't know how much time I can give her." He spoke absently, his gaze abstracted and his face curiously immobile.

Mercy felt a tingle of uneasiness, but said lightly, "I wasn't aware you had some kind of deadline in mind."

Those hypnotic eyes focused on her, unreadable, and after an instant he smiled slightly. "I don't. I'm just naturally impatient. You should know that by now."

What Mercy knew was just the opposite, that he had the patience of a hunting cougar, perfectly capable of hunkering down in utter stillness and waiting as long as it took to get what he wanted.

He always got what he wanted.

What she didn't know was if he had deliberately lied just now or if he honestly had no idea that he had given away that character trait of patience. Either way, it made her uneasiness increase.

Reluctant to question him, she got to her feet and changed the subject. "I have to get some papers out of Duncan's safe before Leigh has a fit, so I'd better go. Anything you need me to do?"

Before Nicholas could answer, there was a soft knock followed instantly by Leigh peering around the door. She had been so quick that if they had been doing anything indiscreet, they would have been caught. But if she had hoped for that, the office manager hid her disappointment well.

She smiled brightly. "Sorry to interrupt—but, Mercy, I really need those papers."

"I'll get them now, Leigh."

"Good. Thanks. Sorry again." She retreated, closing the door quietly.

"Yes, there is something I need you to do," Nicholas said. "I need you to have a lock put on that door."

"Oh, no!" Mercy turned away, adding over her shoulder, "Then she'd know she was right to suspect sinful things going on in here. See you later." She heard Nicholas laugh as she left his office, but thought the sound didn't hold much amusement.

And that bothered her more than anything.

It was Friday afternoon when Rachel decided to go into Richmond. She was planning to do a bit of shopping, more to get out of the house than because there was anything she wanted or needed. Her restlessness had not abated; if anything, it had only gotten stronger. And her vacillation between selling out and returning to New York or staying here was really beginning to bother her.

She got into her mother's Mercedes sedan and drove down to the front gate, which was standing open because Darby's workmen had been hauling attic furniture from the house since early morning.

Rachel turned toward Richmond, and her car began to pick up speed as it moved down a long slope. She reached absently to change the radio station. When she glanced back up at the virtually deserted road, she felt a shock as she once again saw the blond man.

He was standing at the bottom of the slope, still a quarter-mile away, but Rachel knew it was the man she had seen before. Sunlight glinted off his silvery hair, and his lean face was turned toward her. He was just off the road, near a big oak tree and the corner of the brick wall that surrounded much of the Grant estate.

Without arguing with herself, Rachel stepped on the brake, determined not to let him slip away this time. She had to see him, talk to him, had to find out who he was—

The brake pedal resisted for an instant, and then went easily all the way to the floorboard.

The emergency brake proved equally useless, and the gearshift refused to budge.

She couldn't stop the car.

In the space of only heartbeats, Rachel knew that her only choice was to somehow get off the road. Just beyond the bottom of the slope was a traffic light, always busy; she couldn't take the chance of getting through it without hitting another car or a pedestrian.

She waited until the blond man flashed by on her right, then she wrenched the steering wheel to the right, praying desperately that she could avoid the trees.

There was no curb to provide even a nominal barrier, and the heavy sedan barely slowed as it plowed through the spring flowers, weeds, and bushes filling what was essentially an empty lot. Still, Rachel thought she might make it.

Until the rear of the sedan began to fishtail, and she lost control.

Seconds later, the car crashed headlong into an old oak tree.

In those first confused moments, Rachel's mind seemed to function at half speed while her heart pounded in triple time. She found herself sitting behind the wheel, dazed, the air bag deflating now that it had done its job. The car horn was wailing stridently, and the hood was crumpled back almost to the windshield.

Rachel was surprised to be alive and apparently undamaged.

The passenger door was wrenched open suddenly, and a handsome blond man with intense violet eyes leaned in to stare at her. "Rachel, my God, are you all right?" he demanded.

The shock of the accident was forgotten. Her stunned gaze searched that face, as familiar to her as her own, and she was barely aware of whispering, "My God. Thomas."

Then everything went black.

T H R E E

In the hospital, where paramedics had taken her, the doctor who examined Rachel was not happy. He could find no serious injury barring a slight bump on the side of her head where she had apparently hit the window frame of the car, yet she had remained unconscious long enough to raise grave concerns. Rachel tried to explain that the cause had been emotional shock rather than physical, but apparently only she had seen Thomas.

He had vanished once again.

When she had awakened in the ambulance, the paramedic treating her insisted that there had been no blond man at the scene of the accident.

Rachel didn't want to sound like a lunatic by insisting on the reappearance of her long-dead fiancé, so she finally just submitted when the doctor ordered tests and an overnight stay to keep her under observation.

She was ruefully aware that her father's generous endowment to the hospital—and her own possible future interest—was largely responsible for the doctor's caution.

It was more than two hours before she was in a private room and could call the house to inform Fiona and her uncle, and ask that Graham be called so he could find out about the car. She was fine, she told the anxious housekeeper. There was no need for anyone to come to the hospital, because she'd be home in the morning anyway. She just wanted to rest.

But when the silence of the room closed around her, Rachel began to wish she had asked for visitors. Anything to distract her from her muddled thoughts.

Thomas? How could it have been him? He was dead. He had been dead for nearly ten years. And yet . . . it was no ghost that had leaned into her car, no ghost's voice that had called her by name and demanded to know if she was all right. No ghost, but a real flesh-and-blood man. She had even felt the heat of his body, caught the scent of aftershave.

Think it through.

It couldn't have been Thomas, surely it couldn't have. Because if he had been alive all this time, and had let her go on believing him dead . . . No, the man she had loved would never be so cruel.

Unless he hadn't been able to tell her the truth?

He had often been somewhat mysterious about his trips out of the country, so much so that it had bothered her. Yet whenever she had expressed that worry, he had merely laughed and told her she was imagining things. He was a pilot who worked for a shipping company, and he hauled cargo. Normal stuff, he told her. Supplies and equipment.

Yet something in his eyes had made Rachel wonder.

Mercy had often said that her brother loved intrigue and invented it in his own life, that that was why he sometimes seemed mysterious about his activities, but Rachel had not been reassured. She had been certain that he was sometimes in danger, and with a young woman's flair for drama, she had imagined that danger to involve guns and bullets even though there had been no evidence at all to support that.

Now, with an older woman's rationality, Rachel found it difficult to think of any reason Thomas might have faked his own death, any reason he would have needed to stay away for nearly a decade from those who loved him. It just didn't make sense.

But if it hadn't been Thomas she had seen, alive or dead, then who was this man that might have been his twin? He knew her, or at least knew her name. Three times he had been nearby, seemingly watching her, only to vanish before she could touch him, speak to him. Who was he? What had brought him into her life, and why did he stand back as though uncertain or wary of approaching her?

That didn't make sense either.

She was still arguing with herself about an hour later when a hasty knock at the door heralded Graham's arrival. He was carrying a vase filled with her favorite yellow roses and looked very much upset.

"Rachel—my God, are you all right?"

Odd that he used the exact same words the stranger had.

40

"I'm fine, Graham. A little bump on the head and an overly cautious doctor, that's all. Lovely flowers, but you didn't have to."

He set the vase on the table by her bed and stood staring down at her with a frown. "From what Fiona told me on the phone, I expected to find broken bones."

Rachel smiled. "By now you should know how Fiona exaggerates."

"I do. But I also checked on your car. After seeing it, I expected worse than broken bones."

"I'm fine, really. The air bag worked like a charm. Remind me to send a note of thanks to whoever invented the things."

"I'm more interested in what caused the accident." He drew a chair close to the bed and sat down, still frowning. "How did you lose control? The police say there were no skid marks."

"I didn't lose control. Well, I mean, I didn't until the car started to slide all over the place on the grass. I had to steer it into that empty lot because I had no brakes."

"What? You mean they were just gone?"

For the first time, Rachel thought about something other than Thomas, and a shiver of remembered panic crept up her spine. "The pedal felt a little spongy for an instant, then went all the way to the floor. I guess the brake line was somehow broken."

"I don't see how." Graham shook his head. "But I'll have the car towed to a good garage and checked out bumper to bumper. And I'll arrange for another car for you. You don't want to drive Duncan's Rolls, do you?"

Rachel grimaced. "Hardly."

"Didn't think so." He smiled. "Any preferences?"

"Anything but a sports car. I hate them."

"So that's why you never want to ride in my 'Vette."

"That's why," she agreed.

"I'll keep that in mind." Graham's faint smile died, and he added very seriously, "You're sure you're all right?"

"I'm sure." *Just losing my mind, that's all.* "The doctor wants me here for observation because I was . . . unconscious for a little while. But I'm okay. I'll be able to go home in the morning."

"Then I'll come by and pick you up—not in the 'Vette." He got to his feet. "In the meantime, I should go and let you rest."

Rachel wanted to object, because she really didn't want to be left alone with her bewildered thoughts. But she also didn't want to explain to Graham that she had once again seen Thomas's ghost or his twin, and he would certainly wonder if she expressed an unusual desire for his company.

So she merely said, "Will you do me another favor?"

"Of course I will."

"Stop by the house and reassure Fiona and Cam? Tell them I'm fine and I'll see them in the morning?"

"I'll do that."

"Thanks."

"Don't mention it." He hesitated, then briefly touched her hand. "See you in the morning."

She nodded, and held on to her smile until the door swung shut behind him. Then she sighed and turned her gaze to the uninspiring ceiling.

It was going to be a long night.

It was probably after midnight when Rachel half woke from a drugged sleep. The doctor had insisted on the sedative once he'd found no evidence of concussion, saying she needed a solid night's rest. But now she wanted to be awake and the drug was fighting her. She didn't know why she wanted to be awake, not at first. It was very quiet, and the room was dimly lit by the panel light above the head of her bed.

Then he moved out of the shadows near the door and came toward the bed, and Rachel felt her heart leap.

He came to the side of the bed and stood looking down at her for a moment, his face grave. She made a little sound, wordless but urgent, and reached out a wavering hand to him. And when he took her hand in his, the warmth of his flesh touching hers was so solid, so real that it was shocking.

"Who . . . ?" It was all she could get out, and Rachel concentrated fiercely on fighting the drug that was trying to drag her back toward unconsciousness.

He bent down, closer to her, and for a moment Rachel could only stare at that familiar face. Then her heart clenched in pain.

"I'm sorry," he murmured.

His eyes were blue.

Rachel wanted to cry. She thought she might have, but the drug in her system finally won the struggle, and the familiar face of a stranger grew hazy and then disappeared into the dark peace of sleep.

In the bright light of day, the sedative cleared from her system, her nighttime visitor definitely seemed ghostlike at best, and a total figment of her drugged imagination at worst.

Except that she knew he had been there.

She couldn't explain the certainty, but didn't doubt it. The blond man had been in her hospital room last night. He had held her hand, and he had said he was sorry. And his eyes had not been violet as she had thought at the scene of her accident, but pale blue. Despite the dim light of her room last night, she was sure of that.

He was not Thomas.

In one sense, that fact was a relief; at least now she could stop agonizing over whether Thomas had been alive all the time she had believed him dead. He hadn't lied to her, hadn't been cruel enough to hide himself from her.

He had, quite simply, died in a tragic plane crash before his thirtieth birthday.

No, this was another man entirely. A man at least a few years younger than Thomas would have been, maybe thirty-five at most. But the resemblance was certainly uncanny. It made her seriously ask herself if maybe everyone really did have a twin somewhere in the world.

So. There was a stranger who looked like Thomas, a man who knew her name and who had seemingly been watching her for at least several days. The question was—why?

That question remained in Rachel's mind after she went home and all through the weekend, while Fiona fussed over her and Cam exclaimed, and the phone rang with worried inquiries from concerned friends—this surprising her, since she had not realized so many people still thought of her as a friend after she had spent so many years away from Richmond.

She found herself going often to her bedroom window, where there was a view of the front gate, her gaze searching for sunlight glinting off blond hair. But she didn't see what she looked for. Who she looked for. And without information only he could supply, there was no way for her to know who he was and why he had come into her life as he had.

By Monday afternoon Rachel had reached the point of wondering if she should take out an ad in the newspapers asking the mysterious blond man to give her a call. She didn't, but the thought was definitely tempting.

No one seemed to notice her preoccupation over the weekend, or if they did, chalked it up to her brush with near death. Graham was the only one to comment on Monday afternoon when she went to his office to sign yet another stack of legal documents.

"You're very quiet today," he said, leaning back in his chair to study her thoughtfully. "Aftereffects of the crash?"

"Probably." She made her voice reassuring. "I don't know, maybe everybody should crash their car into an oak tree at least once. It sort of puts things into perspective for you."

"What kinds of things?"

Her shoulders lifted and fell. "What really matters. Graham, I don't think I want to sell the house after all. Even to Cam."

He didn't seem surprised. "What about the business?"

"I haven't decided about that yet. But the house . . . Mom and Dad loved it so much, and they're very much there in spirit." Despite control, her voice quivered. "I started cleaning out their bedrooms yesterday, finally going through everything, and I couldn't believe how close to them it made me feel. When I thought of Mom's letters and her collection of lace handkerchiefs being packed away, and all the books Dad loved going into storage because I don't have room for them in my apartment in New York . . . it just hit me what I was thinking of doing."

She hadn't actually begun cleaning out their bedrooms. What she had done was take two steps into her dad's room and then sit in a chair, crying for the better part of an hour. But the result had been the same. She couldn't bear the thought of selling out.

Graham smiled. "Well, there's enough money to maintain the house, no question. Would you move back to Richmond and commute to New York? Keep the apartment in Manhattan and visit here on weekends? Or do your design work out of the house?"

Rachel sighed. "I haven't made those decisions yet—except there's no way I could work totally out of the house and keep my job. To make a name for yourself in the fashion industry, you have to be where it's happening—and that means New York."

"So that's still important to you? It's one of the things the accident put into perspective?"

She thought about it, nodding slowly. "It's not fame I'm after. It's not even success, really. It's . . . being creative the only way I know how. It's the excitement I feel whenever I see an idea actually taking shape in a sketch and then in fabric and on a model."

"You could have that here in Richmond," he said neutrally. "Open a boutique, maybe, with one-of-a-kind designs. The label of Rachel Grant, a Richmond exclusive. I'd say most of the ladies around here would eat it up. In time, New York could come knocking on *your* door."

Even as he spoke, Rachel knew it could work, could be a huge success. She was only surprised she hadn't thought of it before then.

"It's a possibility," she said slowly.

Graham nodded. "Definitely something to think about. I mean, if you're going to keep the house, it'd be a shame to have it go unoccupied for long stretches. Living here, working here. Makes sense to me." And it would keep her in Richmond, which was what he wanted.

She smiled at him. "You should have stayed with trial work, Graham. You can be very persuasive when you want to be."

"That's why I stopped criminal trial work." He smiled slightly in return. "I was able to sway a jury to believe my client was innocent when he was actually guilty as hell. Didn't much like the way that made me feel, so I switched to corporate law."

"I never knew that."

He shrugged. "I didn't run my car into an oak tree, but what happened did put things into perspective for me. I've found life often forces us to make choices, whether we think we're ready for them or not."

"I'm beginning to think you're right about that." Her voice was somewhat rueful. "When I came back here, it seemed there were nothing but choices to make, and I didn't want to make them. Yet, somehow, every time I've had to choose, it's been easier than I expected. More simple and clear-cut."

"Maybe you're getting back on balance. You've had a hell of a rough year, Rachel, don't forget that. Give yourself time. There's no decision you absolutely have to make now, no choice so imperative that it won't wait a few weeks. As with the house, you'll know the right choice when it hits you."

"I suppose you're right."

"Of course."

She laughed and got to her feet. "I'll let the whole situation simmer for a while and see what happens. Satisfied?"

"For the moment." He rose as well, smiling. "How's the car?"

"Drives like a dream, thanks. I meant to ask if it's a rental or leased?"

"Leased. Let me know if you want to buy it."

"Okay." If she lived in Richmond on a permanent basis, she would need to own a car, something she had not needed in New York. Then there would be insurance, and a tag, and maintenance . . . responsibilities. Ties to this place. If she kept the house—and she was fairly certain she would—that would be the biggest tie of all. She felt a tinge of uneasiness but pushed that reaction aside.

"Rachel?"

She looked at Graham, saw his frown, and realized that she must have flinched or otherwise betrayed discomfort. "It's nothing. For a minute there, I let the . . . weight of choices overwhelm me. But you're right. There's nothing I have to decide right this minute. Which reminds me—"

"I'll tell Nicholas you need more time to decide about the business."

"Thanks. I'll see you later, Graham."

"You bet."

Rachel left his office and drove her leased sedan home without incident. Except that she couldn't stop scanning her surroundings in search of the blond stranger. She didn't see him.

That newspaper ad began to seem more inviting.

When she went into the house, it was to discover that Fiona was upset because Darby's workmen had been "tramping" up and down the stairs all day, getting in her way, and Cam wanted to talk to her about buying a rosewood wardrobe that had been found in the attic even though Darby was desperate to have it for her shop, and Darby needed to check with Rachel because she had a list of requested pieces from clients.

Rachel dealt with each of them patiently, soothing, answering, or making a decision—whatever was called for. Fiona was promised fewer difficulties caused by workmen, Cam was promised the rosewood wardrobe, and Darby's list was gone over and selected items agreed upon. Then Rachel retreated to her father's study so she could be alone for a little while.

It was a room she had always loved, a fairly small room off a side hall on the first floor, where her father had spent much of his time when he was home. It was one of the few rooms in the house not furnished with delicate antiques—though the huge Regency table that had served as his desk was certainly an exquisite piece. The remaining furniture consisted of big, comfortable, overstuffed chairs and a sofa that faced the marble fireplace, as well as big, solid end tables and occasional tables. The floor was hardwood, but covered with a lovely rug in muted shades of blue and burgundy, and bookshelves lined the wall between the two large windows.

Rachel had already been through all the business papers her father had kept in this room, but she was still in the process of sorting through his remaining personal papers. He had been quite a letter writer, especially in his younger years, and Rachel was loath to throw away his correspondence without reading it just to make sure nothing important was discarded by accident.

She was sitting at the desk bemusedly reading a letter to her father from a rather well-known sixties actor, when the door opened and Fiona stepped in, a peculiar expression on her face.

"Miss Rachel . . ."

"What is it, Fiona? Darby said she'd speak to her guys, so they should stay out of your way now. Is that it? Or is there another problem?"

"No. That is—I don't know. There's a—a gentleman here to see you." The housekeeper's voice was as odd as her expression, a little shaky and more than a little hesitant.

"Oh? Who is he?"

"He says his name is Delafield, Miss Rachel. Adam Delafield. He says."

Rachel frowned at the housekeeper. "Did he say what it was about?"

"Something about your father, he said."

"All right. Show him in." Since her parents had died, she had been getting calls and visits from people they had known, and in particular from people who had been helped in some way by her father.

"Miss Rachel—" Fiona hesitated, then turned away, muttering something under her breath. And crossing herself.

So Rachel probably should have expected her visitor to present something of a shock. But she didn't. And when the blond man walked into the room a few moments later, she could only stare at him in astonishment.

"Hello," he said, his voice low and curiously compelling. "I'm Adam Delafield. It's nice to finally meet you, Rachel."

His eyes were definitely blue.

He was tall and athletic in appearance, with wide shoulders and an easy way of moving that spoke of an active life. His lean face wore a tan that had obviously come from time spent outdoors over the years. He was dressed casually in dark slacks and a black leather jacket worn over an open-necked white shirt, and looked perfectly at ease.

He also looked, amazingly, incredibly, heartbreakingly, like Thomas.

Of all the questions swirling around in Rachel's mind, the first one to find voice was "Who are you?"

He smiled slightly. "I just told you."

She got up and went toward him, stopping when she could rest her hands on the back of a chair, keeping it between them as a barrier. "You told me your name. But *who are you?* Why have you been watching me? Why did you leave the accident and—and come to my hospital room, and how do you know my name?" *And how is it that you look so much like him?*

"Lot of questions." His smile remained. "Can we sit down while I try to answer them?"

Rachel hesitated, then gestured for him to sit on the sofa while she chose the chair across from it. She couldn't take her eyes off his face, and even as he began speaking in a voice that was—surely it was!—eerily like Thomas's, she realized that he was not as at ease as he appeared. There was tension in him; she could feel it. And those blue eyes held a muted intensity that stirred a new and wordless uneasiness in her.

"My name, as I said, is Adam Delafield." He spoke slowly, consideringly, and his gaze was intent on her. "And the simple answer to all your questions is that I knew your father."

"How did you know him?"

"He invested money in a . . . project of mine."

Rachel frowned, trying to take in what he was saying, to separate his words from the overwhelming confusion of his looks. "I don't recall seeing your name on any of Dad's financial records."

"No, you wouldn't have. The investment wasn't through the bank. He used personal money and there were no records of the transaction."

Her frown deepened. "I know Dad occasionally invested his own money in ventures he considered too risky for the bank, but no records? A handshake deal? How could he report his profits or losses if there was no paperwork?"

"In my case, he didn't expect either profit or loss. The deal was simple, a turnaround of the money. He invested a considerable sum, which I was to repay within ten years."

"Interest free? That sounds like a loan rather than an investment. And a pretty good deal for you."

Adam Delafield nodded. "An excellent deal for me. But he called it an investment because he was sure we would do business together in the future. That was a little more than five years ago. I expect to be in a position to pay off the . . . loan—within the next six months."

"And that's why you showed up here? Why you watched me from a distance for days?"

"You make me sound like a stalker." His voice was light, but that intensity lingered and lent the words shadows. He sighed. "Rachel—I hope you don't mind, but Duncan talked about you and I got into the habit of thinking of you as if I knew you."

She hesitated, then shrugged. "No, I don't mind."

"Thanks. Rachel, I just wasn't sure how to approach you. I intended to introduce myself to you earlier, right after Duncan and your mother were killed, but you had already gone back to New York, and until the estate was settled, or nearly so, you weren't expected back. I didn't want to intrude on your grief. And—I knew about the resemblance."

Taken aback, she said, "You did?"

He nodded. "Duncan commented on it, even showed me a photograph of Thomas Sheridan. So I knew my appearance would probably come as a shock to you. I didn't want to upset you, that's why I hesitated to just come up and knock on the door. At the same time, the investment Duncan made in my project was substantial, and since I knew there were no documents, and that he wouldn't have mentioned it in his will, and possibly not even in his personal papers, I had to see you and explain the situation."

She thought it said something about this man's character that he insisted she know about a part of her inheritance she would never have missed; she couldn't help wondering how many people would have just kept the money and their silence. But all she said was "It doesn't really sound like Dad, investing money with no records. He must have trusted you a great deal."

Adam looked down at his clasped hands. "He was very kind to me at a point in my life when kindness meant more than money. And he had faith in my future, something I didn't have myself. I don't know why he trusted me, but he did. I'll always be as grateful to him for that trust as for the money that put me back on my feet."

Rachel was moved despite both uneasiness and fascination. *Dear God, he looks so much like Thomas!* And sounded like him. She clasped her hands together and made herself concentrate. "How did you know Dad? I mean, how did you meet him?"

"It's a bit involved." He raised his gaze to her face and smiled faintly. "He came out to California, where I'm from, more than five years ago on a business trip. I had, the week before, called up an old friend to ask for help. The friend, as it turned out, was away in Europe. His partner, as it turned out, was Duncan Grant."

"Nicholas Ross?" That surprised her, although she couldn't have said exactly why.

"Yes. We'd known each other a long time and Nick . . . sort of owed me a favor. Anyway, when I couldn't reach him, I spoke briefly to Duncan. I found out when he came out to San Francisco the next week that he had called Nick and asked about me. To this day I don't know what Nick told him, but he came out to California specifically to see me. He listened to my problems and my plans, and offered me the money I needed on the spot.

"Over the next three or four years I flew out here several times to see him. To let him know how his investment was doing. How I was doing. We'd have lunch, maybe even do a flyover of the city in that little plane he was so proud of. And then I'd go back to California."

Rachel flinched a little as she thought of the sleek twin-engine plane her father had loved—and that had taken both her parents to their deaths. Adam obviously saw her reaction.

"I'm sorry. I didn't mean to cause you any pain, Rachel."

"No, it's just . . . I don't like to think about that plane, that's all." Planes had taken all the people she loved. She conjured a smile. "So you know Nicholas. Didn't you assume he'd tell me about Dad's investment?"

Adam shook his head. "No, I knew he'd leave it to me. Nick isn't exactly the most candid of men, you know. I mean, he isn't apt to discuss other people's business."

"Or even his own," Rachel observed dryly.

"Very true." Adam's eyes grew even more intense when he smiled at her, and it made her feel strange. *He isn't Thomas. He isn't! No matter how much he looks like him.* But those logical reminders did nothing to curb her growing desire to reach out and touch him.

Unwilling to let a silence fall between them, she said, "Why did you leave the scene on Friday when I hit that tree? The paramedics told me only the highway patrol was there near the car when they arrived."

"You should have asked the highway patrol about me," he told her with a touch of amusement. "When they reached the scene, they made everyone else stand back. You were in expert care and there didn't seem to be anything I could do, so I left when I heard the ambulance coming."

She half nodded, then said, "Why did you come to my room at the hospital so late? You did, didn't you? I didn't imagine it?"

"No, you didn't imagine it." He hesitated. "I just wanted to make sure you were all right. Didn't expect you to wake up, but you were obviously groggy and went back to sleep almost at once, so I didn't stay."

"You came late. After visiting hours." That still bothered her.

"There were some things I had to take care of first," he said rather vaguely, looking briefly down at his hands in a way that shuttered his gaze for a moment. "It was late when I finished up and got to the hospital. To be honest, I snuck in."

She thought his smile was very disarming. "I see. All right— Adam. I suppose all this makes sense." *But it doesn't, none of it does.*

"But you still have your doubts?"

"Well, let's just say it surprises me that Dad would have done business the way you say he did. However, you didn't have to come and tell me all this, and I can't think of any devious reason why you would have. And I imagine Nicholas will vouch for you."

A flicker of some emotion Rachel couldn't read crossed his handsome face, but he merely said, "I'm sure he will. In the meantime, I just want to assure you that Duncan's investment will be repaid as promised. By the end of the year, I believe."

Realizing suddenly that she had no idea, she said, "I suppose I should ask what kind of business Dad invested in."

"It was more a project than a business, initially. I had dreamed up an electronic gadget that would improve most manufacturing facilities. I had to get the design patented, a prototype built, and try to sell it. It was so successful that I was able to start my own electronic design and engineering firm. All possible due to the investment Duncan made."

"I'm sure he was pleased with your success. Dad loved to see people achieve their dreams." Rachel started to rise to her feet. "How much was the investment, by the way?"

Matter-of-factly, Adam replied, "Three million dollars."

F O U R

R achel sat back down. "Three million dollars?"

He nodded.

"You're telling me that my father invested three million dollars of his own money on a handshake?"

Patient, Adam said, "I've already told you that, yes."

"You didn't tell me it was three million dollars." She was incredulous. "Adam, I've seen Dad's bank records going back years. There was no unexplained withdrawal anywhere near that size, not five years ago and not ever. Every penny has been accounted for."

"I don't know what to tell you. Except—as I remember, he transferred the funds to my bank from a Swiss bank account."

She blinked. "He what? He doesn't have a Swiss bank account."

"He did five years ago. I was sitting in the room, admittedly a bit numb, but I remember the call clearly. He definitely called Geneva."

Rachel had passed bewilderment; now she felt distinctly un-nerved, and not only because the image of her long-dead fiancé was sitting across from her. What would an honest businessman want with a Swiss bank account? And why had no sign of such a thing come to light during all the months countless experts had combed through Duncan Grant's financial records?

It naturally occurred to her that she was hearing this from a virtual stranger, and that she had every reason to doubt what he was telling her. Except that he seemed about to hand her three million dollars, and she couldn't imagine how that could be part of some tangled deception. And—he looked like Thomas. He looked so damned much like Thomas.

"Rachel? Are you all right?"

"No, I'm not."

He hesitated, then said reassuringly, "I'm sure there's no reason for you to be concerned. Duncan may have routed some of his funds through Geneva temporarily for some tax reason. If the account still existed, you surely would have found some record of it among his papers."

"Would I? I found no record of a three-million-dollar invest-ment, so I would say nothing's certain where my father is con-cerned."

Adam hesitated once again before saying, "He wouldn't have wanted you to miss getting part of your inheritance, so I'm sure he would have left some kind of word for you if he had money . . . put aside somewhere you wouldn't expect it to be."

"You mean if he had money hidden somewhere."

"I didn't want to put it that way," he murmured.

"My father," she told him fiercely, "was an honest man. He earned every nickel he had. Every last one. There was no reason for him to hide money."

"I'm sure you're right." Adam shook his head. "Look, Rachel, I'm sorry I've upset you. It wasn't my intention to do that. I just wanted to let you know that Duncan's investment will be repaid this year. You might want to talk to whoever advises you financially. That's a pretty large chunk of money."

"No kidding." It was Rachel's turn to shake her head. "And how do I explain it? How will *you* explain it?"

"Repayment of a personal loan," he said promptly. "It started my business, so I've had to be fairly specific in my own paperwork, but since the repayment is coming out of clear and already taxed personal profit, I don't expect there'll be many questions."

Obviously, his "dreamed-up" design and new company had proven to be enormously successful if he could repay three million dollars from his personal bank account. "Simple for you, but I know enough about finance to be fairly certain that if I can't prove that loan was made to you out of already taxed earnings, I'm going to have problems. Somehow, I doubt that's the way Dad planned it."

"So do I," Adam agreed with a slight frown. "Which means he must have left some record somewhere, if only a notation about making a personal loan and where the funds came from. Have you gone through all his personal papers?"

"Not all of them, not yet."

"There you go. Until you do and nothing turns up, let's not borrow trouble."

Rachel managed a smile, even though too many questions remained unanswered. "I guess you're right. Besides, an hour ago this money didn't even exist for me. Anything realized from it is more than I expected."

"That sounds like a sensible way of looking at it." Adam got to his feet. "And now, since I've taken up enough of your time, I'll be going."

Rachel got to her feet as well, and hoped her voice didn't sound as anxious to him as it did to her when she asked "Back to California?"

"No, not yet. I plan to stay in Richmond another week or two. I'll be at the Sheraton if you . . . need to get in touch." He took a step toward her and held out his hand.

Rachel hesitated only an instant before giving him her hand, and as braced for it as she was, the touch of him was still a little shocking. *He isn't Thomas. He isn't.* But that certainty didn't have the power to change what she felt. She gazed up into his eyes and felt stirrings of sensations she hadn't experienced in a long, long time.

This is wrong. I don't know him. I know only what he looks like.

"I realize I'm a stranger to you," he said abruptly, still holding her hand, "but—I'd like to see you again, Rachel. May I call you, say in a day or two? We could have dinner, see a movie. Something casual."

He isn't Thomas.

"I'd like that." She hadn't planned to say it until the words came out, but once they did, she didn't regret them.

"Good." He smiled at her and squeezed her hand gently, then

released it. "I'll see myself out. It was very nice meeting you, Rachel—at last."

"And it was nice finding out you weren't a ghost or a figment of my imagination," she told him, keeping it light.

He had a nice laugh.

When she was alone in the study, Rachel sat in the chair and stared across the room at nothing, thoughts and emotions swirling within her and her hand still tingling from the touch of his.

"My God," she murmured.

"Three million dollars?"

Rachel nodded, gazing across his desk at Graham's surprised expression. "That's what the man said."

"Duncan lent this man three million dollars on a handshake?"

"Uh-huh."

"I don't believe it."

"Startled me too," she murmured.

"No, I mean I flat-out don't believe it. Rachel, that's not the way Duncan did business. It'd be insane to risk that kind of money with absolutely no written promise of repayment. What if this man—Delafield, you said his name was?"

"Adam Delafield."

Graham made a note on the legal pad on his blotter. "What if he denied getting the money? Or simply decided not to repay it? Duncan would have had no recourse, no legal means of demanding the debt be repaid."

Calmly, Rachel said, "Obviously, Dad thought he could trust this man. And the proof of his good judgment came to see me yesterday. If he hadn't, I never would have known about the loan—

not unless something turns up in Dad's private papers, anyway. All he had to do was sit on the money and keep silent. But he came to tell me the debt will be repaid in the next six months or so."

Graham shook his head. "There's something fishy about it."

"Well, if you can figure out some way a con artist would benefit by promising to pay me three million dollars, let me know. I couldn't think of a damned thing."

"Did he ask you for anything? Anything at all?"

I'd like to see you again, Rachel.

She shook her head. "No."

Graham drummed his fingers on the legal pad. "And you say you saw him watching you before he came to the house? That he was the man you mistook on that street corner for Thomas? And that you saw him just before your car's brakes went out?"

"I told you why. He wasn't sure how to approach me, especially since he looks so much like Thomas." Despite her own uneasiness, Rachel smiled. "Graham, you're so suspicious. Why can't Adam Delafield just be an honest man trying to repay a loan? Why does there have to be more to it?"

Graham reached to open the top drawer of his desk and drew out a sheaf of papers. "I got this just a couple of hours ago. Since you'd already called to say you were dropping by, I decided to wait until you got here to discuss it."

"Discuss what?"

"This is the mechanic's report on the Mercedes. The brake line didn't fail, Rachel. It was cut."

She didn't even blink for a moment, but then drew a deep breath. "Cut. You mean—deliberately?"

"That's what it looks like. The mechanic says it would be difficult to prove in court, that it's *possible* the line could have been cut accidentally, but he knows his job and he believes it was no accident."

"You're saying someone wanted to—to hurt me? To cause an accident?"

"I'm saying we should both cultivate a little healthy distrust, especially where strangers are concerned." Graham's voice was deliberate.

Rachel leaned back in her chair and stared at him. "You think it was Adam?"

"I think it's a damned suspicious coincidence that he turns up mysteriously in your life with a convenient resemblance to your dead fiancé, and a few days later your car smashes into a tree."

She felt a chill, but even so had to object. "What would he have to gain? Graham, he *told* me about the money he owes Dad. Why would he have done that if he wanted to renege on the debt?"

"Rachel, you have only this man's word for it that a debt exists."

"But why would he—"

"Think about it. What better way to ingratiate himself into your life than by claiming that your father helped him when he was down on his luck. That he's so grateful your father's *investment* let him turn his life around. *And* by telling you he's going to pay you three million dollars by the end of the year."

"What could he hope to gain by lying about those things?"

"You're an heiress," Graham reminded her bluntly. "Worth a hell of a lot more than three million dollars."

"So he cut the brake line on my car? That is what you're implying?"

"What I'm *saying* is that his story is damned suspicious, especially following what looks very much like a manufactured accident. Rachel, given where the accident happened—had to happen—the chances were good you wouldn't be driving very fast. It wasn't likely to be a serious crash. He could have planned it that way."

"But why?"

"As a distraction, a diversion of your attention. Or mine."

After a moment, Rachel shook her head. "That's too Machiavellian for me, Graham. A possibility only a lawyer could consider."

He didn't smile. If anything, Graham's grimness increased as he slowly realized something. The crash might have put "things" into perspective for Rachel, but something else had happened since then. She was . . . waking up. Coming out of the deep freeze where Thomas's death had left her. Her features were more animated than he could remember seeing them, her smile quicker, and even her voice held more life.

It was a subtle change—but it was a definite change. A hint of more changes to come. And there was only one reason for it that he could think of.

Adam Delafield.

If Graham had been a man given to shouting and throwing things, he would have done so then. All his patience. All his undemanding, understanding friendship, his help and concern for Rachel all these months, and none of it had so much as chipped her frozen serenity. Then came Adam Delafield, looking, apparently, like Thomas Sheridan's twin—and Rachel was thawing.

Keeping his voice level, Graham said, "There have been more involved plans to gain a fortune, Rachel. Plenty of them."

She stared at him for a moment, then shook her head. "No, I

don't believe that he's—what? Trying to sweep me off my feet? Marry me before I discover he's a con artist?"

"It's been done before."

Rachel couldn't help but laugh. "That's absurd! Graham, I'm not an idiot. Nor am I so trusting that I'd give anyone power over me unless I was absolutely certain that power wouldn't be misused."

"How's he supposed to know that? Until he gets to know you, I mean."

"And I thought *my* imagination was working overtime when I was so sure I'd seen Thomas." She shook her head again, this time bemusedly. "Yours is really overactive, you know that?"

Graham's mouth firmed stubbornly. "Maybe so, but humor me. I'm going to have him checked out, Rachel. His background. Find out if there's really a company out in California."

Her first impulse was to tell him not to, but Rachel knew it would be the sensible thing to do. And since she had just claimed she wasn't foolish, she could hardly object to a sensible and responsible precaution. *Because he's not Thomas, after all.*

"Fine," she said. "And you might want to check first with Nicholas, since they're old friends."

If Graham had expected an argument, it didn't show; he merely nodded. "I'll get right on it. But in the meantime, do me a favor? Park your car in secure places and stay away from Adam Delafield?"

"I'll be careful," Rachel promised. Which was not, of course, quite what Graham had asked for, but he didn't realize that until she was gone.

Swearing softly, he reached for his phone.

. . .

It was almost midnight on Tuesday night when Mercy's pillow moved under her, and she murmured a sleepy complaint.

"Sorry, love, but I can't stay tonight." Nicholas eased away from her and slid from the bed.

"Why not?" She winced when he turned on the lamp on her nightstand, then rolled on her side and blinked owlishly.

"Just some things I need to take care of at my place."

"At this hour?" Mercy raised her head and propped it on one hand, watching as he got dressed. She enjoyed watching him dress. Or undress, for that matter. He had an incredible body, so powerfully muscled there was almost no give to his flesh at all. At the same time, he didn't look like those weight lifters with their exaggerated physiques. He was strong in ways they couldn't begin to match, and his muscles were not for show, but for use. Hard use.

Or so Mercy guessed. She guessed he had needed to be strong more than once in his past, probably for his very survival. The several long scars marking his back, chest, and rib cage told that story.

When she had asked, he had said only that he'd been in "a fight or two" in his past, offering no further details. Wary of asking for more than he wanted to give, she had not brought up the subject again. But his silence only encouraged the sometimes incredible tales she made up to account for his various marks and traits and abilities. It was not an unpleasant occupation.

But wearing a bit thin after five years of knowing him and a year of physical intimacy.

Replying to her plaintive question, Nicholas said, "I'm a night owl, you know that. I work best this time of night." He sat on the edge of the bed and began to put on his socks and shoes.

"You could have warned me earlier. I put out a steak to thaw."

Mercy did not cook for Nicholas since he was perfectly able to cook for himself; in fact, he tended to fix breakfast for them both whenever he stayed over at her apartment or she stayed over at his. And, being a very large man with a correspondingly large appetite, he favored substantial breakfasts such as steak and eggs.

"Mmm. Leave it in the refrigerator and we can have it next time. Okay?"

"Sure." It was, strictly speaking, his steak, anyway—bought and paid for. At least once a week he arrived bearing a bag of groceries, always replacing what he had eaten at Mercy's place, and she had never objected. It was just one more way he had of keeping their relationship on a carefully balanced footing, with neither of them beholden to the other.

Dressed now except for the jacket he had left in her living room, he half turned to look down at her consideringly. "Or . . . I could come back in a couple of hours."

Mercy didn't know quite what she was supposed to say to that; it wasn't a suggestion he had ever made before. So she shrugged and murmured, "Suit yourself. You have a key."

He looked at her a moment longer, his ugly face unreadable, then nodded and got to his feet. "Go back to sleep, Mercy." He turned off the lamp, plunging the room into darkness.

Like a cat, he could see easily in the dark.

Mercy lay back on her pillow, listening to the very faint sounds of him leaving the bedroom and then, moments later, the apartment. She didn't go back to sleep for a long time.

.   .   .

In its heyday, it had been known as The Tavern, a nice restaurant and bar that had served good food and good booze to most of the upper class of Richmond. Its Old English–style sign hanging out front had been a landmark, and it had been the place to be on Saturday nights.

That was then.

Neither the neighborhood nor The Tavern had aged gracefully. Most of the surrounding stores were either vacant or else provided shelter for Richmond's population of homeless and aimless. The rest had thick steel doors and iron bars on the windows, and inside went on the quiet, desperate kinds of business that destroyed lives and souls.

The police seldom bothered to patrol the area, and the denizens had learned to take care of trouble on their own.

As for The Tavern itself, the sign out front had long ago vanished, and nobody had bothered to replace it. The interior had been trashed so many times that the current owner had finally stripped the floors down to the stained concrete and the furnishings to little more than scarred pool tables.

The place was incredibly dark and smoky, to say nothing of being three deep at the bar with most of the worst citizens of Richmond, but no one gave Nicholas any trouble. In fact, men gave way for him instantly and without a murmur of complaint or abuse, even the drunkest ones.

He found Adam Delafield in the back corner, occupying one of only three booths not torn out long ago to provide more room for the pool tables and the clientele—a standing man taking up less space and much less furniture than a sitting man.

"Nice place." Nicholas slid into the booth across from Adam, automatically shifting the unsteady table a bit more toward Adam to make room for himself.

Adam rescued two wobbling glasses as the table rocked, then handed one across to Nicholas. "Have a beer. You sound disgruntled."

"I am disgruntled. You dragged me out of a warm bed."

"The beer's not bad. Honest."

Nicholas sipped, then grimaced slightly. "Okay, it's not bad. But that was a very warm and comfortable bed I had to leave, Adam. Couldn't this have waited until morning?"

"You tell me. Did you get the call?"

"From Graham Becket? Yeah. Asked me if you were on the level with Rachel. If Duncan really had loaned you three million dollars."

"And you told him?"

"That you were, and Duncan had. Wasn't that what I was supposed to say?"

"I hope you managed to sound a bit more convincing, Nick."

Nicholas smiled. "Naturally. Fair warning though—Becket's a suspicious bastard at the best of times, and where Rachel's concerned, he's even more so."

Adam frowned. "Is he that protective of her?"

"He's that in love with her."

"You're sure about that?"

Nicholas shrugged. "As sure as one man can be of another man's feelings. He'd just love to slay dragons for her. Protecting her and her money from an ex-con with a fishy story would suit him right down to the ground."

Adam scowled. "Great."

"I did try to warn you this wouldn't be easy."

"I know. But I'm an optimist." Adam took a drink of his beer, still frowning.

"You'd also better know that Becket will turn up the conviction and jail time in pretty short order. I don't like the son of a bitch, but he's efficient as hell and definitely motivated. So you'd better start planning to look at Rachel with big, sad eyes while you tell her your long, sad story."

Adam grunted.

Nicholas looked at him with cynical amusement. "Pretty long limb you're crawling out on."

"It's no place I haven't been before."

"True." Nicholas studied him across the table. "And this time you've dressed for the part. That's a new look for you, isn't it?"

Adam shrugged.

Refusing to be warned off, Nicholas went on coolly. "Longer hair, more casual clothing. I seem to recall that was Thomas Sheridan's style."

"You don't say."

"You're taking a big chance, Adam."

Once again Adam shrugged, but a frown drew his brows low. "Maybe. But I don't have much choice, do I? She wouldn't have let me in the door otherwise."

"Which door are we talking about?" Nick asked gently.

Adam ignored that question. Instead, he fixed his attention on using his sweating glass to connect water rings on the scarred table, and changed the subject. "How much time do you figure I've got?"

"Before Becket rides to the rescue? A few days, maybe a week. He'll start with the dope on the company, I imagine, and think about a possible criminal record afterward."

"Shit. That isn't much time."

"No. But all you've got, so make it count."

Adam gave him a look. "Cheap advice."

"If you want the more expensive kind, you have to pay for it." Nicholas smiled.

"Yeah, yeah." Adam leaned back and continued to stare across the table at his companion. "What about you, Nick? Just what do you mean to do if Rachel decides not to sell out?"

Wide shoulders lifted and fell in a shrug as Nicholas said indifferently, "I'll land on my feet. I always do."

The conversation broke off for a few moments as a noisy fight erupted at the center pool table and threatened to spill over into the entire room. Adam and Nicholas watched with wary interest, returning their attention to each other only when the tattooed bouncer tossed both combatants out into the street.

"You don't have much time either," Adam noted.

"No, damned little."

"Want me to encourage Rachel to sell to you?"

Nicholas laughed. "Do you plan on having so much influence over her decisions?"

"You never know."

"Take some more cheap advice. Do what you came here to do and don't fuck around along the way."

"I have to get close to her."

"You don't have to crawl into bed with her."

Adam shrugged. "There was a spark. Damned hard to ignore it."

"Do your best," Nicholas advised. "Unless you really do like being a stand-in for another man, and a dead one at that."

Adam smiled a bit wryly. "There is that. She must have been

crazy about him. The way she looked at me when she thought I might be him . . ."

"She was, so they say. Never the same after he was killed." Nicholas took a sip of his beer and added almost absently, "Some people love only once, it's the way they're made."

Adam didn't reply, and after another moment of silence Nicholas pushed his barely touched glass away and slid from the booth. Pleasantly, he said, "Don't drag me out of my warm bed again, Adam. I get cranky when I lose sleep."

Just as pleasantly, Adam said, "I'll remember that. Next time."

Nicholas strode toward the door, the sea of mostly drunken men parting for him the way the Red Sea must have parted for Moses. Adam was amused by the comparison, for a less holy man than Nicholas would have been hard to imagine.

Not that he himself could afford to cast stones.

Amusement fading, Adam went back to using the base of his dewed glass to connect water rings. That occupied him for some minutes, and then he sighed and stopped. He wiped his damp fingers on his thigh and reached into the slightly open neckline of his white shirt, pulling out a small gold locket on a fine chain.

In the center of the elaborate designs on one side of the locket were the initials *RG*, and on the other side the initials *TS*.

Adam used a thumbnail to open the locket. Inside on the left was a silver St. Christopher medal, sized perfectly to fit as a photo would have. On the right side was a photo, protected by a tiny clear shield. A girl smiled radiantly. She was so hauntingly lovely that Adam's breath caught even though he had seen the picture countless times before.

It was Rachel.

The tip of his thumb gently brushed across the picture, and

then he closed the locket and dropped it back inside his shirt. On a long, rough sigh, he muttered, "Goddammit."

Nicholas stood outside the bar for several minutes, his breath misting in the chilly night air. He gazed off in the direction of Mercy's apartment, even took a step that way. But then he halted, swore, and reversed direction.

He called himself a damned fool all the way to his car.

F I V E

hat?" Cameron Grant stared at his niece across the dining table. "You're going to keep the house? But I thought you were planning to go back to New York."

"I was. I changed my mind."

Rachel was still surprised at herself for the decision she had made sometime in the previous twenty-four hours. She couldn't even say what had finally tipped the balance. All she knew was that the decision had been made, and that it felt right.

It was Wednesday evening, and Rachel had spent the day helping Darby with the furniture inventories.

Obviously trying not to sound as unhappy as he was, Cameron said, "So you'll be keeping the breakfront and the Queen Anne chairs?"

Rachel smiled at him. "No, I promised them to you. They're yours. As for the rest, I'm going to let Darby continue to inventory the entire house, room by room. It needs to be done, and since she's started, she should finish."

"What about the pieces you don't plan to use, Rachel? Are you going to let her sell them to strangers?"

"All the extra stuff has been collecting dust for decades, giving no pleasure to anyone." Rachel's tone was reasonable. "There's no good reason to keep what I won't be using."

"But, Rachel—"

"Don't worry, Cam. If there are other pieces you can't bear to see sold, we'll work something out. But how much room do you have in that house of yours?" Cam had been staying here since shortly before his older brother had been killed, but home was a lovely old town house in San Francisco, currently being renovated. Since he was a moderately successful artist, he could live anywhere he chose, and the West Coast had been his home for more than twenty years.

"There's enough room for a few more big pieces. But whether I can display things or have to put them into storage for the time being isn't the point. I just can't bear to see Grant family things going to strangers, Rachel, that's all. One of us should keep them."

A little weary of the argument, she said, "Hanging on to history isn't always the best thing to do."

He hesitated, then smiled and lifted his wineglass in a small salute to her. "So, you've decided to stay in Richmond. And—what? Take Duncan's place at the bank?"

"I haven't decided whether to keep my interests in the bank, but I certainly won't be working there. I don't have Dad's gift."

"You have your own. Some kind of fashion design, then?"

She told him briefly about Graham's suggestion that she open a boutique selling her own designs. "The idea appeals to me. I think I'll give it a shot."

"That designer you work for is not going to like losing you."

"He won't be too upset. He liked my work, but there was some friction between us."

The friction had consisted of Brian Todd's unshakable belief that he was God's gift to women of all ages, but Rachel didn't feel any impulse to confide this to her uncle.

"Your dad always said you'd come back here," Cameron said.

Rachel was surprised. "He did? Was he—were he and Mom upset that I stayed in New York all those years?" Even though Graham had reassured her, it was something about which Rachel still felt profoundly upset.

Before Cameron could answer, Fiona came into the dining room with dessert and said sourly, "They missed you. Of course they were upset."

"You were listening at the door," Cameron accused.

The housekeeper snorted. "How else am I supposed to find out what goes on around here?"

Cameron had made several attempts to charm Fiona in the months he'd been living there, but she had resisted his blandishments. Since then, the two had observed a wary, occasionally bristly, understanding.

They didn't like each other.

Rachel said, "Don't you two get started. Fiona, I know Mom and Dad missed me. But they understood why I stayed away. Didn't they?" *Tell me they understood.*

The housekeeper's face softened almost imperceptibly. "Of

course. And he's right—about this, anyway. They knew you'd come back here to stay sooner or later."

Almost to herself, Rachel murmured, "I thought there'd be time enough. That I'd come back one day, and everything would be the way it was before I left. But . . . the months turned into years. And time ran out."

"They understood, Miss Rachel. Both of them. Your mother especially, I think."

It was a reassurance Rachel needed, and even if she still didn't quite believe it, the housekeeper's words gave her the first really good night's sleep she'd had since coming back home.

On Thursday morning, while Darby continued with the inventory, Rachel excused herself to drive into town. A visit to a real estate agency resulted in a list of several properties she wanted to have a look at, and though the agent had wanted to accompany her, Rachel preferred to be alone in the initial stages of choosing a location for her boutique.

It occurred to her only during the drive that "her boutique" had taken on the solidity of reality in her mind, so much so that she had a very clear idea of just what she wanted to do.

Like the decision to keep the house, the decision to open a boutique, once made, also felt very right. Whether the venture was a success or a failure, Rachel was looking forward to it—and it was exhilarating to find herself looking ahead rather than back.

She had spent too many years looking back.

The first address the agent had provided turned out to be totally unsuitable for what Rachel had in mind. The second one, however, had definite possibilities. It was a fairly small vacant store in a block-long area that already contained several small specialty stores, and foot traffic was brisk even on this weekday morning.

Standing on the sidewalk as she considered the store, Rachel didn't notice a quiet black sedan pull up to the curb behind her, so it surprised her very much to hear Nicholas Ross's harsh voice.

"Good morning, Rachel."

She jumped, but only a little. The sheer size of him was overpowering as he reached her side and loomed over her, but she managed not to back away. "Hi, Nick."

He had always made her feel wary. She hoped it didn't show.

He nodded toward the For Lease sign in the dirty window. "Is that what interests you so much?"

Rachel hesitated, then nodded. "I'm thinking about opening a boutique here in Richmond. One-of-a-kind fashion designs."

Nicholas frowned slightly. "I see. Then I take it you won't be returning to New York."

"No, not for good. I'll have to go back there eventually, of course, and pack up my apartment."

"What about the bank?"

She shook her head. "I haven't decided about that yet. It's why I haven't come to talk to you. But you can be sure I won't be trying to tell you how to run things, Nick, no matter what I decide to do. For all intents and purposes, it's your bank now."

His frown remained, and those pale eyes were unreadable as they gazed at the empty store before them. In an abrupt tone he said, "If you decide to keep your interest, you couldn't go wrong asking Mercy to manage for you."

Rachel was a little surprised. "I hadn't thought about it. I guess I assumed she'd be working for you now that Dad's gone."

"No." He looked down at her. "I've asked, but . . . Mercy

knows I've never wanted an assistant. She's an asset to the bank, though, and I'd hate to lose her. She has a rare understanding of finances. If you're looking for someone to manage all your business interests, I'd put her at the top of a very short list."

Curious, Rachel said, "Where would you put Graham?" She was aware the two men didn't care for each other, but wasn't sure of the cause. Distinctly different personalities, maybe?

"Graham Becket is a fine lawyer."

She waited a moment, then said dryly, "And that says it all?"

Nicholas smiled, and it was not a charming thing. "I think so. I'd trust him with my legal affairs, but I'd want someone else giving me financial advice. It's not his specialty."

"I see. Well, thanks for the suggestion about Mercy. I'll keep it in mind."

"Do that. Can I give you a lift somewhere?"

"No, thanks. I have a leased car I'm trying out." She didn't see any reason to confide in him about the possibly sabotaged brake line. "It's over there. So thanks anyway."

"Off to look at another store, or has this one caught your fancy?"

"This one's a little small, but possible. I've just started looking, though, so no decision is imminent."

"Glad to hear it." He glanced around them. "You wouldn't know to look at it, but this neighborhood isn't the best. A higher crime rate than some of the worst parts of town."

Rachel didn't bother to tell him that she would have researched the crime rate as well as other important elements before making a decision. She merely said, "Well, maybe the third place will be the charm."

"Where is it?"

"On Queen Street. The Realtor was enthusiastic."

"I imagine so. It's pricey real estate. But a good location." He took a step back and turned toward his car. "Let me know if I can do anything to help, Rachel. I'd be happy to."

"Thanks, Nick."

She watched as he got into his car with a grace uncommon in such a big, powerful man, and moments later the black sedan had purred its way out of sight.

She was still wary of Nick.

And she had a feeling it had definitely shown.

Shrugging off a lingering unease, Rachel used the key the agency had provided to go into the store, and spent another ten minutes or so checking it out.

Naturally, her thoroughness had nothing to do with Nick's dismissal of the spot as a good prospect.

But she reached the same conclusion for different reasons, however reluctantly. The layout of the interior was wrong, would require considerable remodeling, and that was not something Rachel wanted to waste time with if at all possible.

So she got back into her car and drove to the next spot, on Queen Street. Nick had been right about this area as well; it was high-ticket real estate boasting some of the most exclusive stores in Richmond.

An area no more than two blocks long, it was designed with foot traffic in mind, with wide sidewalks and handy benches placed near the decorative and functional lampposts. Parking was handy without being intrusive, and a nearby police station was undoubtedly a deterrent to crime.

Rachel was impressed by the store she had come to see. It was slightly larger than she had planned, but temporary walls could take care of that until—hopefully—the need for expansion arose. Other than that she could see no structural problems. There was even a huge office space and storage area in the back, both of which would come in handy.

She was standing in the center of the front part of the store, jotting down a few ideas for colors and a decorating style, when a voice from the open door caught her by surprise.

"Rachel?"

Adam Delafield.

"Hello. What are you doing here?" After the first moment of surprise, her heart rate had returned to normal. Or almost.

"I was going to ask you the same thing." He came in and crossed the space between them. "I was in a store across the street, and thought I saw you come in here."

"I'm . . . thinking of starting a business. Fashions designed by me."

"So you're not going back to New York?"

Rachel realized it was a question she was going to hear a lot. "No. I don't think so. I belong in Richmond."

"Ghosts and all?"

Whether it was the cryptic note in his voice or simply the reminder, Rachel found the question a difficult one to answer casually, and confiding in this virtual stranger was impossible. So she tried to keep it light. "I don't believe in ghosts."

"Don't you?"

"Of course not."

"You thought I was Thomas Sheridan." There was something almost insolent in his voice.

"Yes, I did," she admitted. "Thomas—alive and well. Not his spirit haunting me. I never believed that."

Not for a moment. Right.

"In any case," she added, making her tone brisk, "it's a bright, sunny spring day, and there are certainly no ghosts lurking here." She turned away from him and gestured to the space around them. "What do you think? A classy store selling unique designs? The label of Rachel Grant, a Richmond exclusive."

"I think you'll be a hit. A major hit."

She looked at him, relieved that his voice was casual again but bothered by the intent way he looked at her. It made her feel self-conscious. No, more than that. It made her feel that no one else had ever really looked at her before. And that was disconcerting.

It was also a little scary.

She made a production of putting her notebook away in her shoulder bag. "Well, we'll see. Who knows? Maybe I inherited a little of Dad's business savvy."

"I wouldn't doubt it a bit." He followed her from the store and stood just behind her as she locked up.

"I have two other places to check out," she said as she turned to face him, "so—"

"Why don't you let me buy you lunch? It's after noon, and there's a really good restaurant just down the block. Do you like Italian?"

"Yes, but—I really should take a look at the other stores."

"You can do that just as well after lunch. And you have to eat."

When Rachel hesitated just a moment too long, Adam nodded slightly and a wry expression crossed his face.

"Would it help if I promise not to ask any more dumb questions about ghosts?"

"Not dumb. Just . . ."

"Just not welcome. Especially from somebody who looks like

me." He smiled, but that intensity she had sensed earlier was still in him, lurking just below the surface. "I understand. Have lunch with me, Rachel, please. I'd like to talk about a man I admired very much—to his daughter."

That was an appeal Rachel could hardly refuse, especially since she wanted to hear more about her father's relationship with this man. And he had a point. She had to eat.

"In that case, thanks. I'd love to have lunch with you."

"The restaurant is close enough to walk to. If you feel like it."

"Sounds great."

Adam offered his arm, and Rachel surprised herself by taking it. She was immediately aware of strength and leashed power, of hard muscles beneath her fingers, and other senses whispered to her of force and will. And darkness. *He isn't what he wants me to believe he is. Who he wants me to believe he is.* That knowledge was so strong that Rachel almost pulled her hand away from him. But along with wariness and uneasiness was curiosity.

Who was he, really? And what did he want from her?

Despite Graham's warning, Rachel didn't believe it was her money Adam was after. She had never thought much about intuition, but hers was alive in her now, and it insisted there was much more to this—to him—than simple greed. She was sure of it.

And he looks like Thomas. That has to mean something. Doesn't it?

Nicholas Ross sat in his long black car and gazed down the block, watching Rachel and Adam stroll along the sidewalk toward him. As far as he could tell, they were pleased to be in each other's company.

Then Rachel looked up at her companion and smiled that slow smile of hers, transforming her face into something radiant. Even at this distance, Nicholas could see Adam's reaction, see his free hand reach to cover the one resting in the crook of his arm in a gesture any other man would recognize as possessive.

"Slow down," Nicholas murmured. But nobody heard him, of course. And even if the right person had, Nicholas doubted his warning would make much of a difference.

He understood obsession.

He watched the couple until they disappeared into an Italian restaurant, the door of which was barely twenty feet from the hood of his car. Rachel hadn't appeared to notice the car, and behind the tinted windows Nicholas knew he was virtually invisible.

Adam hadn't so much as glanced this way.

Once they'd vanished into the restaurant, Nicholas started his car and pulled away from the curb. He reached for his mobile phone and punched in a number. The phone rang a long time before anybody answered.

"Yeah."

"Simon, it's Nick. I have a job for you."

In her bed that night, Rachel thought about the interlude with Adam, but she still wasn't sure what she felt about it. Adam was a charming man, no doubt about that, and all her instincts told her he had sincerely liked and respected her father. Though they hadn't talked much about Duncan Grant, now that Rachel thought about it.

They had, she realized, talked mostly about themselves.

Or had she done most of the talking, with Adam asking questions and offering little except agreement now and then?

He was not an easy man to read. There was that intensity she sensed lurking in him, a kind of force that was very much belied by his casual, almost lazy exterior. He struck her as the kind of man who would make a very good friend and a very bad enemy, and she thought he could—and would—be ruthless if the stakes were high enough.

But what were the stakes now?

He had said no more than that he had been "down on his luck" when Duncan Grant had made him the loan. No one else had believed in the design he had invented. So Rachel had no way of knowing what his life had been like then. But if he had built up a prosperous engineering and design company in less than five years, he had clearly worked hard and made all the right business decisions.

He had to be tough, that was certain; he was obviously smart.

In the course of the conversation, it had emerged that they had similar taste in books and movies, shared a love of horses and cats, preferred baseball to football, were staunch independents, loved to look at the ocean, and were vehemently opposed to AstroTurf and the designated hitter. Both liked to sleep with the windows open unless it was too hot—it was never too cold—enjoyed putting together jigsaw puzzles, and loved the sound of wind chimes.

He seemed to smile more quickly than frown, and his voice could be serious one moment and filled with amusement the next, but his blue eyes gave nothing away, and had once or twice even appeared to be shuttered, deliberately veiled with secretiveness.

Rachel couldn't deny to herself that she was attracted, but she was wary. Very wary. Because he looked so like Thomas. And because she didn't trust her own feelings—about him or anything else just then.

A week ago she had been in limbo, feeling little, refusing even to grieve for her parents. But now, suddenly, she was feeling too much. What little Adam had said about Duncan Grant during lunch had pulled the tears so close to the surface that she'd had difficulty holding them back. Twice during the remainder of the day she had found herself crying unexpectedly, once because she'd found one of her mother's old handkerchiefs in a drawer and once because she could have sworn she had caught the scent of the cologne Thomas had always worn, the kind she had bought him for his birthday when she was fifteen and that had become his signature scent.

But the scent was only another ghostly reminder of fact.

Dead. Thomas was dead. Her parents were dead.

Ghosts and all?

She had lived a long time with ghosts. One in particular. And as simple as it was to tell herself that Thomas was long dead, her heart had never been able to believe that. He had lingered in Richmond for her, his memory filling all the corners. And because she had run away rather than face those corners, his memory was still vivid.

How could she be sure that it wasn't his memory coloring her feelings for Adam? Could she trust her own mind and heart not to latch on to him eagerly because he was the nearest thing to Thomas she had found?

That was a creepy thought.

Rachel turned over in bed and told herself to stop thinking. She told herself that several times.

By the time it finally worked and she fell asleep, it was past the witching hour, and she dreamed vivid dreams in which a man wearing a mask of Thomas's face was Adam, and when he removed the mask of Adam there was another mask underneath that was Thomas again. *"I tried to reach you,"* he said urgently. *"I tried over and over. But you shut me out for so long, for so many years. Don't shut me out now, Rachel, please, it's so important. Listen. You must listen to me. . . ."*

And then somebody was laughing, and someone else was calling her name with Thomas's voice, and in the distance she could hear something else, a rustling sound that made her skin crawl.

Then she smelled something like rotten eggs, and the voice that sounded like Thomas whispered, *"Run, Rachel. Get out. Hurry. Don't trust—"*

She sat straight up in bed as the alarm buzzed insistently on her nightstand, and stared around the room with wide eyes.

Morning sunlight slanted in, brightening the room. A slight breeze lazily moved the curtains. The alarm clock buzzed.

She was awake.

Rachel turned off the alarm and got up, trying to shake off the dream. She didn't believe in signs and portents, and certainly not in the clairvoyance of dreams. What she did believe was that her uncertainty about her feelings for Adam, her confusion about two men who looked so much alike, had followed her into sleep.

That was all.

She showered and dressed, and her morning routine soon pushed the dream into the back of her mind. Breakfast, with Uncle Cam and Fiona sniping at each other. The arrival of Darby and her guys, all briskly determined to get as much accomplished as possible on this Friday.

Rachel left them to it. Though she wasn't quite sure how it had happened, she had somehow, during yesterday's lunch, invited Adam to meet her at the real estate office that morning, where more keys awaited her. There were two more stores she wanted to check out, and he was going to keep her company while she did.

Or something like that.

She didn't even bother to chide herself, especially once she reached the real estate office and saw Adam waiting for her.

He isn't Thomas. That isn't why.

"So where are we going today?" he asked when she emerged from the office with keys.

"Two more stores. One on Evans, and the other on Claiborne. Unless you know the city better than I think you do, I'll drive."

"Fine by me," he said agreeably.

They left his rental car parked there, where it would remain until they returned the keys later, and were quickly on their way to the first of the two addresses. As the day before, Adam was a pleasant companion, casual and humorous, keeping her mind occupied with unimportant things. He told her a funny story about the room service waiter he'd had the night before, and another about a hotel message system that had suddenly gone nuts and notified him every ten minutes for more than an hour that he had a call from someone in Cairo.

"I gather you don't know anybody in Cairo?"

"Not the one in Egypt, no. The hotel finally pulled the plug on their system and sent me champagne as an apology. I decided to save it for later. In case I want to celebrate something."

Rachel let that pass. "Good idea. Let's see . . . I think the first address is just ahead. . . ."

It was, and they didn't have to get out of the car. The store was obviously tiny, and the seedy pawnshop next door argued against the sort of upscale image Rachel had in mind.

"I don't think so," she said.

"No, I'd agree. Onward."

More casual conversation occupied them for another five minutes, until they reached the second address.

"Possible." Rachel stood beside the car and studied the storefront. It was just about the right size, and the neighborhood was a good one. The only drawback she could see was that the store, with parking on one side and a narrow street on the other, seemed isolated.

"Which could be a good thing," Adam suggested when she brought that up. "Make you look even more exclusive."

"Umm. Let's take a look inside."

The key stuck a bit, but finally turned with a faint click, and they went into the store. It was a very plain space, virtually unfinished, with concrete floors and white block walls, and their footsteps echoed hollowly. An interior wall held a single door, which presumably led to either office or storage space in the back.

"Not much personality," Adam noted.

"No, but that could be—" Rachel caught a faint whiff of an odor like rotten eggs, and a chill chased up and down her spine. It was what she had smelled in her dream. "Do you smell something?"

Even before he spoke, Adam was grabbing her hand. "Gas. Let's get out of here. *Move,* Rachel."

He hadn't shouted, and didn't seem to move hastily, yet Adam had her outside the store in seconds.

Seconds later, the whole world seemed to blow up.

S I X

T he storage room was bigger than it looked, and it was full of gas." Adam's voice was level. "That's why the explosion was so big even though we barely smelled the stuff."

Rachel winced as the paramedic stuck a small Band-Aid on the cut on her cheek. As hard as she tried, she couldn't quite keep her voice as steady as his. "Will there be enough of the building left for them to figure out what caused the spark?"

Before Adam could reply to that, a plainclothes cop approached them, notebook in hand. "Miss Grant? If you're up to it, I'd like to ask you a few questions now."

He had talked to Adam before, while Rachel was being checked out in the paramedics' van.

"I'm fine," she said, but she was grateful for Adam's quick hand helping her out of the van, and glad he kept an arm around her shoulders. She felt more than a little shaky, and she would undoubtedly be stiff and sore tomorrow from all the bruises, since she and Adam had been thrown to the pavement by the force of the explosion.

Fire department personnel were still milling around, but the explosion had been so ferocious that there had actually been little fire. There was also little left of the store, except for a few yards of the side walls and a very large heap of rubble from the collapsed roof.

"I have Mr. Delafield's statement," Detective James said. "It's pretty clear. Did you see or hear anything unusual, Miss Grant? Before the explosion?"

"No."

"Did you notice anyone lurking around the store, or walking away quickly?"

"No." She frowned, the idea occurring to her for the first time with a sharp chill. "You don't think it was an accident?"

The detective shrugged. "Well, Miss Grant, we've had some arson in this area, and several times the target was a vacant store. That's the most likely answer. We think a valve was opened, and that doesn't happen by accident."

"What about the spark?"

"There are some fairly easy tricks to set up a delayed spark, and most arsonists know them all. We'll find enough evidence to be sure of just how he did it." He shook his head. "Bad luck that you two happened to be looking at the store today."

"Yes." Her voice was hollow. "Very bad luck."

Adam's arm tightened around her.

"I'm going to give you one of my cards," Detective James said, "so you can call me if you think of anything else. You might have seen something you don't remember right now—a person or thing out of place, something like that. Give me a call if you do."

She accepted the card. "I will."

Adam asked, "May we go now?"

"Sure. I have your numbers if I need to get in touch."

Rachel took one last glance at the smoldering ruin, then walked with Adam back to her car, which had narrowly escaped getting a huge dent when a chunk of concrete had fallen near it. She didn't object when Adam took her to the passenger side, and even managed a smile when he spoke.

"This time I'll drive."

He turned the heater on when he got in, and Rachel realized only then that she was shivering.

"I'm all right," she said.

"You're in shock." Adam's tone was quite pleasant, but there was a note underneath that sounded almost savage.

She glanced at him, hearing the latter and wondering at it. "Accidents happen. We were just in the wrong place at the wrong time."

"Yeah—but this was no accident. Some sorry bastard took the idea of playing with matches way too far. A few more seconds . . ."

"We got out," she reminded him. "Whole and pretty much unharmed."

"Yeah." But he was obviously unconvinced of that. He drove only a couple of blocks, pulling over to the curb in front of a coffee shop. "I'll be right back."

"Okay." Rachel watched him get out and shut the door, then turned her gaze forward and her attention to the worried questions in her mind.

Obviously, the explosion had been no accident. But there was no reason for her to assume she had been the target. People committed arson with depressing frequency, and that cop had even said it had happened several times in the area recently.

So it *was* just bad luck that she had stopped by that day to look at the store.

Nothing more than that.

Besides, how could she have been a target? No one had known where she would be today except the Realtor, and since that very nice lady had pulled the addresses out of her file only that morning, there had hardly been time for lethal plans—even if she had been so inclined.

Which was, of course, ridiculous.

Still, Rachel was uneasy. The cut brake line loomed much larger now with this second "accident" following so soon after it.

She didn't know what to think. Or what to believe. All she really knew was that she was very glad Adam had been with her. She doubted she would have reacted so quickly to the gas if she'd been alone. And though it had all happened too fast for her to be sure, she had the hazy idea that he had shielded her as they'd fallen, his thick leather jacket withstanding some flying debris that would have easily torn through her linen blazer.

He had probably saved her life.

And since he had been with her every minute from the time she'd gotten the addresses, he had certainly not been the one to rig the explosion.

The relief of that was overwhelming.

Adam returned to the car just then and handed her a steaming cup. "Tea. Hot and sweet. Drink it, Rachel."

"Good thing I like tea," she murmured, sipping.

He smiled suddenly. "Am I being high-handed? Sorry. I'm not usually a bully, I promise you. Just worried at the moment."

"I'm fine. Really." She did her best to sound convincing despite her awareness that only her death grip on the cup was keeping her hands from shaking visibly.

He looked at her steadily for a moment, then nodded and put the car in gear. "Okay. But I don't want you driving today, so I'll take you home."

"Your car—"

"I'll call a cab to take me back to the real estate office, and I'll turn the keys in. It's no problem, Rachel."

She decided not to argue with him. For one thing, she was pretty sure he'd made up his mind. For another, it was pleasant to let herself drift while someone else made the decisions for a while.

She drank her tea.

They were almost at her house, when Adam spoke abruptly. "I get the feeling something's worrying you about that explosion. Am I wrong?"

Rachel hesitated, but reminded herself that he couldn't possibly have had anything to do with the explosion. "That car accident I had last week. The mechanic thinks the brake line was cut."

Adam shot her a quick, hard look. "Are you saying somebody's trying to hurt you?"

"I don't know. Hurt me, scare me. Maybe. I just can't think of a reason why anybody would want to do either."

"Hurt you or scare you? You could have been killed today, Rachel."

She flinched a little, and stared at her half-finished tea. "You heard that cop. There's been arson in the area. Besides, nobody could have known I'd be there just then. Nobody."

"That makes sense," he said slowly. "Not even the Realtor could have known for sure which store we'd check out first. It took some time for the gas to build up, time to set up some gadget to cause a spark. We were inside no more than a couple of minutes before we smelled the gas."

"So—it couldn't have had anything to do with me."

"I don't believe in coincidence," he said.

"In this case, you'll have to. It can't be anything else." She was arguing with herself as well as him.

"Maybe. Just promise me you'll be careful from now on, Rachel. Very careful."

"You bet," she said lightly, and watched the tea slosh around inside her cup.

"I'd like to know why the hell I had to hear about this from the police, Rachel." Graham was definitely upset, and didn't try to hide it.

Rachel sat on the edge of her bed with a sigh. She'd just been about to go soak in a hot tub in a hopeful attempt to ward off soreness tomorrow, having finally escaped the anxious attention of Fiona and Cam. Adam had remained just long enough for his cab to arrive.

"I'm sorry, Graham. I would have called as soon as I had a chance to catch my breath. But why did the police call you?"

"They always call me whenever anything happens involving the Grant family. Are you all right?"

"I'm fine." She was getting tired of saying it, especially since it wasn't true. "Although, if it hadn't been for Adam, I wouldn't be."

"So he was Johnny on the spot again."

"He probably saved my life, Graham. I wouldn't have moved fast enough to get out of there, not without him."

"I don't trust him, Rachel. And I sure as hell don't like this explosion coming barely a week after your car's brake lines were cut."

"It was just a bizarre accident. No one could have known I'd be at that particular store at that particular moment." She kept repeating that fact like a mantra.

"Delafield was always with you? He didn't excuse himself for a few minutes at any point?"

"No."

Graham was silent for a moment, then repeated, "I don't trust him."

"You checked him out, didn't you? Like you said you would?" She rubbed her forehead slowly and thought longingly of a bath and peace.

Again, Graham hesitated. "I did. The company exists. Delafield Design. It was founded about five years ago. It *appears* to be successful."

"Then he told me the truth."

"Maybe. Or maybe he just told you some of the truth. His background information is too damned sketchy for my taste. I'm going to keep digging."

Rachel sighed. "Fine. You do that. In the meantime, I'm going to go soak a few bruises away. Good-bye, Graham." She hung up without waiting for a response.

She was accustomed to Graham's caution, knew it came from affection and concern, and sincerely valued his opinions—but this time he was taking things too far. She could trust Adam.

He'd saved her life, hadn't he?

Mercy hung up the phone and gazed across the kitchen at Nicholas, who was clearing up the remains of the Chinese takeout they'd had for dinner. "You heard?"

"Your half of the conversation, yeah. So Rachel's all right?"

"I think so. What do you know about this Adam Delafield she says probably saved her life?"

Nicholas dumped several empty cartons in the trash and turned to look at her. "We knew each other a long time ago."

"That's what Rachel said. That you two were old friends." She left it there, but watched him steadily from her stool at the breakfast bar.

Nicholas came to the bar and poured fresh wine for both of them. "It isn't a long story, love. About ten years ago Adam worked for a design firm I did some business with."

"Had you known him before that?"

Nicholas shrugged massive shoulders. "As a matter of fact, I had. We first met about fifteen years ago. He was in college. We had some mutual interests, and a mutual friend introduced us."

Mercy smiled wryly. "You'd think I'd learn."

"Learn what?"

"Not to ask questions about your past."

His brows rose in surprise, carving deep furrows in his forehead. "There's just nothing to say that would interest you, love."

"I have my doubts about that, but never mind. What do you think about this explosion?"

"That they're damned lucky they got out in time."

"Don't you think there's something strange going on? I mean, a week ago Rachel practically wraps her car around a tree, and today she's nearly blown to smithereens. She went twenty-nine years without so much as a sprained ankle—and now this? Am I the only one who thinks this is something more than just a bad week?"

Nicholas sipped his wine for a moment, studying her with one of his more enigmatic gazes. "What are you suggesting?"

"I don't know." Mercy shrugged helplessly. "I can't imagine anyone wanting to hurt Rachel, can you?"

"No."

"Nick, something's going on."

"Two violent accidents in one week is a bizarre coincidence, I admit. But how could it be more than that?"

Mercy hesitated, then said, "Rachel wrecked her car because the brake lines had been cut. Deliberately."

"How do you know that?" Nicholas was intent, but not frowning.

"Rachel told me. Graham's gone all suspicious of your pal Adam, but so far he isn't convincing Rachel, especially after today. But somebody cut that brake line. Somebody wanted to hurt Rachel. Or scare her."

"Scare her? What would be the point?"

"To make her go back to New York, maybe. How should I know?"

Nicholas shook his head. "The explosion might have been arson, but it doesn't appear to have been aimed at anyone in particular. Rachel and Adam were just in the wrong place at the wrong time. As for the cut brake lines—even the best mechanic can make a mistake, and brake lines have been known to fail without helping hands. There's no solid evidence either occurrence was anything more than an accident, love."

Mercy knew when she'd lost an argument, especially with this man. She sighed. "Okay, okay. But I'm worried."

"You told Rachel to be careful. What else can you do?"

"Worry." She smiled.

He came around the bar and lifted her easily off the stool. "I can think of a few better things to occupy your attention."

As always, she felt engulfed in his embrace, blissfully wrapped in warmth and strength. "I'm certainly open to suggestion," she murmured, tilting her head back to smile up at him.

"Good." He lifted her completely off her feet with an ease that never failed to astonish her, and carried her through the sparsely furnished apartment toward his bedroom.

Mercy spared a passing moment to consider the bland color scheme and minimalist decor, and sighed. "You've got to get more furniture."

"Why?"

He had a point. He never entertained here that she knew of, and there were enough chairs—and a big enough bed—for two, so what did it matter?

"Never mind," she said. "The next time I'm out shopping I'll find you a plant or two, and maybe a rug. . . ."

·   ·   ·

When the phone on his nightstand rang a couple of hours later, Nicholas reached over so quickly that he got the receiver in hand before the first ring finished. "Yeah?"

Half asleep, Mercy heard only his side of the brief conversation, but it was enough to bring her fully awake.

"You fucked up," Nicholas said. His voice was low. It was also unpleasant. He listened for a moment, then added, "I'll call you tomorrow." And replaced the receiver in its cradle.

"Trouble?" She made sure her voice was drowsy.

"Nothing I can't handle. Tomorrow." Nicholas shifted slightly and put a hand under her chin to tilt her face up. "Are you going to sleep all evening?"

"I was just resting my eyes," she explained.

"Are they rested?"

"I think so."

He kissed her, taking his time about it. One big hand was wrapped gently around her throat, while the other one pushed the covers down and began a leisurely wandering.

Mercy tried her best not to purr out loud.

"How would you like to spend the whole weekend in here with me?" he murmured, his mouth replacing his hand on her throat.

She heard an odd sound, and thought it was probably her, purring. She cleared her throat. "What? The whole weekend? In bed?"

"Why not?" His mouth moved lower.

Mercy clutched a handful of sheet at her hip. "Um . . . it sounds . . . very hedonistic." The words were followed by another of those throaty murmurs, and she felt a vague embarrassment. Damn the man, did he *have* to reduce her to incoherent sounds?

His laugh against her skin was a caressing rumble. "I like that word. Shall we be hedonists?"

She let go of the sheet and clutched at him. "Nick, for God's sake—stop *talking.*"

With another laugh, he did.

Rachel was in her father's study on Saturday morning, when a still-unnerved Fiona announced Adam and quickly retreated, crossing herself once again.

"Hello," Rachel said. "I didn't expect to see you today."

"I don't want to make a nuisance of myself," he said, coming toward her. "But I thought maybe I could take you to lunch?"

She had been working at the drafting table and sent a surprised look at her watch. "It's nearly noon? I had no idea." After a virtually sleepless night it had taken her hours and another hot bath to work most of the stiffness and soreness out of her body; her unsettled thoughts and emotions had been far less easy to tame, and only fierce concentration on this work had steadied her somewhat. But she knew her control was uncertain at best.

"Looks like you've been busy." He nodded toward the sketches on the table. "Designs for the new store?"

"Yes."

"So you're going forward with the scheme?"

"Of course."

He shifted a bit restlessly and jammed his hands into the pockets of his jacket. "I guess it'd be useless to ask you to put off moving on that for a while?"

"Until?"

"Until the police have the fire marshal's report on the explosion. Until I can nose around a bit, ask some questions."

Rachel frowned at him. "Ask who what kind of questions?"

"I'm not entirely sure. Yet. But I know I'd like to talk to the mechanic who examined your car. Maybe to your lawyer."

"Why him?"

"You come home to settle your parents' estate and things start happening. Maybe there's no connection—and maybe there is. Maybe something your father was involved in has survived him."

"My father had no enemies."

"Rachel, every rich man has enemies."

She shook her head, but instead of arguing, said, "I don't think you want to talk to Graham. He . . . wouldn't be very forthcoming."

"Most lawyers aren't. But I'm sure he has your best interests at heart."

"Adam, I appreciate your concern, but—"

"But it isn't any of my business?"

She hesitated. "I wasn't going to say that. It's just . . . I don't need a watchdog. Or a bloodhound, for that matter. I don't believe anyone's trying to hurt me. Just accidents, that's all."

"Rachel, I know I'm a virtual stranger to you, and there's no reason on earth why you should listen to me. Except one."

"Which is?"

"I'm asking you to."

After a moment, Rachel moved away from him to lean against

the edge of her father's desk. She was still shaky, and hoped he couldn't see it. "Okay. I'm listening."

Instead of coming toward her, he respected the distance she had put between them and remained by her drafting table. "Look, I don't know if there's someone out there who's a threat to you. All I do know is that both of us will feel better when we eliminate the possibility. And the only way to do that is to find a few answers."

She shook her head slightly. "Suppose the mechanic tells you he's positive the brake line was cut. What then?"

"Then we try to find out who had access to the car between the last time it was safely driven and when you got in."

"And if the fire marshal's report says the explosion was arson?"

"Then we try to find out who was seen near the building yesterday morning before we arrived."

"But that won't tell us if I was meant to be a target."

"It will if we find the arsonist."

"Isn't that for the police to do?"

"The police have a city to take care of. We can focus entirely on you."

Rachel shook her head again. "Adam, I'm not a cop. Or any kind of investigator."

"I know that. I'm not either. But I know how to find answers. All I'm asking is that you let me try."

"I thought you were going back to California."

"Not for a while." He looked at her steadily. "A staff I trust is running the company for me. Anything I have to do I can do by phone and fax, or with my laptop. Right now this is more important to me."

Rachel asked the question before she could stop herself. "Why?"

"I could say it's because you're the daughter of the man I owe everything to."

"You could. Would it be true?" At that moment, she forgot about being sore and shaky and afraid.

"Partly."

Rachel shied away from pressing for anything further. She wasn't sure she wanted to know the answer.

"All right, I'll accept that. For now."

"And you'll let me try to find out what's going on?"

She smiled briefly. "I get the feeling I couldn't stop you if I tried. But you can forget about talking to Graham. He wouldn't tell you anything about Dad's business. Or mine, for that matter."

Adam frowned. "Have you gone through Duncan's personal papers yet?"

Rachel glanced over her shoulder at the huge desk. "I barely made a start. A few letters so far. There's an awful lot packed into this desk. I think Dad kept every scrap of paper he wrote a note on. And I haven't even gotten that far with the little desk in his bedroom."

Slowly, Adam said, "I know you want to go forward with your plans for the store, Rachel. And I know it's . . . less painful to postpone going through your father's things. But it needs to be done."

"You're so sure the answer's there? That my father made an enemy so vicious that now he's after me?"

"I think we have to rule it out. Rachel, none of us ever knows all the secrets of the people we're close to. I'm absolutely positive your father was an honorable man, and if he ever broke the law, it would come as a shock to me. But he was a wealthy man who dealt with a wide range of people. It isn't beyond the realm of possibility that he got involved in something that became dangerous. That he might have made an enemy."

Reluctantly, Rachel nodded. "I accept that. But an enemy coming after me now? I can't believe that."

"The explosion—"

"A random arsonist. You heard what the police said."

Before she could continue, the phone on her father's desk rang. With a slight smile of apology, Rachel went around to sit in the swivel chair and answer the call.

"Hello?"

"Miss Grant?"

"Yes?"

"Miss Grant, this is Sharon Wilkins, from the real estate office. I just wanted to call you and say how horrified we are about that explosion."

"A random arsonist," Rachel said lightly. "None of you could have known it was going to happen, Sharon. It's just a shame the building's gone now."

"Yes—but at least it was insured." The agent's voice became brisk. "Miss Grant, I didn't want to bother you, on a Saturday and all, but I did want to assure you that if you do lease a property we're representing, we'll make sure security is part of the package."

"Thanks, Sharon. As a matter of fact, I've made up my mind. I want to lease the store on Queen Street." She was aware of Adam moving restlessly, but didn't look at him. "So if you could get the papers ready?"

"Absolutely. I can have everything ready for your signature by Monday afternoon."

"Great."

"I'll see you then. Oh—and, Miss Grant?"

"Yes?"

"Did your friend find you?"

"My friend?"

"Yes. He called here just after you left yesterday morning, very eager to talk to you."

Rachel felt a slow chill crawl up her spine. "So—you told him what stores I was going to be looking at? The addresses?"

"Well, yes." Sharon's voice became anxious. "I just assumed— He knew all about your plans for a boutique, and I assumed he was somehow working with you. If I did the wrong thing—"

"No." Rachel cleared her throat. "No, of course not. And, yes—he found me. I'll see you Monday, Sharon."

Gently, she hung up the phone.

"Rachel?"

She looked at Adam, vaguely surprised to find that he had come around the desk and knelt beside her chair. "The strangest thing."

"Someone knew where you'd be yesterday? Is that what she told you?" His voice was grim.

"Yes. Someone called the real estate office. A man. He knew about the boutique idea. So she told him."

"So that explosion could have been meant for you."

Rachel drew a breath.

And for the first time, she really believed it.

It was very possible that someone wanted her dead.

S E V E N

A dam wanted to take her to lunch, but Rachel was too shaken by the phone call, and he didn't press her. Instead, Fiona brought soup and sandwiches to the library. Rachel hardly touched the meal, but she was able to get the shakes under control by the time she pushed her plate away.

"Stop watching me," she told him. "I'm fine."

"I wasn't watching you, I was looking at you." He smiled slightly. "Don't ask me to stop doing that. And you're not fine. You wouldn't be human if you weren't scared and worried."

"I just can't quite get my mind around the idea that someone might want to kill me."

"We still don't know that for sure," he said, now playing devil's advocate. "Whoever called the real estate office may have really wanted to see you. Maybe he got there after the explosion, and didn't try to approach you in all the confusion."

"I don't know who it would have been."

"How about Graham Becket?"

Instantly, Rachel shook her head. "He wouldn't have told Sharon he was my friend. He would have said he was my attorney." She smiled. "He likes the sound of it."

Adam leaned his forearms on the desk they were using as a dining table. "Can you think of anyone else? Any reason why someone would have wanted to find you yesterday?"

"No. No one who knew about the plans for the boutique. That's where the list gets really short."

"Me," he said.

"Yes, but—logically—you were with me the whole time. Graham knows. My uncle Cam. Nicholas Ross. Any of them could have told someone else, but why would they?"

"Maybe we'd better ask."

Rachel grimaced. "Why don't you ask Nick? I mean, since you two are friends. He unnerves me."

"I can deal with Nick," Adam said.

"I'll ask Cam later. And call Graham."

Reluctantly, Adam said, "Do you suspect any of them?"

She didn't immediately say no. Instead, she replied with a carefully maintained detachment. "I have a will. Or, rather, a trust. It was updated after Mom and Dad were killed. If I were to die anytime soon, childless, Cam would get the house and contents. Nick would get my shares in the bank. Graham would get a relatively small bequest, some beach property. Is any of that enough to kill for?"

Adam reached across the desk and took her hand. "I don't think that's it, Rachel. This all started when you came home to Richmond to settle your father's estate. I think we have to look there first."

She looked down at his hand and, almost absently, said, "It's taken months to sort out Dad's business affairs at the bank. Sorting out his personal affairs could take just as long."

"I'm not going anywhere."

"You know, you don't have to feel obligated to do this. To watch over me. No matter what Dad did for you, he wouldn't expect—"

"Rachel."

She looked up and met his gaze. That was very different from Thomas, that gaze. The color of his eyes, their intensity. There was something in them that made her breath catch in the back of her throat.

His fingers tightened around hers. "Tell me not to say it. Tell me you're not ready to hear it."

Nobody had ever looked at her like that before. Not even Thomas. For just an instant, she hesitated, almost not breathing. But then she leaned back in her chair and very gently pulled her hand from his grasp. Her heart was pounding, and she didn't know if it was excitement or terror. "I'm not ready. Adam, we barely know each other—"

"I know all I need to know." But he was smiling faintly, that naked look in his eyes gone now. Or hidden. "But I also know you need time."

"Yes. It's an understatement to say there's a lot going on in my life right now. The timing is—"

"Lousy. Yeah, I know. Rachel, listen to me. I won't push. I

learned a long time ago how to be patient. And I am not going to let anything happen to you. All right?"

She nodded slowly, conscious that her heart was still thudding against her ribs, that it was still difficult to catch her breath. "All right."

"Good. Now—why don't I get out of here and leave you alone. We need to start asking those questions."

"Right," she murmured. "Questions."

"Did I tell anyone about your plans to open a boutique?" Graham raised a surprised brow. "Until I heard about the explosion, I hadn't even been aware that you were serious enough about the idea to be looking at property. Why would I have told anyone?"

"It was just a question, Graham." She kept her voice casual, but gazed steadily across the desk at him. For this, she had wanted to be face-to-face, and so had driven into town after Adam had left. Graham was always in his office on Saturday afternoons. "Somebody called the real estate office just after I left there yesterday morning, looking for me. Somebody who knew I was thinking of opening a boutique. So I just wondered if you'd told anyone."

"No."

"And you weren't looking for me yourself?" She knew he hadn't been but asked anyway.

"No. I think I would have mentioned it when we talked after the explosion. Of course, since you hung up on me—"

"I didn't do that."

"As good as. I tried to call you around lunchtime. Fiona said you were shut up in Duncan's library with Adam Delafield."

Rachel had let the housekeeper take that call when the phone had rung partway through their meal. She had still been too upset to talk to anyone, and knew Fiona would have told her if the call had been important. Unfortunately, Fiona had always had a soft spot for Graham and was, Rachel sometimes thought, a tad too willing to tell him everything that went on in the Grant household.

"We had lunch."

"It obviously wouldn't do me any good to ask you again to stay away from him until I get the background information on him."

"That wasn't a question. But the answer is no."

Graham scowled. "I don't trust him, Rachel."

"You've said that before. But, so far, you haven't shown me any reason not to trust him." She kept her voice quiet and even, knowing that Graham's concern was sincere. "Graham, he probably saved my life. Dad trusted him enough to lend him three million dollars on a handshake—"

"Or so he says."

"And I like him," she finished defiantly.

Graham's face closed down into its lawyerly expression of detachment. "Which, of course, has nothing to do with the fact that he could be Thomas Sheridan's twin."

That wasn't something Rachel wanted to hear, but she managed to meet his eyes steadily. "I don't know if it does or not. But I'd like the chance to find out."

"And the fact that during the week after he appeared in your life you had two rather violent close calls doesn't bother you?"

"Of course it bothers me." Rachel kept her voice matter-of-fact, reluctant to encourage Graham in any way to overreact. "In fact, it should relieve you to know that Adam is just as concerned. He thinks Dad may have made an enemy who has some reason to want me out of the way."

Clearly hesitant to agree with Adam, Graham said, "Rich men do make enemies. But even if that were true, I can't imagine why it would carry over to you."

"I can't either." Rachel frowned. "Unless it has something to do with the bank. I haven't decided what to do about my shares yet. Maybe somebody's trying to . . . encourage me to sell out."

"You suspect Nick Ross?"

Rachel barely hesitated before shaking her head. "Not really. He has enough control at the bank to do virtually whatever he wants, with or without my shares. I've told him I won't interfere, and I meant it. I think he knows that. As a matter of fact, he told me that if I intended to keep my shares, he'd advise me to hire Mercy to manage them for me."

"I don't see who else would benefit if you gave up your shares."

"Graham, it's just a possibility. That's all I have right now, possibilities. I can't be sure of anything. I don't know, for a fact, that either of those two . . . violent close calls were specifically intended to injure me. The brake line *could* have failed by accident, and the arson of that building *could* have been completely random. I just don't know."

"You know enough to be careful."

"That's more or less what Adam said."

Again Graham didn't appear thrilled to be in agreement with Adam. "It's common sense, Rachel. You shouldn't even have driven into town alone today. And where's your car parked? In the secure lot, or—"

"Out front," she murmured.

Graham picked up his phone and called a cab. "Leave the keys to the lease here. I'll get another car sent out to you. And when I do, promise me you won't leave it in *any* unsecured area."

Rachel pushed the car keys across the desk to him. "All right."

"Will you also promise me you'll try to stick close to home for a while? Until we know more?"

She avoided the promise by saying, "What do you expect to know? More about Adam's background?"

"Among other things."

"What other things?"

"I intend to go through my copies of Duncan's business papers. Contracts and the like."

"You've been all through those to settle the estate."

"Yes, but I wasn't looking for any reason someone might want you out of the way. This time I will."

Rachel nodded and stood up. "Okay. You do that. I'm due to sign a lease on the store on Queen Street Monday."

"Bring it to me before you sign."

She grimaced slightly, but nodded again. "In the meantime, I'm going to start going through Dad's personal papers. Maybe I'll turn up something."

"Just be careful, Rachel, all right?"

"You bet."

When he was alone again, Graham sat for a long time in his silent office, gazing at nothing. Then he reached for his phone.

When the car pulled over to the curb, Adam moved out of the shadows and got into the passenger side.

"Did we *have* to meet so late?" the driver complained. "I should be at home in bed. And why this shitty neighborhood? Jesus, I don't dare turn off the engine or I'll find my tires slashed. Or missing."

"Will you stop bitching, Mike, and show me what you've got?"

Mike reached inside his dark raincoat and pulled out a small plastic bag. "Here. And if they find it missing from the evidence locker before I can get it back, my job is history. When you call in a favor, you don't mess around, do you?"

Adam ignored the question. "This is what the fire marshal found?"

"That's it. Arson for damn sure."

Instead of turning on the dome light, Adam removed a penlight from inside his jacket and used that to slowly examine the charred bits of metal and melted plastic inside the bag.

"Any suspects?"

Mike shook his head. "Nah. The other arsons in the area were started with plain old gasoline and a match. What's left of this thing shows a lot more imagination, according to the experts. And a lot more expertise. State-of-the-art sparking mechanism, says our guy. And probably on some kind of timer. But those bits and pieces don't match up with any unsolved explosions or arsons in the computer."

Adam grunted.

"You see something different? I mean, I know you're some kind of electrical wizard and all."

"No," Adam said. "I don't see anything different." He turned off the penlight. "Guess there's no chance of me keeping this for a while."

"Hey, pal, I don't owe you *that* big."

Adam returned the bag to him. "No problem. But I would . . . appreciate a copy of the fire marshal's report."

Mike groaned. "Christ, you're gonna get me fired."

"Just a copy. You can get it."

"Yeah, yeah. I'll see what I can do."

"Thanks, Mike."

Mike peered through the gloom at Adam. "You want to tell me what all this is about?"

"I'm just keeping an eye on a friend, that's all."

"Rachel Grant? That's some friend, pal. Most any man in Richmond would just love to be keeping an eye on her."

Adam shifted slightly in his seat, but all he said was "Anybody suspicious of this on her account?"

"You mean does anybody think your girl was meant to end up on a slab?"

"Something like that."

"Not that I've heard. She was just in the wrong place at the wrong time, is the thinking. Why? You know something we don't?"

"No. Just wondering."

Mike grunted. "If it comes to that, I would have thought you were a more likely target for an *accidental* death than Rachel Grant. You've made more than your fair share of enemies."

"Yeah. But not in Richmond."

"Oh, I think you might have one or two even here."

Adam turned his head to stare at him. "Oh?"

"Yeah. Saw an old . . . friend of yours the other day."

"Who?"

"Max Galloway."

"Son of a bitch."

"He's all of that. And a loose cannon into the bargain. I don't pretend to know what he's doing in Richmond, but you can bet your last dollar it's nothing good."

"Can you find out?"

"Only if he breaks the law, draws attention to himself. He isn't likely to do that. The Richmond cops don't know him. Except for me, of course, because I used to work in California."

"Maybe you'd better warn them."

"Yeah. Maybe I will. And you watch your back, Adam. Galloway never made it a secret that he hated your guts. Maybe he followed you here to finally do something about it."

Adam didn't say anything to that, and when he opened the car door, the dome light showed no change in his calm expression. "Thanks for giving me a look at the evidence, Mike. I'll wait for your call about the fire marshal's report."

"Give me a few days."

"Right." Adam got out of the car and shut the door.

Mike didn't waste any time in leaving the neighborhood.

Adam turned up the collar of his jacket, conscious of the chilly mist that was drifting in, and began walking slowly along the littered sidewalk. Blocks away from The Tavern, the area was desolate, mostly deserted. The only sounds were the rustle of trash skittering over the pavement and his own quiet footsteps.

Max Galloway.

Patterns of fate? Threads of destiny? How else to explain it?

And how long had that violent enemy been in Richmond? Maybe waiting. Maybe watching.

Maybe acting.

Rachel.

Automatically, his hand lifted to touch the slight bulge of the locket beneath his shirt. Its presence did nothing to reassure him.

Max Galloway.

Rachel.

Jesus.

Adam quickened his pace.

Rachel came out of her bathroom on Sunday morning and stopped dead in her bedroom. For just a moment she could have sworn she had once again caught the elusive scent of the cologne Thomas had always worn. But even as she sniffed, it was gone.

Oh, of course it was gone. Because it hadn't been there at all.

Just my imagination.

She sat down at her dressing table and began brushing her hair, an unseeing gaze fixed on the mirror. With that imagined scent had come a rush of memories, and she had no choice but to endure them. Thomas, teasing her because it turned out the men's cologne she had fallen in love with was what the TV commercials insisted women dreamed of their men wearing when they came home from the sea. It was not something *he* would have chosen to wear, but he had worn it for her. He had always worn it.

Thomas hiding little notes and presents for her, here in the house and out in the garden, laughing at her when she couldn't find one. His voice whispering words of love. His promises . . .

He wasn't very good at keeping his promises.

When that thought occurred, it felt so much a betrayal that Rachel was jerked from the daydreaming. She focused on her face in the mirror, saw her cheeks were wet. Slowly, she wiped the tears away.

He hadn't been very good at keeping his promises. And not only the last one. Thomas had more than once made a careless promise, only to find himself unable to keep it later. He had always been sincerely apologetic—she thought—but it occurred to her for the first time that the character trait might well have made him a less than perfect husband.

The realization unnerved Rachel. She got up from her vanity table and went to dress, and it wasn't until she was ready to leave the room that she saw the rose. It lay on her pillow, a single yellow rose so fresh there was still a drop of dew on a satiny petal.

Rachel's first reaction as she picked up the flower was simply one of pleasure. She loved flowers, especially yellow roses. But then she realized that there was something very strange about this. Where had it come from? The flower hadn't been there when she had gone to shower half an hour before. So who could have come in and placed it on the pillow? It was still early; Cam was a late sleeper, and Fiona was far too brusque for something like this— even if there had been a yellow rose in the garden to pick. There wasn't.

She stood there, staring at the rose, baffled and uneasy.

It was after noon on Sunday before Rachel could finally bring herself to sit down at her father's desk one more time. She would have preferred to do something else. Almost anything else. But suspecting that somebody was trying to frighten—or kill—her was even more painful than facing her father's memory.

At least, she hoped that was true.

For the first hour or so, she occupied herself by sorting through what she found in the two top drawers and placing them in reason-ably neat piles atop the desk. Her father's day planner was put to one side so she could go through it at her leisure; what looked like personal correspondence was stacked together; pens, paper clips, and other standard supplies; endless scraps of paper with sometimes cryptic notes in her father's hand; quite a bit of business correspondence unrelated to the bank; stacks of business cards.

And two small notebooks detailing deposits and withdrawals.

To and from a bank in Geneva, Switzerland.

Rachel placed one of the notebooks on the blotter and began slowly to thumb through the other. Her hands were shaking.

The deposits and withdrawals went back more than twenty years. Some were fairly small. Most were large, into six and even seven figures.

Millions. Millions had gone through the accounts.

After the first shock had passed, Rachel found a legal pad and a sharpened pencil and began doing some figuring. It took some time, but she gradually realized that there was a pattern to the deposits and withdrawals.

Over the first five years there had been only deposits made, until the total reached just over ten million dollars. After that, each year there was never more than a single withdrawal, though there was sometimes more than one deposit. A million in, two hundred thousand out. Five hundred thousand in, two million out. Two hundred thousand in, a million out.

Slowly, Rachel found the matches. Each withdrawal was matched to the penny by a deposit at a later date. The account never held more than fifteen million dollars, and never held less than five.

When she looked more closely, Rachel saw that the note of each withdrawal contained a series of numbers and letters—always ending in two letters. Initials, she realized. And each set of initials for a withdrawal was matched by a set for a later deposit.

"Loans," she whispered as realization dawned.

The two notebooks contained a history of loans—or, as her father had undoubtedly called them, "investments"—made and repaid. Over the space of twenty years. With no paperwork except these simple figures kept in two little black leather notebooks.

"Rachel, that's not the way Duncan did business."

Graham had said that. And he was right. It hadn't been the way her father had done business, not for the bank. But for himself, it seemed, a handshake and these little notebooks had been enough.

And there it was—five years before, a three-million-dollar withdrawal. And the series of identifying numbers and letters ended with *AD*. It was a series not yet repeated in the notebook, because the loan had not yet been repaid.

Adam had told her the truth.

If he was who and what he claimed to be.

I trust him. Of course I do. And not because he looks like Thomas.

Her own doubts disturbed her as much as the existence of this notebook. And then another realization dawned and she bent over the notebooks and her legal pad and did more figuring.

The sum she arrived at left her feeling a bit light-headed.

Not counting the loan she assumed was Adam's, there were three loans still outstanding. One for a hundred and fifty thousand, one for one and a half million, and the last for five million. The initials were *RS, LM,* and *JW,* and the most recent loan—the largest—had been made just months before her father's death.

So there were three people who had been given loans by her father who had not yet come forward to repay them. The problem was, Rachel had no way of knowing when those loans had been set to come due. Adam had been lent his money five years ago; according to the notebooks, several other loans had run at least that long, and one for six years. For all she knew, these outstanding loans also had lengthy lives and simply weren't yet due to be repaid.

Of course, that didn't explain why those given the money hadn't sought her out, as Adam had, to promise repayment.

She knew what Graham would say, of course. That these three people were taking advantage of her father's trust, not coming forward in the hope that she would have no way of knowing what they owed.

She had no intention of telling Graham about this.

That was not as difficult a decision as Rachel had expected. It seemed to her that her father had kept this quiet and private because that was the way he had wanted it. For twenty years he had apparently helped people like Adam, people who had needed large sums of cash to achieve their dreams.

She doubted that Graham would appreciate that.

But she did.

That was an easy decision. There were several others to be made, however. By her calculations, even if the outstanding loans were not repaid, the account held upward of ten million dollars.

"Oh, wow, Dad. Now what do I do?"

It was a heartfelt question. For all she knew, her father's personal financial dealings, while undoubtedly noble, could well be illegal. She definitely knew that none of this money had been counted in his estate. Although, now that she thought about it, she vaguely remembered a phrase contained in the trust that went something like "deposits in any financial institution other than those in Duncan and Ross Investments, Ltd., to be transferred outright to my daughter, Rachel Grant."

Something like that.

So the money was, she assumed, legally hers. That was to say if any of this was legal . . .

She definitely foresaw a confidential visit to a specialist in taxes and estates in her near future.

She pushed that aside to be dealt with later. Until her father's estate was finally settled, the problem of this money could wait. What most concerned her at the present was the question of whether any of this held the answer to why someone might want her dead.

Maybe someone *really* didn't want to repay his or her loan.

Her first thought was that only the five-million-dollar loan might be motive enough for murder. But when she thought about it as dispassionately as possible, she realized that even the smallest loan, for a mere hundred and fifty thousand, could be worth murder.

It was all a matter of perspective. And from the right perspective, killing for a hundred dollars or even less could make sense.

That was a chilling thought.

Slowly, she circled the three outstanding entries on her legal pad.

Three people, any one of whom could have decided that killing Rachel would cancel their loan.

Three people with nothing to identify them for her except initials.

Three people with nothing to lose and everything to gain by her death.

Rachel opened the big black iron gate, its hinge creaking loudly, and began to follow the path toward the woods. It was misty, the fog rising from the ground and swirling as though stirred by a restless hand.

It was very quiet.

She was happy. Around her neck she wore the locket she had given Thomas, the one containing her picture and the St. Christopher that she had hoped would keep him safe.

She followed the path, oblivious of the mist. Of the chill. Her eyes were fixed ahead on the edge of the woods, where a figure waited.

He took shape out of the mist as she neared, a tall man with fair hair gleaming in the strange light. He smiled a welcoming smile. He held out his arms to her.

Rachel laughed and ran toward him.

But then, close enough to really see him, she faltered and stopped.

His face had become a mask of cracked porcelain, the eyeholes dark and empty. And from the gaping hole of the mouth, a hoarse voice whispered, "Don't trust him, Rachel. Don't trust him."

Worms began to ooze from the eyeholes of the mask.

Rachel screamed and screamed. . . .

Adam bolted upright in bed, a cry tangled and trapped in his throat. His heart was pounding violently, and his breathing rasped audibly. He looked around, his gaze stabbing into every corner of the hotel room that was lit by dawn's gray light.

Slowly, very slowly, he lay back on his pillows, lifting his hand to grasp the locket he wore.

"Oh, God, Rachel," he whispered.

EIGHT

F iona? You didn't leave a rose on my pillow yesterday morning, did you?"

The housekeeper looked blank. "A rose? Why would I do that, Miss Rachel?"

"Never mind." Rachel tried to laugh it off. "My imagination has been working overtime recently." Except that she hadn't imagined it. That rose was very real, and in a bud vase on her nightstand.

Fiona frowned, then shrugged and asked what she wanted for breakfast.

Rachel talked to Sharon at the real estate office after breakfast, and to save time had her messenger the lease agreement to Graham's office. Unless he found something wrong when he went over it, she could still sign it that day, and then the store would be hers. And during that process she wouldn't have to leave the house, which definitely appealed to her.

Whether someone was after her or not, remaining close to home for the time being seemed like a good idea.

In the meantime, with only a slight hesitation she called Adam. She considered calling Mercy, since her friend had always been the one she'd confided in, but something stopped her this time. Mercy didn't know about the loans. She knew that Adam claimed to be on the verge of repaying a private loan, but she had no idea of the extent of Duncan's private loans. And just as she had decided not to tell Graham, Rachel decided not to tell Mercy. Not until she could feel more certain of doing what her father would have wished.

But Adam, bent as he seemed to be on finding out who and what represented a threat against her and already in Duncan's confidence to the tune of three million dollars, seemed the best person in whom to confide this new information. It would have been too much to say that she trusted him completely, but Rachel's instincts told her to tell him this much, and she listened to them.

It isn't because he looks like Thomas. It isn't.

He arrived at the house within half an hour, and once again Fiona announced him and quickly retreated after crossing herself.

"Why does she always do that?" he asked, coming into the study.

"Because you look like Tom," Rachel answered as casually as she could. "It unnerves her."

Adam smiled slightly. "It unnerves her. How about you?"

Rachel, standing behind her father's desk, gazed at him. "No, it doesn't unnerve me. Now." She paused, then added honestly, "But it isn't something I can forget, Adam. You do look like Thomas."

"Is that the only reason I'm here, Rachel?"

She hesitated, then shook her head. "No."

He nodded. "Good."

Deciding that enough had been said about that, Rachel handed the two small notebooks to Adam. "Look what I found. It seems you were right about that bank account in Geneva." She sat down behind the desk and watched as he took the visitor's chair and frowned over the notebooks.

"Loans?" he guessed, looking up at her.

Rachel nodded and pushed the legal pad with all her notes across the desk.

It didn't take Adam long to see the pattern. "My God. Nearly twenty loans of varying sizes over twenty years."

"Almost all of them repaid to the penny," Rachel said. "My dad obviously had great judgment about whom he could trust. See the initials? At the end of each series of numbers. Yours are there."

Adam smiled at her. "I see. I'm glad he left you this, Rachel."

"I'm not so sure I am. Take a look at that last page of figures."

He did, and a frown quickly replaced his smile. "Three loans other than mine outstanding?"

"That's what it looks like."

"Goddammit," he muttered. "That means three people with a potential reason to want you out of the way."

"That's possible. But I've been thinking about it. Adam, what threat am I to those people? All I have are their initials, so I don't know who they are. And even if I did, there's nothing legally binding about this setup, not that I can see. Any of those people could knock on my door and say the loans wouldn't be repaid, and there's nothing I could do about it. If it comes to that, they could claim the money was a gift."

"That's a good point." He considered it for a moment. "Still, there could be something we don't know about all this."

"What do you mean?"

"I'm not quite sure. Except that it makes me damned uneasy that none of these people have been in touch with you since your father's death."

"Maybe their loans aren't due to be repaid."

"Maybe. And maybe they have other reasons to stay anonymous."

Rachel shook her head. "I don't know how we can find out what those reasons are. None of the initials tells me anything."

Adam put the legal pad and the notebooks on the desk. "You found the notebooks in this desk?"

"Yes."

"Did you find anything else? Anything that might give us some clue as to who these people are?"

"I don't know, Adam. About a ream's worth of scrap paper, all of it with notes in Dad's hand. I haven't gone through it all yet."

"Maybe we'll find an answer there. Or at least a hint." He looked at her steadily. "I'll help."

"It could take all day. And then there are two more drawers here I haven't even opened, and the secretary in his bedroom . . . Adam, what if your company needs to find you?"

"I have a pager. Rachel, I want to help. Let me. Please."

Rachel wasn't entirely sure that spending the better part of a day in Adam's company was the wisest thing to do. But it was what she wanted to do.

"I'd welcome the company," she said.

.   .   .

"Do I expect to have total control of the bank? I have that now. No, it hardly matters whether Rachel Grant sells me her shares. I have the authority to act in any way I see fit." His tone was very pleasant as he spoke on the phone.

Very pleasant. And completely ruthless.

It made goose bumps rise on Mercy's bare arms. She hadn't heard the beginning of the conversation, but came into his office in time to hear that much. It was enough to disturb her.

She shut the door behind herself and crossed the room to sit down in his visitor's chair, pretending to thumb through the papers she carried rather than listen in on the conversation.

"I told you that last week," Nicholas said. "No. No, I don't see any reason to do that. I imagine the problem will resolve itself fairly quickly."

He paused. His gaze was fixed on Mercy. She could feel it.

"I can come up with ten million."

She looked up in surprise, and felt herself flush when he smiled at her sardonically.

"No, I don't need Rachel's shares to do that. I've told you. I have the authority. Yeah. Yeah, you do that. See you there." He hung up.

"But you don't have the authority," Mercy protested. "An investment that size needs Rachel's approval. In fact, it needs the approval of the board."

Nicholas smiled. "Love, do you intend working for me as my assistant?"

"You know I don't."

"Has Rachel hired you to manage her interests?"

"The subject hasn't come up. I'm not even sure she means to keep her shares."

Softly, he said, "Then don't concern yourself with whatever decisions I make in running the bank."

He had never warned her off quite so bluntly before, and coming now, this warning served only to make her more worried. He was up to something. She could sense it. She just didn't know what was going on.

"I don't mean to meddle in your business, Nick."

"I know you don't, love."

"It's just—ten million dollars is a hell of a lot of money. Even for a bank this size."

"I know what I'm doing, Mercy."

His record with the bank bore that out, so all she could do was nod. "I know."

He smiled, then nodded toward the papers forgotten in her grasp. "Are those for me?"

She got up and handed them to him across the desk. "Some things you need to look over and sign—"

Nicholas grasped her wrist. It was a warm, strong, inescapable hold. "Sure you don't want to work for me?" he murmured seductively. "Be right at the seat of power? Know all my secrets?"

She leaned her free hand on the desk. "I have a feeling I'll never live long enough to know all your secrets, Nick."

His eyes gleamed at her. "But it's something to strive for, surely."

"Oh, it's at the top of my list."

He let out one of those short barks of laughter so characteristic of him, and released her wrist. "Could you pander to my ego at least once, love?"

"I have a sneaking suspicion your ego is remarkably healthy as it is," she said, still leaning on the desk.

"Perhaps." He glanced down at the papers he held. "Do you need these right away? I need to go out for a while."

"They can wait until tomorrow. I didn't see an appointment on your calendar." She kept her voice casual.

"A last-minute arrangement." He got up and came around the desk, and when she turned to face him, he lifted a hand to lay alongside her neck. He bent his head and kissed her, taking his time about it and totally ignoring the unlocked door.

Then again, she thought hazily, maybe he had a sixth sense about such things. They'd never been interrupted—and he had provoked greater intimacies than this in the past.

When he finally drew back far enough to speak, he murmured huskily, "Trust me, Mercy. I really do know what I'm doing."

It took her a moment to remember what they'd been discussing. "I do. Of course I do."

"Do you?" His fingers caressed her throat. "Then why are you so worried?"

"Because— How do you know I'm worried?"

"I know."

Well, *that* was certainly unnerving. Up until then she'd thought she had a great poker face.

This time his laugh was a deep rumble. He kissed her again, then released her and stepped back. "Mind the store for a couple of hours, will you, love?"

"Of course."

But he was no sooner out the door than Mercy made an impulsive decision. With a hurried order to Leigh to mind the store, she grabbed her purse and dashed out before the office manager could do more than sputter in surprise.

Mercy wasn't at all sure she could follow him without his knowledge, but she intended to give it a damn good try. He had asked for her trust, and she had said it was given—but Mercy had lied. He seemed to her more secretive than ever these days, and she didn't like it. There had been too many cryptic telephone conversations, too many evasions, too many enigmatic gazes and inexplicable silences.

Her best friend had survived two so-called accidents, a fact Nick seemed almost totally disinterested in, even though he stood to gain by her death. And soon after the second one, he had told somebody on the phone that they had "fucked up."

Damned straight, Mercy was worried.

She had no idea if the man she loved was a man she could trust.

Fiona brought them lunch on trays since they didn't want to stop going through Duncan's private papers. But by two o'clock Adam firmly called a halt.

"My eyes are beginning to cross, and that's the third time you've rubbed yours," he told Rachel. "We need a break."

"Maybe you're right." She rubbed the back of her neck instead, finding it a bit stiff. They had moved from her father's desk to the leather sofa and big, square coffee table. Adam sat on the sofa, while Rachel had ended up sitting on the floor on the other side of the table with a big pillow to lean on.

Not because she wanted to avoid sitting beside him, but because . . . because they'd needed the entire coffee table on which to spread out papers, and it was easier to work from both sides.

That was all.

Adam got up and came around to offer her his hands. "Come on. Why don't we go outside and take a walk or something."

She took his hands and allowed him to pull her up, wincing as her left leg protested the sudden change in position.

"Did I hurt you?"

"No, no. Just a slight cramp in my leg. It's easing off." She released his hands and stepped away, unnerved by his closeness. At such moments she was always aware of that leashed power in him, that hidden strength. It bothered her in some way she could hardly put a name to.

Realizing suddenly that she had been silent just a moment too long, she said casually, "If there's no furniture barring the way, I'll show you through a bit more of the house on our way to the back. We have a kind of informal garden, and it's a pleasant place to walk."

"Sounds good to me."

They closed the study door when they left, and Rachel locked it, sliding the key into the front pocket of her jeans.

"Have you been keeping the room locked?"

"No, just the desk. But with all those papers spread out, locking the door seems best for now."

"A sensible precaution."

They encountered a barricade in the hallway outside the formal dining room. And encountered her uncle Cameron, who was not happy.

Since he'd already met Adam, he simply acknowledged his

presence with a nod, launching immediately into complaint. "Rachel, Darby says she found three rolltop desks in the basement, and she won't let me go through the contents."

Soothingly, Rachel said, "That's because I asked her just to box up the contents for now, Cam. We can go through all that later. Anything that's been down there for decades can wait a while longer."

He seemed satisfied, but said, "We don't want her throwing away something important thinking it's trash." Not as distinguished-looking as his older brother had been, Cameron carried the added burden of cupidlike features, which tended to make him look pouty even when he wasn't.

"She won't do that, Cam. She's boxing up the contents of everything she finds, no matter what. Don't worry. Darby knows what she's doing."

A crash from the basement caused her uncle to wince in horror and bolt.

"I hope," Rachel murmured.

Adam grinned at her. "Want to go see what ended up in splinters, or shall we go on to the garden?"

"I'm tired of sorting furniture and old boxes." She shrugged. "Let Darby handle it. And Uncle Cam."

"He does seem worried," Adam noted as Rachel let go of his arm so she could pick her way through the furniture barricade.

"He hates the idea of non-Grants having a say in the disposal of family things. Not the family tradition, you see. But I don't see any reason to keep most of the stuff in storage, and Darby is the fairest, most trustworthy antiques dealer I know."

"Why's he so worried about the contents?"

133

"Because a few days ago Darby found a diamond cocktail ring tucked away in a little drawer of an old dresser. Thirties design. I'm almost afraid to have it appraised."

Adam whistled. "So every piece is a potential treasure chest?"

"Well, to Uncle Cam. He always did love poking into corners, so this really does seem like a treasure hunt."

They emerged at last from the forest of furniture, and Adam casually took Rachel's hand. "Which way now?"

"We'll go through the sunroom," she decided, trying not to be so conscious of that warm, strong hand surrounding hers. "Fiona's already working on dinner in the kitchen, so if we go that way, she'll burn something."

"She has her own methods of letting her displeasure be known?"

"Definitely. This way."

The sunroom, a bright and plant-filled space that doubled as a breakfast room, opened onto a tile veranda. Steps led down to a lawn, from which a path paved only with stepping stones wandered off into a lush landscape of bright flowering shrubs and spring greenery.

Large trees towered to either side of the garden area, offering a sense of being closed off from the world outside. The air was mild, and heavily scented from all the flowers.

"Nice," Adam commented as they began strolling along the path.

"Most of the homes in this neighborhood have more formal gardens than we do. But this was designed two hundred years ago, and so far everybody's kept it casual. I mean to as well."

"I like it." They strolled for a few minutes in silence, and then Adam said abruptly, "Tell me about Thomas Sheridan."

Startled, Rachel stopped on the path and stared up at him. "Thomas? Why?"

"I'd just like to know."

"You said Dad talked about him."

"He did. But he wasn't in love with Sheridan. You were."

Rachel pulled to free her hand. "I don't want to—"

"Rachel." His free hand lifted and touched her cheek, making her go still. "I said I wouldn't push, and I won't. But I . . . I need to hear you talk about him."

"Why?"

"Because he was so important to you. Because I look like him, and I need to know that *you* know I'm not him."

She turned and continued walking slowly. But she pulled her hand gently from his, breaking the connection and making them both conscious of the loss. "All right. What do you want to know?"

"Whatever you feel comfortable telling me."

"I loved him from the time I was ten years old. Is that what you want to hear?"

Adam's voice remained steady. "If it's the truth."

"It is." She drew a breath. "He was out of high school when I started—there were ten years between us—but I wore his ring for four years, and never dated anyone else. We got engaged when I turned eighteen, but Tom insisted I go to college for at least a year before we married.

"So I did. But I lived at home, and we saw each other every weekend." She paused. "I didn't like his job."

"He was a pilot, wasn't he?"

"Yes. He flew cargo planes for a company based here in Richmond. It wasn't usually dangerous work. He said."

"You didn't believe that?"

Rachel shrugged, and her voice was a bit tense. "I had a romantic imagination. So I imagined things. Once or twice I got the feeling there had been close calls, just from something he'd said. But he'd only laugh and tell me not to worry. I did, of course. Worry. I gave him the locket on his twenty-ninth birthday."

"The locket?"

Rachel nodded. "A small gold locket. I had our initials engraved on the outside, and a St. Christopher put inside. To protect him. He had my picture put inside as well." She paused. "Neither one protected him very well. His plane vanished just a few months later."

They walked in silence a few minutes, and then Adam said quietly, "Did you bury your heart with him, Rachel?"

"I thought I had."

They stopped, and when she turned to face him his hand reached up to touch her cheek again. This time it lingered. "Did you?"

There was a long silence so intense that even the sounds of the garden seemed to have stilled. Then Rachel took a jerky step away from him, that instinctive retreat making her words unnecessary. But she said them anyway. "I don't know. I just don't know, Adam."

A little flatly, he said, "And I look so much like him."

"It isn't something that's going to go away," she reminded him. "You look like Thomas. But Thomas is dead. And I know that."

"But you haven't said good-bye to him, have you, Rachel?"

He didn't wait for a reply, but reached for her hand, tucked it into the crook of his arm, and began walking along the path once more. For several minutes, they walked in silence.

"Adam?"

"Yes?"

"For a long, long time, I never really believed he was gone. For . . . for years I woke up from dreams about him. He was always trying to tell me something, and I could never quite hear him. I finally realized he was trying to say good-bye. And one day the dreams just stopped."

Adam looked down at her, his face without expression. Then he said, "It's all right, Rachel. I understand."

"Do you?" She shook her head a little. "I'm not so sure I do."

Adam didn't respond to that. But a moment later, as they rounded a bend in the path, he stopped suddenly. "What's that?"

She gave him a curious look. "There's a path through the woods to the river. That gate is the way out of the garden."

Adam stared at tall black wrought-iron gates, at the winding path beyond. His voice sounded strange even to him when he said, "I didn't know it was here."

"No, you wouldn't have seen it except from here—or from the river. Adam, is something wrong?"

"No. No, of course not." He got hold of himself, and walked on, putting the gate behind him.

They completed the circuit of the garden in silence, and it wasn't until they'd almost reached the house again that Rachel spoke.

"You aren't a stand-in for a dead man, Adam."

"I'm glad."

"You don't believe me?"

He hesitated. "I don't believe you've said good-bye to him yet, Rachel. Until you do, you can't be sure."

She didn't reply to that. But she didn't remove her hand from his arm, not even when they went inside and a truculent Fiona met them at the door of the sunroom.

"Mr. Graham has been waiting in the front parlor these fifteen minutes and more, Miss Rachel!"

Mildly, she said, "I'm sure he didn't mind, Fiona."

The housekeeper snorted, shot Adam a dark look, and stomped away.

"Makes a lot of noise for such a little thing," he observed.

Rachel couldn't help but smile, but all she said was "If we go this way, we can avoid the furniture blockade."

They did, and shortly afterward walked through the double doors of the front parlor with Rachel's hand still tucked into the crook of Adam's arm.

Graham didn't like what he saw.

"You two haven't met officially," Rachel said. "Graham, this is—"

"The man who lied to you," Graham snapped.

NINE

Mercy was more than a little worried to find that Nicholas was heading for a decidedly bad part of town.

It hadn't been easy, keeping her small car behind his without making it obvious he was being followed, and as they left the heavier traffic behind, she had to drop farther back to avoid discovery. So she was barely within sight when he finally pulled over to the curb at what looked like a deserted warehouse.

She pulled her car to the curb and killed the engine quickly.

For about ten minutes, nothing happened. Then a tall man who seemed roughly dressed from where Mercy was sitting appeared seemingly out of the shadows of the building and got into Nick's car.

Mercy would have given a year's salary to be a fly in that car.

The meeting lasted no more than five minutes. The stranger got out of the car and melted once more into the shadows. Nicholas's car pulled away from the curb and went on.

Mercy followed.

"What are you up to?" she muttered to herself, her gaze fixed on that big black car. "Dammit, Nick, what are you up to?"

His actions for the next hour offered Mercy no clue. He met twice more with unsavory-looking men who appeared and disappeared into shadow. These meetings were a bit longer, but still were clearly furtive in nature.

Frustrated, Mercy followed him to yet another seemingly deserted warehouse and parked half a block back from him. This time Nicholas left his car and headed for the warehouse. He didn't look to the left or right.

Mercy didn't actually see him open a door; he just appeared to vanish into the shadows as all his grungy pals had done.

She drummed her fingers on the steering wheel and debated getting out and going to look for him.

The passenger door opened suddenly.

"Hello, love. I hope I didn't make it too difficult for you to keep up."

"What did he lie about?" Rachel asked quietly.

"The man's a convicted felon, Rachel." Graham's voice was heavy with satisfaction. "He served five years in prison."

"Well, since I never asked him if he'd been in prison, I don't see that he lied about it, Graham."

"Rachel, for God's sake!"

"Well, I don't."

Adam looked down at Rachel with a slight smile. He led her to the sofa facing the fireplace, and when she sat down, he went to the hearth opposite where Graham stood and faced the other man.

"Tell her the rest," Adam said.

For the first time, Graham looked a bit discomfited. "I don't know what you mean."

"Sure you do. Tell her what my crime was, and where I served my time." Adam shoved his hands into the pockets of his pants and lounged back against the mantel.

The physical contrast between the two men was a stark one. Graham, inarguably good-looking and elegant in his business suit, appeared curiously tame standing so near Adam. He lacked Adam's height and visible strength, but it was more than that. Less formally dressed, his hair a bit shaggy, and his pose a lazy one, Adam radiated leashed intensity in the alert tilt of his head and the sharpness of his gaze, and his slight smile was not so much polite as it was inherently dangerous.

For the first time, Rachel saw a man who might well have spent time in a cage.

She looked at Graham, hiding a sudden anxiety. "Well?"

Reluctantly, Graham said, "He was in prison in South America."

"And my crime?" Adam prompted softly.

Through gritted teeth Graham said, "Crimes against the state."

Adam looked at Rachel through shuttered eyes. "That's a nice little euphemism used by tinpot dictators after they've successfully instigated a coup. A blanket charge to throw over any perceived enemy of the new regime. That's what was happening in San

Cristo, about a week after I arrived. Since I was there to help close down an American-owned business that the new regime promptly nationalized, and since I spoke out against them, I was perceived as an enemy of the state."

He paused. "The *trial* lasted about five minutes. The sentence was life. I got out early only because the tinpot dictator got himself shot almost five years later, and there was a new regime. One that didn't consider me an enemy of the state." He turned his gaze to Graham. "And I think that's all you need to know, Becket."

"I agree," Rachel said.

Graham frowned at her. "Rachel—"

"Did you bring the lease by for me to sign?"

"Yes."

"Is everything in order? All the I's dotted and T's crossed?"

He sighed. "Yes."

"Then I'll sign it now. And you can drop it off at the agency on your way back to town. I don't want to take up any more of your time." She kept her voice quiet, unwilling to get into any discussion with Graham that would lead to her defending Adam.

Graham shot Adam a look and opened his briefcase on the coffee table to get the lease. "Rachel, listen to me. No matter what his story of the imprisonment is, the fact is that I can't find out anything about his background beyond a few sketchy facts. You know only what he's telling you, and it could all be a pack of lies designed to win your trust."

Rachel signed the lease and handed it back to him. "Thank you for going over this, Graham. As for the rest—I've always depended on you for advice. So what do you advise?"

"Don't trust him."

She looked at Adam, leaning silently against the mantel, then returned her gaze to Graham. "I'll have to make up my own mind about that, Graham."

"Rachel—"

"Well, what else do you expect me to say? He landed in a South American prison through actions that neither of us would consider wrong. Once he got out, he convinced a man we both respected to give him a loan in order to start his own company, and five years later that company is thriving, the loan about to be repaid in full—"

"He says," Graham interrupted.

Adam watched and listened in silence, offering nothing.

Rachel shook her head. "All right—he says. You haven't offered any evidence that he's lying, or even any reason why he would. So far, in fact, you haven't given me any reason at all not to trust Adam, aside from your suspicions. I don't happen to share them."

"Because he looks like Thomas. Don't you see, Rachel? He walked into your life looking like Thomas, and you've given him the benefit of every doubt because of that."

Is that really it? Is that why I trust him? Rachel hesitated, then shook her head. "I think you've said enough, Graham. You can show yourself out."

Graham looked at her for a moment, wondering dimly if she had yet realized what was happening to her. He did. And it was a bitter thing to Graham to see her waking up, coming out of the state that Tom's death had left her in, and to know that where he himself had failed, another man had succeeded.

He hesitated only an instant, knowing also that nothing he could say just then would change what was happening. Not unless he could find evidence that Adam Delafield was not who and what he claimed to be. Graham shot another look at Adam, then gathered up his briefcase and strode from the room.

Still lounging back against the mantel, Adam said quietly, "You were pretty hard on him."

"Was I? Maybe."

"He seems to have your best interests at heart."

"Even so." Rachel looked at him steadily. "I'm sorry."

"About what?"

"Graham's attitude. And . . . about what happened to you. It must have been terrible."

Adam came to the sofa and sat down a couple of feet away, turning toward her. "I want to tell you about it."

"You don't have to."

"I know. But I want to." He smiled slightly. "The way I told your father."

Rachel nodded. "All right."

"I was working as an electrical designer at an engineering company in California." Adam spoke slowly. "In that work, I developed a more efficient version of an electrical component already in wide use. It was sort of like inventing a better mousetrap. There was a built-in demand for the gadget, a huge one. Both the company and I stood to make a lot of money."

Rachel nodded again, and waited.

"What I didn't know at the time was that my superior in the company wanted to take the credit—and the money—for himself. All unsuspecting, I gave him my diagrams to look over. The next day I was handed plane tickets and told to get down to San Cristo, close down our manufacturing plant, and get our people out of there before the rumbles of a coup became reality."

"Why was there a plant down there?"

"Cheap labor. And God knows what kind of tax breaks and kickbacks they'd been granted from the old regime. In any case, there was a plant running three shifts, and dozens of American supervisors and office personnel. I had to get them out."

"You must have been very young for such an assignment."

"I was twenty-five. But I'd traveled a great deal during my college years, I could fly a plane, and I spoke Spanish like a native. At the time, it made perfect sense to me that I was the one to go."

"I see." *Another pilot. Like Dad. And like Thomas.*

Adam shrugged. "Getting the others out was a major headache, but nothing I couldn't handle. The company had sent two planes, one for the people, and a cargo plane for all the equipment I could get out."

She frowned. "This was—ten years ago?"

"Not quite. It was in November of eighty-eight."

Six months after Tom's plane had vanished somewhere in South America. Rachel sighed. "So you got everybody out?"

"Yeah. But my superior had been insistent that I be the last man out, and that I do a final check of the plant to make sure nothing valuable had been left behind. Hell, I could practically smell the army coming, and I still went back there." He paused. "I was barely able to get off a call to the cargo plane and tell the pilot to get out before they grabbed me."

"So the new leader wasn't too happy with you."

"Not much, no. He could have used a lot of the equipment I'd managed to get out of the country. So, he gave me a five-minute trial and sentenced me to life at one of his country clubs."

Rachel winced. "It must have been horrible."

"It wasn't fun." He smiled faintly, but his eyes were still shuttered and he didn't offer details.

Rachel decided not to ask. Instead, she asked another question. "But didn't anyone here try to get you out? An American citizen being held like that on trumped-up charges—"

Adam shook his head. "I had no family. When the president of the company tried to find out what had happened to me, the new dictator in San Cristo claimed I'd been killed. He even had a body to ship home—conveniently burned beyond recognition. Seems the plant caught fire, and I didn't get out in time. Terrible accident." He paused, then added, "There's a grave in California, a nice headstone all paid for by the company. And my name on it."

Rachel shivered. "You mean still?"

"Oh, I went through the official process of having myself declared legally alive again. But nobody got around to digging up that poor bastard and finding out who he was. Another enemy of the state, I guess."

"My God."

Adam lifted a hand as though to touch her, then let it fall. "When I got home, I found out that my former superior had made a fortune on the gadget I'd invented, him and the company. There was no proof, of course, just my word against his—and five years later, nobody believed me. Nobody wanted to believe me.

"They offered me a job, but I couldn't take it. To prevent me from suing for five years' back pay, they offered a cash settlement—which I did take. It wasn't enough to start my own company, but it was enough to live on while I drew up the plans for a new design I'd dreamed up in prison. That was about the time I called looking for Nick, and talked to Duncan Grant instead. You know the rest."

"How did you know Nick?" Rachel asked. "I've wondered."

"We met while I was in college. I was bumming around in Europe the summer after my sophomore year. Nick was"—Adam eyed her thoughtfully for a moment, clearly hesitant, then sighed— "I gather you didn't know he had done some intelligence work for the government?"

Rachel blinked. "I certainly didn't."

"He'll skin me if he finds out I told you. I don't know if he likes to keep his past murky or if he feels he should because of the government work. Whichever it is, I've learned to respect his wishes. So, for Christ's sake, don't tell him I told you about the cloak-and-dagger stuff."

"How did he get involved in something like that?"

"You'd have to ask him. All I know is that during that particular summer, he was involved in a . . . situation in Rome. Don't ask me for the details. I'm still hazy on them, and I was there. The only thing I can tell you for certain is that totally by accident I found myself caught up in an international incident involving a Turk, two Frenchmen, an Italian, and Nick. And everybody had a gun but me."

Rachel didn't know whether to laugh or gasp. "What happened?"

"I got shot." He smiled. "It wasn't too serious, but it so happened if I hadn't stopped the bullet, Nick would have been in deep, deep trouble. Somehow, he managed to finish his assignment successfully, and get a wounded American back home without arousing too many questions."

"And after that he owed you a favor."

"A big one." Adam shrugged. "We kept in touch for the next

few years, while I finished college and started working with the company. Saw each other a few times. But it wasn't until after the San Cristo trouble that I called him to collect on the favor."

"And got Dad instead."

"And got Duncan instead."

Rachel shook her head. "That's . . . quite a story."

"I'm sure Graham Becket would say it's all lies. I know he's suspicious of me. But he couldn't find anything much in my background because there isn't anything to find, Rachel."

"I know."

"How can you?"

"Because Dad trusted you. And because I do."

Once again Adam lifted a hand and touched her face gently. His own face was very still, revealing nothing of what he was feeling. "Don't trust so quickly, Rachel."

"How can I not?"

His hand fell, and his smile was a bit strained. "It might be better for us both if you didn't."

"Why?"

Adam shook his head. "Never mind. Would you like to return to Duncan's scraps of paper? We still have some time today, and we need to find those answers."

Rachel wasn't at all sure she liked the way this conversation was ending, but Adam was already getting up, and she had little choice but to follow suit. It bothered her, though.

It bothered her that Adam wasn't quite comfortable with her trust.

. . .

"Okay, I admit it was wrong." Mercy felt like a scolded little girl and Nicholas hadn't even said anything yet. He just sat there behind his desk, staring at her. She wanted to throw something at him. Other than his unpleasant smile and sardonic comment when he'd surprised her in the car, all he'd said was a brief order to meet him back at the bank.

So, there she was. And there he was.

And things were not looking good.

"I'm sorry, Nick. Is that what you want to hear?"

"I want to hear a reason, Mercy. Just what the bloody hell do you think you were doing?"

"My curiosity got the better of me. You were being so damned cryptic and—and I just wanted to find out what you were up to."

"It didn't occur to you to ask?"

She sat up straighter. "You would have told me?"

"No." He smiled for the first time. "But you might have made the attempt before resorting to TV-private-eye tactics."

"Dammit, Nick!" She scowled at him.

"Mercy, I asked you to trust me. You said you did."

"Yeah, well—I do. Almost."

"Almost is not good enough." His pale eyes were very serious now. "Either you trust me, or you don't. If you trust me, then believe that I know what I'm doing."

"Nick, I believe you know what you're doing. I just want to know what that is."

"I'm not going to tell you."

"Why not?" she almost wailed.

Nicholas smiled again, but his eyes remained grave. "Because you have a lousy poker face, love. And I can't afford to risk the chance that the wrong person is a better card player than you are."

"Well, if that isn't cryptic, I don't know what is." She glared at him. "Just tell me this—are you up to something illegal?"

"Would it surprise you if I said yes?" He sounded honestly curious.

Mercy thought about it. "I don't know. For a good enough reason, I think you'd go to just about any lengths. Maybe even breaking the law. Is that what you're doing?"

"No. As a matter of fact, I'm playing strictly by the rules." Now he sounded mocking.

Mercy wasn't reassured. "How about the law?"

"The law is on my side."

She had a feeling he had somehow evaded her question, but she wasn't sure exactly how. She sighed. "And I'm supposed to just accept that."

"I wish you would, yes."

She hesitated, then blurted out, "Just tell me you aren't doing anything that might hurt Rachel."

Nicholas leaned back in his chair and laced his fingers together over his flat middle. "I am not doing anything that might hurt Rachel." His voice was level, every word precisely pronounced. He wasn't smiling any longer.

"I'm sorry."

"Why? You said you didn't quite trust me. Now I know what you think I'm capable of."

This was going from bad to worse. He was angry.

He was very angry.

"I didn't say you were. I *asked* if you were."

"Somehow, I don't get the distinction."

On the defensive and floundering, Mercy said, "Well, there is one. To me. I'm not saying you'd deliberately hurt Rachel. But some of these deals of yours are incredibly complex, and the results might not be good for her interests."

"Oh, I see. It's her *interests* you're worried about. I thought I was being accused of blowing up a building with her in it."

"Nick, for God's sake! I never even thought—"

"Didn't you?"

She stared at him and, very quietly, said, "No. Not that. Never that."

"You just thought I was the sort of ruthless bastard who'd take advantage of her."

After a moment, Mercy got to her feet. "Look, this isn't getting us anywhere. You're mad and I'm getting mad. I'm going to go to my office and finish up for the day. Then I'm going home."

"Good idea," he said flatly.

She turned around and left the office, closing the door with exquisite quiet behind her.

Nick stared after her. Then, softly, he said, "Shit."

Adam sat back and raked a hand through his hair. "Okay, so we think most of this is not going to help us a bit."

Rachel nodded, then reached out to tap three small scraps of paper lying alone before them. "These are the only ones that look even remotely helpful. And we're not sure they mean anything. Just the same initials."

Written on small, irregularly sized pieces of paper in Duncan Grant's neat hand, the notes were as cryptic as any clue ever left to a puzzle.

Only the initials printed there offered a possible connection to what Rachel had found in the notebooks.

RS called.
Wants my opinion
on the new design.

LM called from TX.
Return call soonest.

JW called.
Have to put him off.
Must consider what to do.

"They look like just ordinary notes to himself," Adam mused. "What to do about phone calls, or what they were about. He doesn't say whether he means to offer an opinion on the new design mentioned in the first note. In the second, he means to return the call, no subject noted, but we can assume LM lives or works in Texas. And in the third he seems . . . hesitant, or reluctant."

Rachel looked at the notebook open at her elbow. "If it's the same JW, he's the one who got the big loan. Five million."

"The initials don't mean anything to you?"

She shook her head. "No. We don't even know if this JW is local. LM is apparently in Texas, you were in California. Dad traveled a lot, so these people could be from anywhere in the world."

"This is not narrowing the field," Adam muttered.

"No kidding."

He sighed. "Well, we haven't delved into the other desk drawers yet. Or that secretary upstairs. Maybe we'll find more scraps of paper that make these mean something."

"Maybe." Rachel started to say something else, but then Fiona opened the door and stuck her head in.

"Supper in ten minutes, Miss Rachel." She sent a hostile look toward Adam. "I suppose *he's* invited?"

"Yes, he is," Rachel replied serenely. "Set another place, please, Fiona."

"I don't want to wear out my welcome," Adam said when the housekeeper had withdrawn, muttering.

"You won't." She smiled at him. "You've been helping me all day. The least I can do is feed you."

"I'd love to stay, but I'll leave right after we eat. You need to get some rest this evening, Rachel. Put all this out of your mind. Curl up with a good book or something."

"That could be a plan."

"In the meantime," he said, "is there a copier around?"

"In that cabinet over there. It pulls out. Why?"

"If it's all right with you, I'm going to make copies of these notes, and the relevant pages of the notebooks. I'd like to go over them again tonight, think about them. You should put the originals in a safe place."

"I have a safe in my room."

"Sounds good. May I?"

"Of course." While he was making the copies, Rachel gathered up the scraps of paper they had decided were irrelevant and put them in a file box. "I'll keep these a bit longer. Until we're sure."

"That's probably wise." He handed her the original notes,

notebooks, and one copy of each. "I made you copies too, just in case." He folded his set of copies and went to put that in the pocket of his jacket, which he'd left lying over a chair.

"I'll take this stuff up to my room. And show you where you can wash up before supper."

"Will Fiona examine my fingernails?"

"She just might."

Adam followed her from the room, chuckling.

She showed him to the upstairs guest bathroom across the hall from her bedroom, and then went into her room to put the notes and notebooks away and make use of her own bathroom.

It had been so long since she'd used her safe—hidden in a conventional way behind a painting on one wall—she had almost forgotten the combination, but a minute of thought brought it to mind. There was nothing in the safe at the moment. She had never cared much for jewelry, and so had only a few basic gold pieces she kept in a jewelry box on her dresser. Her mother's jewelry was in a vault at the bank.

She put the notes and notebooks away, then went into her bathroom to wash up. As she stood before the vanity running a brush through her hair, she found herself thinking about Adam and his behavior today.

In the garden he had been so intense. Asking her to talk about Thomas. Asking if she had buried her heart with him.

He wouldn't be a stand-in for a dead man; she understood that. He knew that she had not yet said good-bye to Tom.

Rachel put down the brush and went to the doorway of the bathroom, gazing into her bedroom without really looking at anything there. She thought that nearly five years in a hellish South American prison would have changed any man. But how had it changed Adam? He had gone in an idealistic young man, unaware that he was about to be betrayed, his design and years of his life stolen from him. How had he come out?

What else had he lost there?

"Ready to go down?" He stood in the doorway of the bedroom, smiling at her.

"I'm ready," she said, and went to join him.

T E N

It was still well before midnight, but The Tavern was fairly crowded on this Monday night, and at least half the patrons were well on their way to getting falling-down drunk. Even so, the drunkest of them made way when Nicholas walked through.

He found Adam sitting in one of the booths, two beers sweating on the rickety table before him.

Joining him, Nicholas said, "Becket called me late this afternoon, breathing fire. He can't believe the ex-con story didn't wash with Rachel. So she bought your version?"

Adam nodded.

"Well, just so you know, Becket is hell-bent on finding something damaging in your past. Can he?"

"Not if you did your job."

"I always do my job."

"Then I'm clean."

Nicholas picked up his glass and sipped the beer for a moment. "Okay. We'll assume he comes up with zip. It won't stop him, Adam. In fact, it won't hold him for long. He sees Rachel slipping away from him. And he does not want to let her go."

"Maybe I can use that to distract him."

"Maybe. Dangerous, though. Jealousy can be a violent thing."

"You mean if he can't have her, no man can?" Adam frowned. "Would he go that far?"

"I honestly don't know."

"I'll have to stick close to her."

Nicholas smiled wryly. "Like you haven't been up till now?"

"I know what I'm doing."

"Do you?"

"Yes." Adam met those pale eyes unflinchingly. "I know what I'm doing, Nick."

"You planned carefully, didn't you?" Nicholas looked at him thoughtfully, unsmiling. "From the very beginning. Including putting me where I'd do you the most good."

"I just made a suggestion," Adam said lightly. "We both know nobody's going to *put* you anywhere you don't want to be."

"Richmond wasn't even on my short list."

"Maybe not, but it all worked out. Didn't it?"

"For me? Sure. For you?"

"It will. Eventually."

"But what will it cost you?"

Adam shrugged, and his voice roughened. "Like I said. I know what I'm doing."

Nick accepted that with a nod. "Well, it's your hand to play out. In the meantime, on *my* side of the table, things are getting tight. Without Rachel's shares, I can't control enough of the bank's assets to make Jordan Walsh eager to do business with me."

"If she knew what you were doing—"

Nicholas shook his head. "No. No way. We play this out without involving her. Without involving . . . anyone else. If we go down, we go down alone."

Adam nodded slowly. "I agreed to that from the start."

"So—I have to find a way around having control of Rachel's shares."

"What are you doing right now?"

"Bluffing."

"And if Walsh calls the bluff?"

"Damned if I know," Nicholas said. "I'll figure out something."

There was a moment of silence, and then Adam drew a sheaf of papers from inside his jacket. "Take a look at this."

Nicholas bent forward over the table, squinting in the dim light to study the copies Adam had made earlier at Rachel's. "JW," he said softly. "Unless you believe in coincidence—Jordan Walsh."

"That was my take. If so, he was on the hook to Duncan for five million."

Nicholas looked over the remaining copies, including the ones from the notebooks. He shook his head. "I knew Duncan was handing out money, but I had no idea it was this extensive."

"Neither did I. He left Rachel with a hell of a financial headache."

"Maybe not. When all his papers have been gone through, you may discover that he planned carefully to make sure she wasn't harmed by this. I never met a smarter man about finances."

"We'll see. There's still plenty to go through at the house."

"And Rachel is welcoming your help?"

"I think so. I was invited back for tomorrow."

Nicholas sat back and looked at him for a moment, then tapped the papers on the scarred table between them. "You do realize that Walsh is just a possibility? That any one of these three people could have enough to hide to want to make these loans disappear?"

"I know that. But you have to admit, finding initials matching Walsh's name tells us we're on the right track."

"I hate to admit anything. And there is one huge question about this, if the five-million loan was made to Walsh."

"Why."

Nicholas nodded. "Why. Duncan wouldn't have done business with the man. Especially not a handshake deal."

"So?"

"So there's more to this than we know about. Maybe a lot more."

"And in the meantime, someone wants Rachel out of the way."

"So it seems."

Adam scowled at him. "I'm not happy about that, Nick."

"Do you think I am?"

"For all I know—"

"Don't even finish that sentence."

After a moment, Adam nodded. "Okay, okay. I'm a little tense about the subject."

"No shit."

"Look, keeping Rachel occupied in going through Duncan's private papers is also keeping her close to home, and right now that house looks like the only haven she's got. So she's safe—and out of the way. But she's leased the property on Queen Street, and she's going to want to get to work on her boutique. She'll be out in the open, Nick. And that means trouble."

"I know, I know."

"We're running out of time."

"Then we'll have to pick up the pace, won't we?"

Adam said, "There's something else."

"Oh, great. What?"

"Max Galloway's in Richmond."

Nicholas said softly, "Son of a bitch."

"Yeah."

"A wild card." Nicholas shook his head in disgust. "Are you ever involved in *anything* where a wild card doesn't turn up?"

"Not so you'd notice."

"This is getting old, Adam."

"Tell me about it. And don't shoot the messenger. I didn't invite the bastard to visit, you know."

"Any idea why he's here?"

"We haven't talked. But I'd be willing to lay you good odds that he's here to even the score."

"I don't suppose you could ask him to wait his turn. Maybe put off revenge until next year?"

Adam laughed shortly. "Not likely. As long as I watch my back, though, he shouldn't be able to get close. Sneaking up from behind is his favorite tactic."

Nicholas sighed. "Okay. So that's another complication in an already dizzying situation."

"Agreed."

"I'll see what I can do. In the meantime, you be sure and watch your back."

Adam nodded. "Yeah." He paused, then added absently, "By the way, I was supposed to ask you if you told anybody about Rachel's plans for the boutique. You didn't, did you?"

"Not a soul. So unless Becket did—or somebody at the house, I suppose—you've got a very short list of people who could have mentioned it to that real estate agent. Always assuming, of course, that it *was* mentioned, and she didn't say so just to cover her ass."

"I hadn't even thought about that."

"That's your trouble, Adam. You assume people tell you the truth."

"And you assume they lie."

Nicholas smiled. "That assumption, my friend, has saved my skin many times. And yours, once or twice."

"It's a hell of a way to live, Nick."

"Don't waste any time feeling sorry for me. My life is just the way I want it."

"I'm glad. Mine could use some work."

"Then after we get this situation taken care of, work on it."

"More cheap advice."

"Which is the easiest kind to take." Nicholas pushed his half-finished beer away and slid out of the booth.

"One more thing," Adam said casually.

"Yeah?"

Adam cleared his throat and sent Nick a somewhat guarded look. "In the course of my confession earlier today, I sort of mentioned that you'd done some work for the government."

"Oh, you did, did you?"

"Sorry. I guess I got caught up in the narrative."

"Don't get caught up again," Nicholas warned grimly.

"I won't. And I doubt Rachel would say anything about it, except to you or me."

"Sometimes," Nicholas said, "I wish you'd never stepped in front of that bullet in Rome."

"I imagine so."

"Just be careful, will you?"

"I will. You too."

"Always." Nicholas turned and walked back through the bar, along the wide path drunken men made for him.

The warm day had become a chilly night. Nicholas stood outside The Tavern and let out a long breath, watching it turn to mist. A crash from behind him in the bar made him look over his shoulder briefly, but he didn't go back inside to find out what had happened.

Despite his propensity for stopping bullets meant for other people, Adam was more than capable of taking care of himself.

But the deck was stacked against them this time. They were running out of time. And, as usual, there was a wild card in the game.

Max Galloway.

Nicholas swore, watching his baleful words turn to mist. Then he walked slowly to his car. He got in and started the engine, but for a long while just sat gazing off in the direction of Mercy's apartment, his hand idle on the gearshift.

"I'm a fool."

He pulled away from the curb, and at the corner hesitated again.

Then he turned the car toward Mercy's apartment.

"I'm a goddamned idiot."

It was still a little before midnight, but Mercy was nevertheless surprised to look through the peephole and find Nicholas at her door—considering the way they'd said good-bye at the office. But she opened the door and stood looking at him, wondering if she would ever be able to read his face. Not tonight, that was for sure.

"Hi."

"Hi. May I come in?"

"Sure you want to? I mean, I might accuse you of trying to blow up my best friend."

"Not without evidence, I hope."

She stepped back and gestured for him to come in, but kept her face expressionless. She hoped. Since she hadn't been expecting him, or company of any kind, she was already dressed for bed in a long, football-jersey-style sleepshirt, which she felt put her at a distinct disadvantage.

But at least she wasn't wearing her damned fuzzy pig slippers.

"I was having a glass of wine," she told him. "Want one?"

"Please."

She left him in the living room, returning a couple of minutes later with the glasses to find he'd loosened his tie but hadn't removed his jacket, and had not sat down. Definitely not the usual drill. Nicholas never seemed to take their relationship for granted, but they had reached a level of ease with each other, and he usually made himself at home in her apartment.

Then again, they'd never gotten as angry with each other as they had that day.

She handed him his glass and then curled up in the big arm-chair at a right angle to the fireplace, leaving the sofa for him. "Have a seat."

He did, and sipped his wine. He didn't take his eyes off her. "I suppose I should apologize," he said. "But I'll be damned if I know why."

"If you don't know, it wouldn't be worth much."

"I got mad. I had reason. I wasn't the only one at fault, Mercy. You had no business following me."

"Granted. I apologized for that."

"And then asked me if I was trying to kill Rachel."

"That's not what I asked. And I won't apologize for it," Mercy said steadily. "You ask for my trust and offer nothing. I've known you for five years, Nick, and I don't have a clue what you're about outside the walls of the bank. Are you trustworthy in business? Absolutely. Honest? I'd have to say yes. Good with finances? No question. Enigmatic and secretive as hell? You bet. Do I know your favorite color? No. The music you like? No. Whether you would do something not in Rachel's best interests *for a good enough reason?* No. I don't know that, Nick. So I asked."

"You never asked before," he said. "Not about my favorite color, or the music I like. Or what I'm about outside the walls of the bank. It didn't seem important to you, Mercy. You didn't ask, I didn't answer."

"You didn't want me to ask."

He was silent for a moment, his gaze now fixed on the wineglass that he rolled back and forth slowly between his palms. "Maybe."

"Maybe? Be honest, Nick. You weren't about to let me get that close."

"Is that what you think?"

164

"I think it's obvious."

He set his wineglass down on the table and got to his feet. Then he crossed the space between them and went down on one knee beside her chair, his arms reaching for her. "I want you as close as I can get you," he said, his voice low, almost harsh.

Mercy wasn't at all sure she would have protested, but in any case she wasn't given time to say a word. He was kissing her, his arms so tight around her that it was almost painful. She supposed he must have taken her glass away from her, or maybe she'd dropped it, but either way her hands were free, and her fingers were tangled in his hair.

Against her mouth he murmured huskily, "My favorite color is green."

Mercy tried to catch her breath when his lips left hers, and she tipped her head back when he began to explore her throat. "It is?"

"I love classical music, especially piano concertos."

"Do . . . you?"

"And I can't think of a good enough reason to do anything that would hurt Rachel."

She tightened her fingers in his hair and tugged until he drew back and looked at her.

"Good," she whispered.

Nicholas picked her up and carried her to the bedroom.

"You are a wonderful lover," Mercy observed a long time later.

"I know."

She grinned at him. "Modest, aren't you?"

Raised on an elbow beside her with his free hand lying on her stomach, Nicholas smiled slightly. "I figured out by the time I was sixteen that if I wanted women, I'd have to be good enough in bed for them to look past this ugly mug of mine."

That startled her. She was wary of asking, but raised her brows in a questioning expression.

Surprising her again by answering readily, Nicholas said, "When you're a teenage boy enslaved by your hormones, you'll do just about anything to get laid. Girls my age wouldn't look twice, not even on a bet. But I was lucky. There was an older woman in my neighborhood who was interested in things other than looks. She wanted a young lover, I needed a teacher. It lasted about a year. She taught me how to please a woman, and gave me confidence in myself. I'll always be grateful to her."

Mercy reached up a hand and slid her fingers into his dark hair. It was his one beauty, thick and shining, a little longer than was fashionable, incredibly sensuous and silky to the touch. "I imagine there have been quite a few women since your teacher."

"A few. I'm forty, Mercy. And I've been on my own since I was seventeen. There's a lot of road behind me."

"No relationships? Just women along the way?"

"More or less. I've never lived with a woman. Never fathered a child as far as I know. Until I came to Richmond, I'd never spent more than a year in any one place."

"You never wanted a family?"

"I never thought I'd have one." He shrugged, and his voice was not quite careless when he said, "I'm a realist, love. Being good in bed is one thing, but the prospect of spending thirty or forty years staring at this mug across a breakfast table is enough to daunt any woman. And that's okay. I don't mind being alone. Sometimes I even prefer it."

"Do you?"

He smiled. "One thing my life has taught me is to live day to day. And night to night. Tonight I have you. A beautiful, warm, giving woman beside me in bed. Some men have passed through their entire lives never knowing that."

Mercy wondered why her throat was hurting, why it was difficult to hold her voice steady. "We've never talked like this before. You've never talked like this before."

"You never asked, love." He caught her hand against the side of his face and pressed his lips to her palm.

Somewhat fiercely, she said, "You're damned sexy, in case you didn't know that."

He chuckled, the bedroom rumble of the laugh much softer than his usual harsh one. "I'm glad you think so."

"And I've looked at your face across many a breakfast table. It hasn't bothered me so far."

"I'm glad of that too." He leaned down and kissed her, his lips playing lightly with hers in a teasing seduction that instantly sent her senses whirling and her entire body throbbing.

Mercy put her other hand up and pulled at his hard shoulders until she could feel his weight on her. He was wonderfully heavy.

And he definitely knew how to please a woman, how to touch and taste and caress, how to bring her body alive. More than knowledge, though, was infinite patience and empathy. He had very quickly learned all Mercy's most sensitive spots, learned to read her responses and build her desire until she burned in his arms.

But for the first time, Mercy didn't allow herself to be merely a passive lover, accepting his astonishing skill and the control it demanded of him. She didn't want him to feel that he had to give some extraordinary performance, that he had to remain detached, critical of what he was doing, striving to be the perfect lover. She wanted a mutual passion.

And she knew how to get it.

He wasn't the only one who had learned from a lover. Mercy had paid attention as well.

Her fingers and lips found the most sensitive spots on his hard body, and she used all the skill and passion at her command to arouse him past his ability to control what he felt, to push him beyond his detachment. She used the fire in herself to make him burn.

She had the dim awareness that what she was doing was dangerous, that Nicholas with his control in splinters just might be more than she or any woman could handle. But she didn't care.

For once, just this once, he was going to be as ensnared by her as she was by him.

"God, Mercy, what are you doing to me?" His voice was hoarse, almost gone, and his fingers bit into her shoulders.

"Making love to you," she murmured huskily. "You don't want me to stop, do you?" Her lips moved slowly down his hard stomach.

He groaned. "Christ, no."

Mercy had learned a lot. And by the time his control shattered and his heavy body covered hers, she was so wildly aroused herself, she could only hold him and cry out in a pleasure so intense she wasn't sure she would survive it.

And didn't care.

.   .   .

The lamp on her nightstand burned low, but Nicholas didn't bother to turn it off. He didn't want to let go of her long enough to move.

They were on their sides facing away from the light, curled up back to front. Spooning, he thought it was called. Mercy's silky back pressed against his chest, her warm bottom curved into his loins. His arms were wrapped around her.

She was sleeping.

Careful not to wake her, he rubbed his cheek against her hair and breathed in the sweet scent. He loved the way she smelled. Her hair, her skin. He wanted to absorb the smell of her, make it his own.

Make a memory.

Something had changed tonight. He had been so careful, and still it had happened. She had made it happen, had made him lose control. So now she knew.

She had to know.

It was only a matter of time now. Maybe not tomorrow or next week, but it was inevitable. He had known that from their first night together.

He rubbed his cheek gently against her hair and listened to the soft sounds of her breathing.

Making another memory.

It was very quiet.

All she heard was that soft rustling sound, the sound that made her skin crawl and terrified without definition.

Rachel walked on.

She didn't know where she was going.

She was in a building, one with many hallways and rooms, and doors that were locked. She tried some of the doors, but most remained stubbornly closed. Then one opened for her, and she blinked in surprise.

Just a brick wall with a mask hanging on it.

Rachel closed the door and walked on. She passed by a room that held odd lights and shadows, and when she paused to look in, she found more masks. Hanging on the walls. Dangling from the ceiling.

Rachel walked on.

Another room she looked into had windows covered with brown paper, blocking the light.

She went on, and around the next corner there was a door that seemed to have a great deal of light behind it. At first Rachel thought it was locked, but she tugged and tugged, and finally it opened.

For a moment, she was blinded by all the light pouring from the room. That's all there was—light.

"Rachel."

She took a step back.

"Rachel." He stepped out of the light, smiling at her.

Adam. Happily, she held out a hand to him.

He took off Adam's face, and it was Thomas.

Rachel's hand fell, and she took another step back, suddenly frightened.

"Don't trust him, Rachel." Thomas took off his face, and it was Adam again.

"Don't trust him."

The Thomas mask fell to the floor, and when she looked down at it, it was horribly broken, the ragged edges dripping blood. . . .

·   ·   ·

Rachel woke up with a cry tearing free of her throat. Her heart was thundering, her breathing so hoarse that each gasp stabbed her.

She sat there, her knees drawn up and her arms wrapped around them, shivering, staring around at the morning-bright room, trying to reassure herself that it had been only a dream.

Slowly, her fear and panic faded, but anxiety lingered. She had never in her life dreamed like this. Masks. Thomas and Adam, seemingly interchangeable, one or both of them warning her not to trust . . . someone.

Who?

Was it only her own subconscious warning her to be very sure of her feelings for both men—the living and the dead?

Or was it a different kind of warning?

E L E V E N

When Rachel came back into her bedroom after her shower, she paused while getting dressed and gazed at the yellow rose in the bud vase on her nightstand. It should have been wilting at least a little, she thought.

It wasn't.

She reached out and touched a silky petal, then withdrew her hand and stared at her fingers. On two of them were crystal drops. As if the flower were so fresh, it still held morning dew.

Rachel sank down on the side of her bed and stared at the rose. Flowers didn't just appear out of nowhere and then freshen themselves every night. So there had to be an explanation.

Except she couldn't think of one.

Even if there had been nothing else, Rachel would have been unsettled. Added to her dream, it was profoundly disturbing.

"Don't trust him, Rachel."

Dreams were seldom straightforward, instead presenting symbols and signs that had to be interpreted based on what was going on in one's life at that moment. She knew that. So what was her subconscious trying to tell her? Not to trust Adam? Or not to trust her growing feelings for him?

Rachel didn't know, and not knowing was painful.

She finished dressing and went down to breakfast, pleased to find that Mercy had stopped by, as she sometimes did. Their lives had been so busy that they had not had much time to talk lately, but during the past weeks Mercy had made it a habit to stop by once every few days for coffee and conversation.

On this morning, Mercy was a bit preoccupied, but she did note a change in her friend. "Bad night?" she asked as she joined Rachel at the table.

Rachel grimaced. "Does it show?"

"Yes," Mercy replied slowly. "It does."

"Just unsettling dreams," Rachel said.

"About?"

Rachel hesitated, then shrugged. "Tom. Adam."

"You still dream about Tom?"

"I hadn't for a long time. But lately . . ."

"Since Adam came?"

Rachel nodded. "I guess my subconscious is trying to work out how I feel about them both. Adam's coming over this morning, so you may see him, Mercy. Be warned. He's the image of Tom."

"Maybe that's it," Mercy murmured.

"What?"

"Why you're different."

"I didn't know I was."

Mercy smiled. "Look in the mirror. It isn't a drastic change, but this morning you look a lot like that girl I knew as a teenager. Your whole face seems more alive somehow. Expressive of what you're feeling."

Rachel knew that Tom's death had changed her. What she had not realized was that Adam's arrival had wrought another change. "And you think it's because Adam looks like Tom?"

"Isn't it possible? You lost the love of your life, and ten years later his double shows up. I can only imagine that he would be easy to love."

Rachel gave herself a moment, sipping her coffee, then spoke slowly. "I can't deny that Adam looking so much like Tom might have influenced me in the beginning."

"Might have?"

"All right—did. But, Mercy, I know he isn't Tom. He looks like him, even sounds like him, but there's something in Adam I never saw or sensed in Tom."

"What?"

"A toughness. A danger. Tom was always more careless and carefree than anything else. Friendly, charming. You never got the feeling that Tom could be dangerous, that there was anything especially powerful or tough inside him." Rachel shrugged. "He loved fast cars and fast planes, and he laughed more than he frowned. He'd make promises blithely, with every intention of keeping them, but somehow . . ."

"Somehow they always got broken."

A little hesitantly, Rachel looked at Tom's sister. "He always tried to keep his promises, I know that."

Mercy smiled. "Of course he did. He was my brother, Rachel, and I loved him. But he was a lot like our father. His charm took him through life, and it succeeded so well for him that he never really had to work at anything. Never had to fight for anything that mattered to him."

"You've never said anything like that before."

"You weren't ready to hear it." Mercy shook her head. "He loved you, and I like to believe he would have made you a good husband, but those fast cars and fast planes would have kept him away from you a lot. Just the way they've kept Dad away from Mom."

Rachel had been vaguely aware of Tom and Mercy's parents as a child, and had gotten to know them a bit better during her engagement to Tom, but she had never really considered them as a couple. Thinking about it now, she realized that Alex Sheridan traveled a great deal and was seldom home, and that Ruth Sheridan—like her own mother had—occupied her time with charities and other social duties and responsibilities. To all appearances, it seemed a content marriage, just as her own parents' marriage had seemed content. On the surface.

"I never thought," she said slowly.

Mercy's smile held a touch of ruefulness. "Charming men have a way of discouraging thought."

Rachel looked at her. "Is that why you've tended to date men who were—"

"Not charming?" Mercy laughed. "I guess you could say that. I learned to value other qualities more." Then she sobered and gazed at her friend steadily. "The point is that you can't believe you're being disloyal to Tom because Adam has come into your life. Whether anything develops between you or not, Tom shouldn't be part of the equation. He had his share of faults, just like the rest of us, and you have no way of knowing—really knowing—if the two of you would have been happy together. But even that isn't important. He's gone, Rachel. Let him go."

Rachel managed a smile. "That's easy for you to say. You haven't met Adam yet."

"Looks can be deceptive, as the man said. At least, I think it was a man. Anyway, just keep reminding yourself that Adam is not Tom. Sooner or later you're bound to get them separated."

"Umm. I hope you're right."

"I am. Which entitles me to ask one nosy question."

"That being?"

"Why is Adam Delafield coming over this morning?"

Rachel's hesitation was brief. "To help me go through Dad's private papers."

Mercy raised an eyebrow. "Oh? Rache, I hate to sound too much like Graham Becket, but is that a good idea?"

"I don't know," Rachel replied frankly. "Yesterday I would have said I trusted him. In fact, I did say it. Today . . . I just don't know."

"Then maybe you should ask him not to come. Give yourself a little more time to make up your mind about him. With everything that's happened to you recently, it would probably be a good idea."

Rachel shook her head. "No. Dad trusted him, Mercy. He trusted him enough to lend him a lot of money on a handshake."

"You're sure of that?"

"Reasonably sure. Maybe as sure as I'll ever be. In any case, I can't see how his helping me would be a mistake on my part."

"You hope."

Rachel sighed. "Yeah. I hope."

There didn't seem to be much to say after that, and in a few minutes Mercy took her leave. She was preoccupied once again as she walked toward her car, but that abstraction vanished as she watched a strange car pull up beside her own—and the living image of her dead brother get out.

"My God," she whispered. Until that moment "he looks like Tom" had been a statement she only vaguely understood, but now Rachel's confusion became all too clear.

He saw her, saw her shock, and came toward her slowly. His expression was as enigmatic as Nick's had ever been, and that veiled look sat oddly, she thought, on her brother's open face. The disparity freed her from the paralysis of astonishment.

"My God," she repeated.

He stopped an arm's length away and slid his hands into the pockets of his jacket. "You're Mercy Sheridan," he said. "Rachel described you."

Tom's voice. Yet not quite. "And she described you. But I didn't . . . quite believe her."

"I'm sorry," he said. "I know it must be a shock."

"You could say that. You could certainly say that." Mercy shook her head, her eyes fixed on his face. "You really could almost be his twin."

"So I've been told."

"No wonder Rachel is . . ." She didn't finish that sentence, and if there was any reaction from Adam, it was so subtle, she missed it. Mercy drew a breath. "Well. I would say it's nice to meet you, but you'll have to let me get used to the idea."

"I understand."

She wondered if he did. "Rachel's expecting you. And I have to get to work. So—I guess I'll see you again."

"I hope so," he said, the words conventional and his tone light. He stepped back onto the walkway and watched her until she reached her car and got in. Then he turned and headed toward the house.

Mercy had a lot on her mind these days, but the shock of Adam's appearance stayed with her all the way to the bank. And she wasn't sure which bothered her more. That Adam looked so much like her dead brother, or that his familiar face held a secretiveness Tom's had never displayed.

"Here's something." Rachel was at her father's desk, going through the contents of the bottom drawer while Adam sat on the sofa with the contents of the other remaining desk drawer spread out on the coffee table before him. "Another scrap of paper with a name and phone number, and the notation *call about JW*. Those were the initials beside that largest loan." She kept her tone casual, just as she had since he had arrived.

"Is it a Richmond number?" Adam asked.

"There's no area code, so it must be."

"What's the name?"

"John Elliot. Doesn't ring a bell with me."

Adam came to the desk and looked at the paper for a moment, then reached for the phone. "One way to find out."

He punched the number, listened for a few moments with his brows rising, then gave his and Rachel's names and her number and asked that the call be returned to either of them as soon as possible.

"Voice mail?" Rachel asked as he hung up.

"Yeah." He frowned. "John Elliot is out of town for an unspecified length of time. Rachel, he's a private investigator."

She leaned back slowly in the desk chair and stared at him. "So Dad wanted this JW investigated?"

"Looks like it."

"But the bank has an investigator on retainer. Why would Dad use another one?"

"Maybe because this was one of his private loans."

Rachel shook her head. "There's no date on the note. We have no way of knowing if this JW was investigated before or after Dad lent him the money. Or even at all. It could be a plan he was never able to put into motion. Until John Elliot gets his messages and calls us . . ."

"We just have another question."

Rachel took the note and said, "So I guess we just copy this, put a copy in the file with the rest of our bits and pieces—and keep looking while we wait for Elliot to call."

Adam perched on the corner of the desk. "You sound discouraged."

"Well, it's like putting together a jigsaw puzzle when we don't know what the picture is supposed to be. *And* half the pieces are missing. I'm afraid I'm going to look right at something vitally important and not realize it. Why the hell did Dad have to be so cryptic?"

"He was a very . . . discreet man." Adam smiled.

"To a fault."

"If you want to put off finishing this, Rachel—"

"No, no. It has to be done."

"Yes, but not necessarily today. I know this is hard for you, and not just because we're putting together a jigsaw puzzle. Maybe we need to take a break. Why don't I buy you lunch, and then maybe we can take a closer look at that store you leased yesterday."

Rachel smiled slightly. "You're not going to let me off the leash, are you?"

He grimaced. "That obvious?"

"That you don't want me leaving this house by myself? Oh, yes, it's fairly obvious." *But is it for my safety, Adam? Or for yours?*

"Rachel, until we know more than we do now, it's better to be safe than sorry. That explosion last Friday was too close for comfort."

"I know, but, Adam, the mechanic admitted the cut brake line *could* have happened accidentally. And even though the police said the explosion was definitely arson, it's happened more than once in that neighborhood in the past months, and nobody in the area saw anything."

"We still don't know who called the agent looking for you," he reminded her.

"I know. And I mean to be careful. But I won't be a prisoner. Even in my own house."

He nodded. "Okay. But that aside, I still want to take you to lunch, and I'd like to hear your plans for the store. You're not going to abandon me today just to prove a point, are you?"

"Of course not." Rachel looked at him, wishing, for the first time that he didn't look like Tom. But he did, and because he did, how could she trust the instincts telling her she could trust him?

"Good. Then why don't you go grab a jacket and tell Fiona we're leaving, and I'll straighten up in here."

"Okay. I won't be a minute."

"Take your time."

When he was alone in the study, Adam hesitated, then picked up the phone and quickly punched a number. When the call was answered briefly, he said merely, "We're leaving," and hung up.

He quickly gathered up the scattered papers on the coffee table and put them into a box where they were keeping the items that didn't mean anything to either of them. He locked the file with the new note and copies of the other notes and notebooks in the top center desk drawer.

He was about to close the desk drawer Rachel had been slowly emptying when something down at the very bottom caught his attention. It looked like the corner of another small black notebook.

When Adam dug it out, that was exactly what it was. But this one was filled with numbers more cryptic than anything they'd yet found. And something that looked to him like some kind of code.

Adam hesitated, then swore under his breath and put the notebook into the inside pocket of his jacket, then locked up the drawer.

When Rachel came downstairs, he was waiting in the foyer, lounging back against the newel post and watching two of Darby's men wrestle with a rather fine barrister bookcase. It was taking up much of the hallway leading toward the rear of the house.

Darby appeared with her ever-present clipboard, and Rachel said, "We're going out for a while. If you need anything while I'm gone, just ask Fiona."

"And hope she's feeling charitable?"

"I've spoken to her. She promised to be polite and helpful."

"Uh-huh. Well, we'll see."

A few minutes later, as they headed toward Richmond in Adam's rental car, he said, "So Fiona's rough on other people as well, huh? I thought it was just me."

"No, she's pretty democratic in her dislikes. Actually, though, she's just slow to trust and hates change. But she's been with my family a long time."

"I gathered as much."

There was a short silence, and to Rachel it felt a bit strained. If Adam had noticed her reserve, he hadn't commented, but she couldn't get last night's dream and her doubts about him out of her mind. She cast about for something to say to break the silence. "We'll have to go by Graham's office before going to the store. He called last night and said he got the keys from the agency when he took the signed lease by."

Adam frowned slightly. "Rachel, I think you should arrange to have security in that store right away. A top-notch alarm system for sure, maybe even a security service to make regular patrols."

"That's what Graham said."

"It's a sensible idea."

"I know. I'll call and make the arrangements tomorrow. But I also have to arrange for some preliminary remodeling. At night we can lock everything up, but security won't be very tight with workmen coming in and out during the daytime."

Adam frowned, but didn't comment.

Rachel wondered what disturbed him. The possible threat to her safety? Or something else? She wished she had the courage to ask.

When she spoke again as they reached the restaurant, it was to change the subject. "Have you talked to Nick lately?"

"I asked him if he'd told anyone about your plans for the boutique. Did you ask your uncle Cam, by the way?"

"Yes. He'd forgotten I'd even mentioned the plans. All he has on his mind these days is furniture. What about Nick?"

"Didn't tell a soul."

"Then it really is a short list of people who knew."

"Unless . . ."

"Unless?"

"Unless the agent added that part when she realized you were upset. So she wouldn't sound so irresponsible in telling a stranger where you'd be."

"I never thought of that." She sighed. "Why is nothing ever as simple as you think it is?"

Adam didn't answer until he'd parked the car and come around to open her door. Then he said, "To keep us on our toes, maybe?" He was smiling, but his eyes weren't.

"As good a reason as any, I guess."

"Come on," he said, offering his arm. "Let's forget all about it for an hour or so."

"That I definitely agree with," Rachel said so cheerfully that she almost convinced herself.

The phone conversation was brief.

"You wanted to know where they went."

"Yes."

"A restaurant first. Then a quick stop at the lawyer's office. She went in, he didn't."

"And from there?"

"Looks like they're heading to the store."

"All right."

"Do you want me to—"

"I want you to follow your orders."

"Right."

"And this time don't fuck up."

"I'm surprised Becket didn't insist on coming along," Adam commented as Rachel unlocked the front door of the store and they went inside.

"He did make a suggestion."

"That he come along?"

"It might be a good idea, he said. Just to look the place over and hear about all my plans. So he could advise me about business permits and so on."

"Which you're perfectly capable of finding out on your own."

"Exactly what I told him."

Adam looked at the big empty space surrounding them. "Still, this is quite an undertaking. Maybe he *could* advise you."

"You're more charitable about him than he is about you." Rachel kept her voice casual.

"I'm a nice guy."

Are you? Are you really? "And not a suspicious lawyer."

"I guess it's an occupational hazard for him."

"Definitely more charitable than Graham." Rachel shook her head, then said, "I want to go check out the back. I didn't take more than a quick look last time."

"Hold on a second." Adam slipped around her, moving quickly

enough to catch her off guard, and went through the door into the back areas of the building.

By the time Adam reappeared, Rachel had managed to remind herself that all kinds of appearances could be deceptive. Maybe Adam really was worried about her safety.

Or maybe he just wanted her to think so.

God, I hate this!

"Satisfied?" she asked lightly.

Equally lightly, he said, "Just because you're paranoid doesn't mean someone isn't out to get you. Being careful never hurts."

"What did you expect to find back there?"

"A clear space and a locked rear door. Which is what I found."

"You do realize this place doesn't even have gas heat? It's electric."

"I realize it now—after seeing the furnace in the back."

"May I go back there now?"

"Yes, ma'am."

They were, she thought, both being polite. Very polite.

"I need to get a rough estimate of the space back there."

He followed her this time. "So you can get the work started?"

"That's the idea." She stood beside a tall stepladder left behind by the previous occupant, opened the small notebook she'd brought along, and used one of the steps as a makeshift desk.

While he watched, she paced off the dimensions of the office space, then did the same in the storage area behind it, and recorded the rough measurements in her notebook. "Plenty of space."

"I'd say so."

She looked at him quickly, the hair on the nape of her neck stirring suddenly. "What's wrong?"

Adam was looking slowly around. "Nothing."

"There is something. I can hear it in your voice."

He shook his head. "I thought I heard something, but I guess not. Are you about done?"

Rachel closed the notebook and put it in her shoulder bag. "I have enough to get started with."

"Then let's go." He took her hand, and she could feel his tension as they walked through the big, echoing space of the store.

Because he thought something might happen? Or because he knew something would? As Graham had pointed out to her earlier, just because Adam was with her when something happened didn't necessarily acquit him of being responsible, as Rachel had assumed. He could, Graham had suggested, be working with a partner.

The suggestion made Rachel feel a bit sick.

When they stood outside on the sidewalk and Rachel had locked the door behind them, she realized she'd been almost holding her breath. It sounded a little shaky when she let it go.

He looked down at her. "I'm sorry, Rachel—I didn't mean to worry you. I guess I'm just jumpy."

She shook her head, too relieved that nothing had happened to hide it. "I'll have a good security system installed tomorrow, and find out when I can get a contractor in to inspect the place from end to end."

"Good idea."

They had to walk about half a block to Adam's car. But they were no more than twenty feet from the store when the sudden roar of an engine jerked both of them around.

It was a huge black car, the windows tinted dark, and it was coming straight for them.

Fast.

For what seemed like an eternity, Rachel stared, frozen, at the car bearing down on them. She saw it shear off a decorative lamp-post as it jumped the curb and roared onto the sidewalk toward them.

Fast.

So terribly fast.

A hard arm locked around her middle.

Rachel felt herself yanked off her feet, and then the car was gone from her vision and only the ungodly roar of its laboring engine filled her ears. Adam had literally swept her out of the path of that juggernaut.

Then they were on the hard pavement, the momentum rolling them over and over, and the engine of the black car screamed.

Rachel felt the hot breath of its passing.

The paramedics treated Rachel for a sprained wrist and one ugly abrasion just below her elbow. They said she was in shock.

She agreed with that assessment.

Once again, Adam's thick leather jacket had protected him somewhat, even though he had taken the brunt of the punishment in trying to shield Rachel. But he, too, had been treated, for several abrasions on his hands and a scrape along one cheek.

They were both lucky, the paramedics said.

The cops said the same thing, and were very unhappy to find that none of the witnesses to the scene could tell them much.

"A big black car," one of the cops said to Adam while Rachel was being patched up. "Tinted windows, no way to see the driver. And nobody got a license plate." He eyed the shattered lamppost and what was left of a bench the car had taken out before leaving the sidewalk, and shook his head. "Damned thing must have been a tank."

"It was big and heavy, no question," Adam said. "I didn't get the make or model. It just happened too damned fast."

"Do you think it was deliberate? Was the car driven onto the sidewalk in an attempt to get you two?" It seemed an automatic question; this officer seemed to have no awareness of Rachel's previous close calls.

Adam hesitated, then shrugged. "Like I said, it all happened too fast to be sure of anything. It could have been a drunk driver, I suppose, or somebody who just lost control." He didn't mention that laboring engine, a sound he suspected would linger in his memory for a long, long time.

And in Rachel's, no doubt.

He saw one of the paramedics helping her out of their van, and said quickly to the cop, "I need to get Miss Grant home. You know how to get in touch if there are any more questions."

"Sure, go ahead."

"She's in shock," the paramedic told Adam flatly when he reached them. "But she won't go to the hospital. Keep her warm and get something hot inside her."

Adam hesitated, on the point of overruling Rachel. But then she looked up at him with pleading eyes, and there was no way he could withstand that. He took off his jacket and put it around her shoulders, then took her to his car and put her inside. He turned up the heat, full blast.

And he got her away from there.

"More hot tea?" she murmured when he pulled over in front of a café five minutes later.

"I think so. Unless you'd rather have something else?"

"No. Tea's fine."

Adam didn't want to leave her for a minute, but her pallor and the darkness of her eyes bothered him. And she looked so small with his jacket enveloping her.

He brought the hot, sweet tea back quickly, and put the cup into Rachel's hands.

"Thank you," she said politely.

"Drink it, Rachel."

Obedient, she sipped.

She didn't say anything else until they were almost at her house, and when she did speak, her voice was unnaturally steady. "In case you're wondering, I believe it now."

He looked at her quickly and saw a single tear fall.

"Rachel . . ."

"Someone wants me dead." She drew a breath, and a tremor shook her voice. "Someone really wants me dead."

T W E L V E

L isten to me, Rachel. I am not going to let them succeed."

She sniffed, then murmured, "That's twice you've saved my life. How can I ever thank you for that?"

He didn't like the way she sounded. Almost mechanical. "Don't," he said. "Just . . . don't."

"We have to find out who it is, Adam. We have to finish going through Dad's papers."

"Yes. But not today."

Rachel was silent while he parked the car near the house and came around to help her out. For a moment, she stood there, looking at the house, and then she said, "I won't be a prisoner."

"I know. Come on." He put an arm around her and took her into the house.

He saw her safely into the anxious care of Fiona and Darby, both of whom seemed to know exactly what Rachel needed. They took her upstairs at once, Darby saying something about a hot bath and Fiona promising hot soup.

Adam briefly explained the day's events to Cameron, who was appalled, then promised he'd return the following day to check on Rachel. Then he drove back to Richmond, to Duncan and Ross Investments.

As he strode rapidly through the lobby and toward the offices, Adam thought one or two people had the idea of asking him his business, but he didn't give anyone the chance. He went into Nick's office and closed the door behind him.

Behind his desk, Nick immediately looked up and asked, "How is she?"

Adam wasn't surprised by his knowledge. "Shaken. Scared. It's a miracle she isn't dead."

"You're why she isn't dead, according to what I heard."

Adam waved that off. "Have you found Galloway?"

Nicholas eyed him somewhat warily. "I have a few possibles. Why?"

Adam came forward and put his hands on Nick's desk, leaning toward the other man. "Because I want to talk to him."

"Adam—"

"I have to know. I have to know if it's Galloway."

"And if it is?"

"Then I have to make damned sure he doesn't kill Rachel trying to get to me."

"And you propose to do that how?"

Adam laughed shortly. "Break his neck?"

"The law frowns on that."

"I don't really care."

"For Rachel's sake, you'd better." Nicholas paused a moment and watched that sink in, then went on calmly. "I agree, we need to have a little talk with him."

"We?"

"Well," Nicholas said, rising, "your hands already look pretty beat up. Mine are nice and fresh. Let's go."

"He left his jacket," Rachel murmured.

"I'm sure he'll be back for it tomorrow," Darby said. She removed the tray from Rachel's lap and added, "You should try to rest. I'll be glad to sit with you—"

"No, Darby, you've already done enough. I'm okay, really. The bath helped, and so did the soup. I'll probably be able to sleep in a little while. You go on home."

"Sure?"

Rachel smiled. "See you tomorrow."

But when she was alone in her bedroom, Rachel felt the shakes start up all over again. She was bundled in a thick robe as well as pajamas, but still she shivered. She was already so sore that getting comfortable in bed was impossible, so finally she got up and took a couple of aspirin from her bathroom medicine cabinet.

That didn't help the shakes.

She went to the chair where Darby had left Adam's jacket and sat down there, using it as a blanket. It smelled of him, and she inhaled slowly, glad that whatever cologne or aftershave he used was not what Tom had worn. Very glad.

The shakes stopped after a little while despite the insistent inner voice reminding Rachel once again that just because Adam had been with her, just because he had seemingly saved her life once more, she still couldn't be sure he wasn't involved in this.

No. How can I believe that? He could have been killed as well, and surely that makes him innocent? Surely . . .

A few minutes later, she found the notebook in the inner pocket.

And recognized her father's handwriting immediately.

The shakes came back.

Max Galloway had a long history of dealing with his victims by remote control. Call someone and give an order; plant evidence to be found eventually; set explosives to go off when he was far away.

He seldom stood close. Rarely looked them in the eye.

Which was one reason he hated Adam Delafield.

Another reason was that he really hated getting slammed against a hard tile wall.

"I'm not going to ask again, Max." Adam's voice was quite gentle, in stark contrast to the hands threatening to make Max's next breath an arduous challenge.

Max sent one glance past Adam's shoulder, and wasn't reassured. Nicholas seemed indolent as he leaned against the closed door of the dingy men's room. He held the gun with indifference.

But it was a big gun.

"All right," Max gasped, coughing once in an effort to get those iron fingers around his throat to loosen.

They loosened. A bit.

"Talk," Adam said. "You followed me from San Francisco."

"Hell, what did you expect?" Max allowed his honest indignation to surface. "Jesus Christ, Adam, you fucking ruined my life! I've got a price on my head because of you."

"You went renegade, Max. You almost blew up two square blocks of the city. Did you expect me to just let you do that?"

"It wasn't any of your business, Adam! You were out, how many times did I hear you say it? Just wanted to run your company and be left alone. So I left you alone! Your company wasn't in that area, so—"

Adam tightened his fingers, and Max choked.

Easing off just a bit, Adam said, "I'm not here to listen to you try to justify wholesale murder, Max. All I'm interested in right now is what you've done in Richmond."

"Nothing," Max said sullenly.

"Oh, no? You didn't try to blow up a building with me in it?"

Max looked bewildered. "Somebody try to blow you up, Adam? You just make friends everywhere, don't you?"

Adam applied a bit of judicious pressure, and Max choked again. "You're saying you didn't call the real estate office trying to find Rachel and me? Get there ahead of us and set a timer?"

Max coughed. "It wasn't me, goddammit! I haven't been in town long enough to be able to lay my hands on—my usual supplies. Especially not with this fucking price on my head!"

Adam glanced at Nicholas, who lifted a brow and shrugged.

Returning his attention to Max, Adam said, "But you were driving that car today, weren't you?"

"Car? What car?" This time his bewilderment wasn't convincing.

Adam slammed him against the wall again, making it perfectly obvious that he didn't care if he cracked Max's skull open.

Max groaned. "*Shit.* Okay, okay."

"It was you?"

"Yeah, it was me. I saw you with the girl and—it just seemed like a good idea at the time."

"Bullshit. You came here planning to get me."

"Well, yeah," Max said. "But not with a car. That was a great car too, and I had to ditch it right after."

"Another black mark against me?" Adam asked dryly.

"I really liked that car, Adam."

"How were you planning to get me?"

Vaguely, Max said, "I hadn't decided. Something painful."

Adam glanced at Nicholas, who was smiling slightly, then looked back at Max and tried not to smile himself. It wasn't that Max wasn't dangerous; he was definitely that. But he also possessed a kind of cockeyed charm that had more than once saved his skin.

Still, Adam wasn't about to let him off that easily. And remembering what had happened to Rachel today made his fingers tighten on Max's throat once more. "You made a big mistake today, Max. I wasn't alone when you aimed that car at me. Because of you, the lady got hurt. That makes me very unhappy, Max."

"Stop talking to him," Nicholas advised calmly. "Just kill him."

When he was allowed to breathe again, Max muttered, "I know the good cop–bad cop routine."

"Yeah," Adam said. "But you also know we aren't cops. And neither one of us is very good. Now, give me one convincing reason why I shouldn't collect that bounty—which is, as I recall, for your body dead or alive."

"You don't want to kill me, Adam."

"That's up to you. But I'll sure as hell turn your ass in."

Max groaned. "Might as well kill me. You know they will."

"That," Adam said, "is not my problem."

"Wait! I have something that might be worth listening to."

"I doubt it."

"I swear, Adam!"

"Then let's hear it."

Cagey, Max said, "You'll let me go? Give me a head start before you call out the dogs? That's all I'm asking, Adam."

"That depends on what you have to say, Max."

"I say kill him," Nicholas offered, supremely indifferent. "If you let him go, he'll just turn up somewhere else and pull another stunt like today."

"No, I won't, I swear."

"But you want to get even, Max," Adam reminded him. "I ruined your life, remember?"

"Yeah, but if you let me go now, you'll sort of be giving it back to me. And I'd appreciate that, Adam. We'd be all square."

"Now, do you really expect me to believe that?"

"I wish you would," Max said earnestly.

Nicholas let out a short laugh, which Adam knew was more amused than it sounded. It sounded derisive, and Max flinched.

"Adam, I swear I'll get out of your life and stay out. I swear."

"Let's hear what you have to say, Max."

Max cleared his throat. "If you could let go of me, it'd be easier."

"No."

"Well, okay. I just thought—"

Adam tightened his fingers for a moment, then eased off. "Max, pretend you're talking for your life. Because you are."

"Right. Right. You know I've sort of been watching you. Not every day, just sometimes."

Adam merely nodded, not admitting that Max's greatest talent—an ability to blend into his surroundings—had prevented Adam from noticing the surveillance.

"Well, I saw something else while I was watching you."

Nicholas barked suddenly, "Spit it out, goddammit!"

Max jumped. "Okay! Somebody else has been following you. I saw two different guys at different times."

"Following just me?"

"Well—you and the girl."

Adam stared at him. "Who were they?"

"One looked like a crook," Max answered. "Scruffy as hell. The other one . . . I dunno. Too polished to be a crook or a cop. Maybe a spook. Hard to say. They stayed well back. Knew what they were doing, both of them. It didn't look like a hit, Adam, honest. Surveillance."

Adam glanced at Nicholas, then looked back at Max. "What did the polished one look like?"

"Well, big, blond. Built sort of like you. As a matter of fact, he reminded me of you a bit. Way he moved, I guess, like he wouldn't have made a sound. I never got a good look at his face, Adam, he kept to the shadows mostly."

"Okay, Max. You just bought yourself a head start. Twenty-four hours. Got it? Twenty-four hours and you better be out of here." He let go of Max's throat and stepped back.

"I'm leaving right now, Adam, I swear." Max didn't even bother to straighten his crumpled shirt. He sidled away from Adam and studiously avoided Nick's gaze as he hurried out the door Nick held open for him.

Adam flexed his hands, which were in even worse shape than they'd been earlier, and went to one of the stained sinks to hold them under cold running water.

Closing the door behind Max, Nicholas thumbed the safety on and put the gun inside the waistband of his pants at the small of his back, where it was concealed by his jacket. "I told you to let me," he said.

"You were more effective just standing there holding that gun."

"Do you think Max is on his way out of town?"

"I think so, but I'll stay alert just in case he has a brave moment."

"He'd be less trouble all around if you turned him in, Adam."

"I know. But he's right. They'd kill him."

"Which is, as you said, not your problem."

Adam shrugged. Changing the subject, he said, "I'm surprised nobody came banging on the door while we were in here."

"I'm not. Every soul in the bar saw us drag Max back here. Nobody was going to risk getting in the middle of that. Not in a place like this."

"I suppose." Adam dried his hands gingerly on a paper towel. "The scruffy one's Simon, right?"

"Nobody'd ever call him polished, so we can assume so."

"Then who the hell is the other one?"

"You never saw him?"

"No. I saw Simon, but I was looking for him." He tossed the paper towel toward an overflowing trash can and turned to stare at Nicholas. "Goddammit, I was hoping it was just Max. Just me."

Nicholas shook his head. "The odds always favored Rachel being a target, you know that."

"I'm not liking the odds very much, Nick. That explosion was meant to kill her, not frighten her. I told you about the timer. The police don't have a clue, but I recognized it. It's the same kind of thing Walsh used before. Designed to leave nothing alive."

"Then we'll have courtroom evidence against him. If I can maneuver him into the net."

"I just don't get his motive for going after Rachel. Even if he did owe Duncan five million, there's no way she could have gone after it. She doesn't know what we suspect, doesn't even know who the JW in her father's notebook is. So how does she threaten him? How could he even imagine that she could threaten him?"

"I don't know."

"Shit. Let's get out of here." Adam didn't say anything else until they'd made their way back through the bar and into Nicholas's car.

It was nearly midnight; it had taken them hours to find Max.

As Nicholas started the car, Adam said suddenly, "My jacket."

"You haven't been wearing one."

"I left it at Rachel's." He paused, then repeated hollowly, "I left it at Rachel's."

Wednesday morning was bright and sunny, so Adam wasn't too surprised when Fiona told him Rachel was out in the garden. But he was surprised when the housekeeper politely showed him as far as the sunroom.

Either Fiona was mellowing toward him, or she was having a really good day.

Adam didn't push his luck by questioning. He just thanked her and went on into the garden in search of Rachel.

He found her near the center, sitting on a teak bench as she gazed absently into a koi pond, where bright flashes of color spoke of active fish. Adam paused for a moment before announcing himself, watching her. She looked none the worse for her close call the day before, but her long-sleeved silk blouse hid both the abrasion on her arm and most of the elastic bandage wound about her sprained wrist.

Even as he watched, she lifted that wrist and used her right hand to massage it gently, wincing.

"Are you going to tell Rachel she wasn't the target?"

"I don't think so. We know she's still in danger. She needs to believe it too. If I tell her that car was aimed at me, she'll go back to doubting that explosion was meant for her. She won't see any reason to be cautious."

"And explaining why you were a target would lead to so many questions, wouldn't it, Adam?"

Questions. God.

Adam walked slowly to Rachel and said, "Good morning."

She looked up at him, and the wariness in her eyes went through him like a bullet. "Hi. I didn't know if you were coming by."

"I didn't even get the chance to say good-bye yesterday, much less make plans. You were obviously in good hands with Fiona and Darby."

"Yes, I was."

She hadn't invited him to sit down, but he did anyway, in a chair at a right angle to her bench. "How are you?"

"Okay. A little sore." She glanced at his hands and frowned. "I didn't know your hands were that bad."

"They look worse than they feel." Since he had iced them the night before, there was little swelling. But they were sore from numerous abrasions and bruises, and still stiff as hell.

"I know you were protecting me when we hit the pavement. Otherwise, I'd be a real mess."

"Rachel—"

"I just want to thank you. I have to." Once again it was said mechanically, with more resolution than anything else.

He drew a breath. "You found the notebook, didn't you? In my jacket?"

She was staring at the fish, her profile still. "Yes."

"Rachel, I saw it in the bottom drawer of your father's desk just before we left the house yesterday. I was going to tell you about it."

"Were you?"

"Of course I was."

"All right."

That wariness again. It tore at him.

"Rachel, you said you trusted me."

"And you told me it might be better for both of us if I didn't trust so quickly."

"I was wrong. You have to trust someone. Trust me. You have to know I'm not trying to hurt you."

She turned her head and looked at him for a long while. Her eyes remained wary. "I believe you've saved my life twice. How can I not trust you?"

Adam wished it weren't a question. He reached over and covered her hands with one of his. "Rachel, I shouldn't have taken the notebook and not told you about it. I'm sorry. But, I swear, with everything that happened later, I simply forgot all about it."

"All right. Did you look in the notebook, Adam?" Her voice was steady.

"Just a glance. Numbers. And what looked like some kind of code."

"His own private code. He taught it to me when I was a child, and we used it in notes to each other. It was a kind of game. I still use it myself whenever I need to take notes."

"You can read the entries?"

Rachel nodded. "Yes."

"And?"

"And it's what we've been looking for, Adam. It's the journal Dad kept detailing his private loans. The recipients are identified."

"All of them?"

"All of them."

If Mercy expected things to be different between her and Nicholas after the greater intimacy of Monday night, she was not disappointed. But she was disappointed—and frustrated—to find that the difference did not appear to be a positive one.

She had a strong feeling that Nick was cautiously withdrawing, that he regretted even the tiny step they had taken from a casual relationship to something closer.

He'd been gone when she woke up the previous morning—which had given her the chance to stop by Rachel's—and he'd busied himself for most of the day in his office, not even taking a break for lunch. Then Adam Delafield had stalked into the bank, looking as if he wanted to take something major apart with his bare hands, and they had left together just moments later.

Mercy didn't find out about Rachel's latest brush with death until she had called her last evening. Rachel had sounded shaky enough, so Mercy didn't mention Adam's arrival at the bank or his subsequent disappearance with Nicholas.

But she wondered. Jesus, what was going on?

And when Nicholas showed up at his usual early hour today, she wondered even more. He was perfectly pleasant as he greeted the few staff members there so early, then shut himself in his office once again. The lights on Mercy's phone told her he was on his private line for much of the morning, and when she ventured to stick her head into his office once and ask if he wanted coffee, she was waved off with no more than an absent smile.

She had an uneasy hunch that he and Adam had gone hunting the driver of a black car last night, though she had no way of knowing whether they had been successful. And while it relieved her to believe neither of them wanted to hurt Rachel, she couldn't get past the idea that both men knew a lot more about the situation than they were willing to admit—at least to the women in their lives.

And despite telling Nicholas she didn't mean to meddle in his private affairs, she couldn't just sit by and wait for him to deign to tell her what was going on.

If he ever did.

Not that she had any intention of following him again. No, that wouldn't get her anywhere. Besides, Mercy's strength wasn't in TV-private-eye tactics, as Nicholas had so mockingly called them.

Her strength was in finances.

If this involved Nicholas, Adam, and Rachel, then the common denominator was obviously Duncan Grant. And what Nicholas either didn't know or chose to ignore was Mercy's familiarity with most areas of Duncan's life.

Since she had been executive assistant to the senior partner of the bank for five years, Mercy not only had all the computer access codes to bank records, but also access to at least some of Duncan's private records. And none of that had been cleared from the computer because Mercy had not yet been told to do so.

Nicholas wasn't the only one who could be secretive.

Mercy made sure Leigh and the rest of the staff were occupied, then shut herself in her own office and got down to work.

If there were answers in numbers, she'd find them.

Sooner or later.

"He kept pretty complete notes," Rachel said.

On the other side of her father's desk in the visitor's chair, Adam said, "Oh? How complete?"

Rachel looked at him for a moment, then began to read aloud from the small black notebook open on the blotter before her. " 'He strikes me as a fine young man with an exceptionally bright future ahead of him. The betrayal of his former employers coupled with his unjust imprisonment has left him wary and disinclined to believe anyone would help him without expecting something in return. I also believe he has placed himself in dangerous situations since he was released from prison several months ago, possibly in an attempt to exert control over his life, but more probably because his own experience left him with a keen understanding of cruelty and injustice.' "

Adam was looking down at his hands. "I had no idea he had given me so much thought."

"Was he right? About the dangerous situations?"

Adam finally met her gaze, and smiled faintly. "Let's just say I could have taken fewer chances along the way."

Rachel nodded, accepting that for the moment. She was more relieved than she wanted to show that Duncan Grant had indeed lent Adam Delafield all that money five years ago, that he had recorded the loan and his impressions of the man in his notebook. But even with that reassurance, the wariness she felt toward Adam wouldn't quite go away.

He was hiding something. Every time he looked at her, she could feel that intensity in him, and though she wasn't sure what it meant, she had the uneasy feeling that Adam definitely wanted something of her. That he had always wanted something of her.

She just didn't know what that was.

Returning her attention to the notebook, she said, "I don't think we need to concern ourselves with most of this. All the loans except these last three have been repaid. We have to start there, don't we?"

"I'd say so."

"Okay." She drew forward a legal pad, turned to the right page in the notebook, and spoke aloud as she began translating the notes onto the legal pad. "RS, lent a hundred and fifty thousand dollars, is—Robert Sherman. He's apparently from Kansas City, where he has a small graphics design business. His partner left him in the lurch, and that's why he needed the cash to reinvest in the business, get some new equipment and whatnot. According to his notes, Dad gave him the money—outright."

That surprised Adam. "Outright? No repayment?"

"No. He told Sherman that when he was a success in years to come, to pass on the favor." Rachel looked at Adam with a slight frown. "You know, I wouldn't be surprised if he'd done that more than once with some of the smaller amounts. I'll have to check on that later. In the meantime . . ."

She found the next entry that interested them. "LM, lent one and a half million, is Lori Mitchell. She lives in a small town in Oregon, where the loan helped her start her own newspaper. Seems her father had known Dad, and that's why she turned to him for help when the local banks refused her loan application. The loan from Dad isn't due to be repaid for another three years. That may be why she hasn't contacted me—if she even knows Dad was killed. He notes here that he told her to concentrate on getting her paper going and not waste time keeping in touch with him."

"Oregon," Adam said. "We can check, just to make sure she's where she's supposed to be. But I think we can probably cross her off the list."

Rachel made a note, then turned a couple of pages of the notebook and began translating again. "JW, lent five million dollars, is—Jordan Walsh. It says he lives in D.C." She glanced up at Adam. "Close enough."

"I'd say so. What does it say in Duncan's notes?"

"Let's see. . . . The money was lent to start a business, though what kind isn't mentioned. Dad was hesitant, but he was asked as a personal favor to lend the money."

"Asked by whom?"

"Doesn't say."

"What does it say *exactly*, Rachel?"

She glanced at him again, then slowly translated aloud,

" 'Walsh is very persuasive, and the company he means to start could help countless people. Still, I'm not entirely convinced this is the best way to finance his efforts. But as a personal favor to an old friend, I am willing to take the risk.' " She looked at Adam. "That's it."

"Nothing more?"

"Not here." She thumbed through the remaining pages slowly. "I don't see his name come up again."

"When is the loan to be repaid?"

"Doesn't say. But . . ."

"What?"

"Dad transferred the money to Walsh just a couple of months before he and Mom were killed. It was the last loan he made."

"And one of the largest."

"Yes."

Adam frowned. "Then I'd say we need to find out a bit more about Jordan Walsh."

"How?"

"Nick can probably help us."

"And what do we tell him?"

"Rachel, he knows about the explosion. He knows about yesterday. It won't surprise him to hear we're going through Duncan's papers looking for an answer." He paused. "You said you didn't suspect Nick. If he isn't a suspect, then maybe he can help us."

"All right."

"Why don't I go and talk to him? After what happened yesterday, you could probably use a quiet day. Stay in, maybe work on the floor plan of your new boutique. Forget the rest of this for a while."

While you do what, Adam? Talk to Nick? Or something else?

Rachel looked down at the notebook, hating her own suspicions.

Adam got up and came around the desk. He took her uninjured hand and pulled her gently to her feet, then reached for her other hand as well. Looking at the elastic bandage wrapping her wrist and hand, he said, "Until we know absolutely that you're safe, you shouldn't be out alone. You've already been hurt enough. If something else happened to you, I don't think I could stand it."

She wanted to believe that. He was looking at her, that intensity unshuttered, explicit hunger in his eyes, and Rachel found it hard to breathe suddenly. "Adam—"

"Oh, I know. You don't quite trust me, do you, Rachel, in spite of saying you do. So much is happening right now, and I'm still a stranger. A stranger who looks like a dead man." There was a tinge of bitterness in his voice. "Jesus, Rachel."

"What do you want me to say? That it doesn't matter? I wish I could, Adam. I really wish I could. But I can't. Not yet. I'm sorry."

"Do you think that helps?"

"I think I don't want to talk about this anymore. Not now."

Adam stared down at her for a moment, then swore beneath his breath. "I'm not Thomas Sheridan, Rachel."

"I know that."

"Do you? Maybe what you need is proof."

Rachel opened her mouth to ask him what he was talking about, but before she could make a sound, she had her answer.

His head bent, and his mouth touched hers. Softly, gently, as if he feared to damage something unspeakably fragile. His mouth was warm and hard, and disturbingly unfamiliar.

She let her eyes drift closed, mesmerized by the butterfly sensations of his lips caressing hers. The heat came slowly, welling up from some core she hardly recognized, rising inside her, swelling until it filled all the places in her that had been cold and dark and empty. She felt a tremor ripple through her body.

He felt it too.

In a moment, she was gathered against him, surrounded by powerful arms, held in an inescapable embrace. Yet still his kiss remained feather light and tentative, his mouth toying gently with hers. Until finally Rachel heard a wordless plea escape her, and her arms slid up around his neck.

His arms tightened around her, and his mouth slanted across hers, finally taking what she offered him.

It shook Rachel as she'd never been shaken before. When she had last felt real desire, it had been the tremulous, yearning passion of a girl for the man she trusted implicitly, the man she had known virtually all her life. Safe in Tom's arms, she had felt no uncertainty, no fear, no anticipation of pain or loss.

In Tom's arms, she had been totally, completely innocent.

Ten years later, grief and loss and pain had taught Rachel there was no safety in loving or being loved. And maybe that sharper awareness of how fleeting and uncertain life could be opened the floodgates containing a passion she had not known herself capable of feeling.

Maybe it was that.

Or maybe it was Adam.

The only thing she knew for certain was that it had nothing to do with Thomas Sheridan.

Adam kissed her in a way she understood not from experience

but only because comprehension sprang from primitive instinct. And she responded with the same all-consuming hunger, the same need to possess, to mark as her own the man who belonged to her.

And it was she who cried out in disappointment when he wrenched his mouth from hers.

"Rachel . . ." His forehead pressed against hers, and his ragged breathing was warm on her face. "Christ, Rachel—"

"Don't stop," she murmured, touching his face with shaking fingers when he drew back just a little and stared down at her.

"I have to." His voice harshened. "I won't win like this, Rachel. I won't take you away from Thomas simply because I can carry you off to my bed—and he can't."

Her hands fell away from him. "You think—"

"I think this is a decision you have to make, and not in the heat of desire. I want you. But I have to be sure it's me you want. You have to be sure. Or it'll destroy both of us."

Adam released her and stepped back. His face was still, his eyes once more shuttered. "I'll go and talk to Nick."

He left her there, staring after him.

THIRTEEN

After Adam left, it was a long time before Rachel could get her thoughts organized. And, even then, they didn't make much sense. She felt shaky, and wasn't sure if it was aftereffects of yesterday's brush with death or what had just happened.

A brush with . . . something else.

Too restless to just sit, needing desperately to be busy, Rachel locked up her father's desk and left the study. Lunchtime was still more than an hour away, and she wasn't sure what she intended to do, but when she reached the foyer, she encountered Darby.

"Hi. I was just looking for you."

"What's up?"

"Well, I was going through that lovely little mahogany secretary—the one that you said used to be in one of the upstairs bedrooms? And I found something I thought you should see."

"I thought you were going to just box up whatever you found when you cleaned out drawers."

"Oh, I am. That's what I've been doing, in fact. But since this has your name on it—literally—I thought I'd better give it to you."

"What?"

Darby pulled a small blue envelope from her clipboard and handed it to Rachel. "I suppose there's no telling how long it was in that drawer—"

"At least . . . ten years."

"Ten years? How do you know that?"

"Because this is Tom's handwriting." She stared at the envelope, at her name scrawled in Tom's sprawling hand, hardly surprised that she remembered his writing so vividly.

"Tom? Tom Sheridan?" Darby looked concerned. "Jeez, maybe I should have just dropped it in the box with the rest of the stuff. I had no idea it'd bring back bad memories, Rachel, I'm sorry."

"No, it's all right." Rachel smiled at her friend. "Good memories, not bad ones. Tom used to leave me little notes and presents hidden in the house. I always suspected I'd never found them all, but he'd never confirm that when I teased him to tell me."

Darby hesitated, then asked, "Are you going to read it? Should I go away and leave you alone?"

Alone with my dead lover. Rachel wasn't surprised that Darby would expect her to be upset; what surprised her was that all she felt was a slightly wistful sadness that hardly hurt at all.

"Of course I'm going to read it. And, no, there's no reason why you should go away and leave me alone." Rachel opened the envelope and withdrew a folded sheet of blue notepaper, which contained only a few words sprawling over the page.

Look in your jewelry box, Rachel.

She showed it to Darby, smiling. "He must have left me a present there. I seem to remember finding one or two over the years."

"Romantic." Darby was smiling as well.

"Yes, he was. Or maybe just playful. I never was quite sure."

Darby chuckled. "Well, I'll keep an eye out for more of his notes to you. And whatever else he may have left for you."

Rachel put the note back into the envelope and slid both into her pocket. "That would be a good idea. In the meantime—could you use some help? I'm not in the mood to do nothing today."

"Sure, if you feel up to it. Do you? With all the bruises you collected yesterday—"

"Moving around a little will do me good. Besides, if I go ahead and start cleaning out drawers, you can get finished faster."

"In that case, you're on. We have more stuff from the basement parked out in the hallway near the kitchen, if you're interested. I had just started to go through the drawers, when I found the note."

Rachel was interested, and a few minutes later was sitting on a borrowed dining room chair while she emptied the drawers of a tallboy. Darby left her to it, retreating once more to the basement to continue her tagging.

Rachel didn't really know what had prompted her to help Darby, when she had resisted doing so before. Maybe it had been

Tom's letter, with the implicit promise of more hidden in the house. More from him—and perhaps from others. Not that Rachel believed the answer to why someone apparently wanted her dead was hidden in some drawer last closed years ago. But given her father's secrecy about the private loans, it was possible that useful information could be found.

Then again, maybe she just wanted her hands and thoughts occupied.

By the time Fiona announced lunch, Rachel had filled one cardboard box with a variety of trash from drawer liners to old church bulletins, used greeting cards and crumpled stationery, and had another half-filled with yellowed linens and yards of unused material. And that was only from the tallboy.

She went upstairs to wash her dusty hands before the meal, pausing to run a brush through her hair and then pausing again as she came back through her bedroom. The rose on her night-stand looked as fresh as it had that morning. As it did every morning.

She wondered what Adam would make of that. She didn't know what to make of it, and every time she considered it, her mind shied away. *It's as if someone places a fresh rose in the vase while I sleep, so fresh there's still dew on the petals. . . .*

"I'm losing my mind," Rachel murmured, and it seemed as good an explanation as any.

She sighed and pulled Tom's note from her pocket. A note from a long-dead lover. A rose that wouldn't wilt. Definitely the stuff of madness.

She carried the note to the little desk near the window and opened the top drawer to place it inside. Then she stopped, aware of a niggling unease. There was something not quite right here, she thought. Something that was . . . something that shouldn't be . . .

She opened the drawer farther and looked at the neat stack of stationery and envelopes, the small notecards. Small blue notecards. Slowly, she compared Tom's note to what lay in the drawer. The stationery was the same. There was nothing wrong with that. Except for one thing. This was stationery she had brought with her from New York.

Ten years ago, there had been none like it in the house.

Look in your jewelry box, Rachel.

Rachel found herself crossing the room to her dresser without thought, but when she stood before the closed leather jewelry box, she went still. Absurd. It was, of course, absurd to think she'd find anything inside. She'd had the box open only yesterday, after all. There was nothing unexpected in there, certainly nothing Tom could have left for her. Not ten years ago.

Not even yesterday.

Drawing a breath, she reached out and opened the box. There was nothing new in the top tray. Her familiar jewelry, nothing more, the everyday things she often wore. She lifted that tray out and set it aside. In the second compartment was also her jewelry, pieces less often worn. A few gold chains, some simple earrings, and—

A delicate gold identification bracelet that had not—surely had not—been there the day before.

Rachel lifted it out slowly. Her name was etched in script on the front. On the back, also in flowing letters, was another inscription.

To my beautiful Rachel
Happy, Happy Birthday
All my love, Tom
August 16, 1988

A birthday present. Except that her birthday had fallen three months after Tom's plane had disappeared. And this was a gift she had never received.

Until now.

Ghosts.

She turned quickly, the bracelet clutched in her hand, and stared around the room. It looked just the same as always. Pretty and neat—and empty of anyone except her.

"Tom?" she whispered.

She listened, her senses straining, but there was nothing to hear.

Of course there was nothing to hear.

Rachel returned the bracelet to the jewelry box and replaced the top tray, telling herself that this, too, could be explained. Tom could have brought stationery from outside the house, the similarity to what she owned now mere coincidence. She had been so in shock and numbed by grief after Tom's death that she could have missed a gift already left for her to find. Could have overlooked it in the bottom tray. Of course she could have.

But for ten years?

Maybe she really was losing her mind.

·　　·　　·

For the rest of the day, Rachel pretended that nothing out of the ordinary had occurred. She went back to going through the furniture that Darby and her men had brought up from the basement, and it was nearly four that afternoon when Fiona summoned her to the study, where Graham waited for her.

"Rachel, are you all right? Why the hell didn't you call me?"

For just a moment, she wondered how on earth he had found out, but then she realized what he must be referring to. Leaving the study door open behind her, she came into the room and perched on the arm of a chair near her father's desk. "I'm sorry, Graham. I was so shaken up, I just didn't think about it. How did you hear?"

He thrust a folded newspaper toward her. "This."

It was a brief article on an inside page and below the fold. A couple was injured slightly when a car came up onto the sidewalk and nearly struck them. The driver fled the scene of the crime. Her name and Adam's, but virtually nothing else.

Rachel shook her head and handed the paper back to him. "Well, at least they didn't make a big deal about it."

"Is that a bandage on your hand?"

"It's just a sprained wrist, Graham. I'm fine. A bit sore today, but I'll recover. Thanks to Adam."

Graham took a couple of steps away and turned to face her, leaning back against her father's desk. "It's always thanks to him, isn't it, Rachel?"

"I would have been killed if he hadn't been there."

"Yeah? Maybe it wouldn't have happened at all if he hadn't been there."

"You're still convinced he's the one who's trying to hurt me? Just your suspicions, Graham? Or something more?"

He drew a breath. "Rachel, there's something fishy about this."

"I know you think so."

"All this started when he came to Richmond. And he's always *there,* Johnny on the spot, ready to be your hero. These *accidents* always just miss you."

"Would you rather they didn't?" she snapped, her own doubts and worries suddenly raw on the surface.

"That's not what I'm saying, and you know it. Rachel . . . a man comes to you. He's ready—he says—to repay a huge loan your father gave him—he says. He looks amazingly like the fiancé you lost ten years ago. And he keeps playing hero and saving you from death, in the best melodramatic tradition."

"Thanks a lot," she said dryly.

"You know what I mean. It's a con, Rachel. He's after your money."

"Graham, for God's sake, you found the information yourself. He has a company doing well out in California."

"That doesn't mean it couldn't do better with more money to spread around."

She shook her head. "You're wrong."

"I don't think so, Rachel."

She didn't know why she didn't tell him about the notebooks and journal they'd found. Maybe because she wanted to keep her father's secret. Or maybe because she didn't want to defend Adam to Graham.

"I trust Adam," she said instead, the declaration slow and firm and hiding her doubts.

"Do you? Then ask him why he's been out of the country more often than in during the last five years. Ask him if he can run that company of his by remote control, because he sure as hell hasn't spent much time there."

"You're still checking his background? Graham—"

"I won't apologize for it, Rachel. Your father would turn in his grave if I didn't do my best to look out for you. And I'm telling you, there's something strange about a man who takes regular trips to places they warn the tourists to stay away from."

"I believe he has placed himself in dangerous situations since his release from prison. . . ."

She crossed her arms and stared at him. "Graham, I know you have my best interests at heart. And I appreciate your concern, I really do. But I am almost thirty years old, and I can manage my own life. Whatever is between Adam and me is between *us*. Stay out of it, please."

His mouth hardened. "I see."

"I wish I believed you did."

"Oh, no, I see well enough. I see more than you do. Tell him to dye his hair black, Rachel, and then see how you feel about him."

"I am not mistaking my feelings because he looks like Tom."

"Aren't you?"

"No. Maybe I did at first, but not anymore. Tom's dead." *Even if he is still giving me presents . . .* "And Adam is alive. And I know the difference."

"Rachel—"

She drew a deep breath to steady her voice. "If that's all you came to say, Graham, then I wish you'd go. I am really sorry you and I don't agree about Adam, but you have to realize that nothing you could say would change my feelings for him."

Slowly, Graham said, "Yes. I see that."

Without another word, he turned and left the room.

Rachel was dimly aware of the angry sounds of his powerful Corvette roaring away from the house, but she didn't really listen. Graham's anger barely touched her.

"Nothing you could say would change my feelings for him," she whispered in realization.

How ironic, she thought dimly, that on the day she had discovered a lost gift from Tom she had also discovered she was beginning to love another man. A man she still wasn't sure she trusted.

"It doesn't tell us much that's new," Nicholas said.

"I know." Adam shrugged. "But at least now we see that Walsh did owe Duncan five million. And that Duncan wasn't easy in his mind about the loan. That jibes with what he told me."

"And no word yet from that P.I.?"

"No. I checked, and he's still out of town. He doesn't have regular office help, and his landlady doesn't care where he is because he paid for the month before he left."

"So we have no way of knowing if he did any looking into Jordan Walsh's dealings."

"Not as far as I can see. I, uh, checked the office. His filing system is something of a mystery, but I couldn't find anything on Duncan or Walsh. That doesn't mean it wasn't there. I didn't have a lot of time."

"Did you find out if he had a security system before you picked his lock?"

"I took a chance."

Nicholas shook his head and leaned back in his desk chair. "I just know I'm going to be bailing your ass out of jail before this is over."

"Think positive. Are you any closer with Walsh?"

"Maybe. Finessing that guy is a lot like dancing with a tiger. One wrong step and the music stops for good."

"Rachel is going to ask me questions about him. I'm supposed to be finding out the answers from you."

"Tell her only as much as you have to—but keep it vague. Because we don't know why Walsh would come after her, and we don't know for sure that the loan Duncan made him has anything to do with it. The ultimate answer may still lie among Duncan's private papers."

Adam sighed. "Well, there may be more information, but I think it's doubtful. What else would he have?"

"A copy of the P.I.'s report, if he made one?"

"That's a big if."

"Granted. But possible."

Adam nodded. "I'll go back to Rachel's tomorrow."

"Yeah, well, get some sleep tonight, will you? No offense, friend, but you're looking a little ragged around the edges. You won't be any good to Rachel if you don't shut it down for a few hours."

"I will."

If the dreams will let me.

"She has more lives than a cat."

"It's that watchdog of hers. Get him out of the way, and—"

"Never mind Delafield. I'm getting sick of this bullshit."

"She's going through her father's papers. Do you really want to take the chance that she won't find something?"

"I'm telling you, he didn't know."

"And I'm telling you, he might have. Duncan Grant was no fool. If he knew, he would have left information or evidence behind. The risk of her finding and understanding it is too great."

"I've taken bigger chances."

"Well, I'm not willing to take this one. I've worked too long and too hard to see this thing fall apart now because of Rachel Grant. And I'm telling you to take care of the problem."

Rachel was back inside the house with all the hallways and doors, and she didn't like it.

She wished she could find a safe place and just wait, but an overpowering urge she didn't understand kept her moving. The hallways were illuminated only by sconces on the walls, and as she walked deeper into the house, the sconces became wrought iron and held candles, and they were fastened to walls of rough stone.

It was getting cold, cold and damp.

Dimly, Rachel could hear sounds, sounds she didn't want to listen to. Something was hurt. Something was hurt, and it groaned and whimpered its pain. As badly as Rachel wanted to escape the sounds, they grew louder as she approached a door at the end of the hallway.

It was a cold metal door, massive in size. A heavy padlock secured it. And there was a small access opening in the door, fastened only by a sliding bolt.

The sounds came from inside.

Groans. Whimpers. And something else, something terrible.

Rachel wanted to turn around and leave. She wanted to run. She wanted badly to run.

Completely against her will, she saw her trembling hand stretch slowly out toward the small access door. She could hear her own breathing, rapid and frightened, and beyond that the sounds from inside the cell.

"No," she whispered, "I don't want to see. I don't want to know."

"Open the door, Rachel." Tom's voice.

"No."

"Open it and look inside."

"I don't want to."

"You have to."

"No."

"You have to know where he's been, Rachel. You have to understand."

"Please . . ."

"Open the door."

She saw her fingers hesitate, then grasp the bolt and slowly draw it back until she could open the access door.

"Don't make me."

"Open the door."

Almost sobbing, she opened the access door.

And cried out.

They had hung him from a heavy beam across the ceiling, his wrists lashed together and stretched above his head, bearing his entire weight. His back was to the door, and he was stripped to the waist. Two men stood on either side of him, and one of them held a whip.

That was the other sound Rachel had heard.

As she stared in horror, the man with the whip used the entire strength of his arm to bring the whip across the back of his victim. A back already crisscrossed with bloody welts.

A muffled groan.

Rachel beat her hands on the door, crying out, "No! Stop! Stop hurting him!"

One of the two men turned his face toward the door, but his face was a featureless mask, and his laugh was hollow.

The man with the whip turned a matching mask toward her, then reached over and slowly turned his victim until he was facing the door.

"No!" Rachel screamed.

The Adam mask the tortured man wore was horribly crushed and bloody, almost unrecognizable. Scarlet dripped from underneath the mask, painting ghastly tracks down his throat and over his bruised chest.

"No! Adam!"

One of the torturers laughed and reached out to his victim, his fingers curling into the eyeholes and the mouth hole of the mask as he jerked it away from the face beneath.

"Look! Look what we've done to him!"

But Rachel couldn't look. She covered her face with her hands and screamed and screamed. . . .

The screams were only whimpers, but Rachel's throat ached as though she had been crying out in agony for hours.

She turned on the lamp on her nightstand and sat huddled against the headboard of her bed, shivering. It took a long time for her heartbeat to slow to its normal cadence, and even longer for the shivering to stop.

It was two o'clock in the morning.

The thought of going back to sleep was too awful to contemplate.

Rachel got up and took a long, hot shower. It eased the lingering stiffness in her body and warmed her up so that when she got out, she felt almost human.

And the only person in the world awake at this hour.

The house was silent, and she wasn't willing to risk waking Cam and Fiona by going downstairs. But it was a long time until morning. And she really didn't want to think about that dream.

She turned on her television to CNN, the volume low, then looked around her room for something else to occupy her mind for a few hours. She found her father's datebook, and it took her a moment to remember that she'd brought it up days before, meaning to go through it when she had time.

Now she had time.

She curled up in a chair and began looking through the last year of her father's life. All his appointments, professional and private. Notes he'd jotted while on the phone. Addresses and phone numbers.

It was hard for Rachel to turn the pages, to see his last days play out before her. She cried a little, her emotions closer to the surface than they had been in a long time. And then she got to the day of his death.

And went cold.

"Oh, my God," she whispered.

When he heard the knock on the door of his room, Adam was only mildly surprised, even though it was four A.M. Room service had delivered coffee and rolls an hour before, and all Adam thought as he went to glance through the security spyhole was that somebody downstairs was bored and had come to collect the tray.

It wasn't room service.

Adam started to open the door, then stopped. He quickly unfastened the chain from around his neck and slid it and the locket into the front pocket of his pants. Not long out of the shower, the pants were all he was wearing.

Then he opened the door. "Rachel, what in God's name are you doing out this time of night? And alone, dammit—"

"Sorry if I woke you," she murmured.

He didn't like the stillness of her eyes. "I was up. Come in."

She did. "I remembered your room number, and—" She gasped.

Realizing his back was to her as he closed the door, Adam turned around quickly. "Rachel—"

"My God," she whispered.

"It wasn't as bad as it looks." He got a shirt from the closet and shrugged into it, leaving it unbuttoned. "Just scars, and those will fade away until they're hardly visible. Eventually."

"How could they do that to you?"

He said lightly, "They were the bad guys."

"Oh, Adam . . ."

He took her hand and led her to the sofa in the small sitting area. "Here, sit down. Good thing the coffee's still hot. Your hand's like ice."

She sat there, her eyes never leaving him, and when he fixed the coffee the way she liked it, she accepted the cup and wrapped her hands around it. "I don't understand people like that."

"Good." He smiled.

"They did that to you . . . for five years?"

"No, most of it came in the first few months. After that they got bored with me. Besides, given the methods of the new government, there were plenty of prisoners coming in every day. I became a very small and unimportant target." He sat down in the chair across from her, not daring to get any closer.

"But why? Why did they want to hurt you like that?"

Adam shook his head. "It was a brutal regime. All they knew was violence. They wanted to make sure I didn't have any information that could benefit them. And . . . I had to be punished."

"For what?"

"For doing what I'd been sent there to do. Getting those people and that equipment out of the country."

"It was your job."

"I never said they were fair, Rachel."

"I'm sorry. I'm so sorry."

"It was a long time ago. I healed."

"Did you?"

He managed another smile. "More or less. Rachel, what are you doing here? To come into the city this time of night, alone . . . What were you thinking?"

She seemed to shake off her horror. Adam was glad. But he was also wary.

"I was thinking I needed to ask you something," Rachel said.

"Something that couldn't wait until morning?"

"Yes."

"Why didn't you just call me?"

"I needed to see your face when I asked. When you answered."

That watchful stillness was back in her eyes. It made him feel cold. He was afraid this was going to be bad. "Okay. You're here. What's your question?"

Rachel leaned forward to set her cup on the coffee table between them. Her gaze never left his face. "Why didn't you tell me you were with Dad the day he died?"

He'd been right.

It was bad.

FOURTEEN

How did you find out?" Adam kept his voice level.

"Dad's datebook."

"And he'd noted a lunch appointment with me just a couple of hours before he and your mother got in that plane."

"Yes." Rachel shook her head. "Why didn't you tell me you were with him?"

Adam drew a breath and let it out slowly. "Because . . . it might have led you to ask other questions I wasn't ready to answer. I didn't want to say anything until we had proof."

"Proof? Proof of what? And who is 'we'?"

Adam answered the last question. "Nick and me."

"Nick was with Dad that day?"

"No. But he believed me when I went to him and told him what

I suspected. What I knew. So we've been working together. Looking for proof."

Rachel sat back on the sofa and stared at him. "Proof of what?"

"Proof that the plane crash wasn't an accident."

"Dad's plane? You're saying you think somebody deliberately rigged it to crash?" She felt an icy chill sweep over her. "That somebody wanted to kill them?"

"That somebody wanted to kill Duncan. Your mother wasn't scheduled to fly with him that day. I don't know why she was on the plane."

"She . . . sometimes went with him when she was in the mood," Rachel murmured. "Adam—the FAA concluded that an electrical spark ignited fumes. That it was an accident."

"I know."

"Then why do you think it wasn't?"

"Because I was there, Rachel. At the airport when he took off, waiting for my own flight back home. Because I was able to see the wreckage a few days later, and I found something. The FAA investigator should have found the same thing, because it was fairly obvious. But his report stated that the crash was an accident. Maybe because he was inept, or maybe because he was corrupt. I don't know—yet. But I found enough to convince me that Duncan's plane was brought down deliberately."

"What? What did you find?"

Adam leaned forward, elbows on his knees, and looked at her steadily. "I know electronics. And even more than most pilots, I know what electronics are found on a plane. What I found didn't belong there. The explosion destroyed most of it, but there were a few pieces of a device that must have been fixed to the altimeter. A kind of timer. That, and a package of explosives hidden near the fuel tank, must have caused the plane to explode when it reached a certain altitude."

"But you don't know that for sure."

"I'm sure, Rachel. In my own mind I'm positive. And those pieces I found are being kept safe by your father's mechanic out at the airport. He agrees with me. And he'll testify. When we have more evidence."

"Why didn't you go to the police?"

Adam hesitated. "Because while I could prove the plane was brought down, I was also fairly certain that the guilty party couldn't be identified by what's left of that timer. Going to the police would just alert him that he was under suspicion, and we'd never get him. I thought Nick and I stood a better chance on our own. It . . . isn't the first time we've done this sort of thing, and I trust us more than I trust the cops."

Rachel was trying to let it sink in, let it make sense to her. "Why would anyone want Dad dead?"

"That's something we haven't been able to find out." Adam paused, then said, "At lunch that day, Duncan seemed preoccupied, unusually distant. So I asked him if anything was wrong. He said it was nothing, just that he was somewhat troubled by something he'd found out about a recent business venture—with a man named Walsh."

"Jordan Walsh?"

"We think so. It's the only clue Duncan offered, the only trail we had to follow."

"Then—you knew about him before we found Dad's journal?"

"We've been concentrating on him for months. The note about the loan just gave us a more concrete reason to suspect him."

"Adam, even if you had only suspicions, surely the police

would be better able to investigate than you two. They must have more resources."

"Maybe. But sometimes belief counts for more. Rachel, Jordan Walsh has ties to the underworld. The police suspect, but can't prove, that he was involved in more than a dozen murders during the past few years. They suspect, but can't prove, that he ran a multimillion-dollar money-laundering operation for a New York crime syndicate.

"And even though the police would no doubt investigate him on your father's behalf, we don't have enough proof to give their investigation the weight it deserves. If we go to them now, they'll just have another unsolved homicide on their books—and Walsh will know we're on to him."

"Adam, I don't understand this. Jordan Walsh doesn't sound like the kind of man my father would do business with."

He nodded. "We think the same thing. It's the most puzzling question in all this. One thing—Walsh was operating out of D.C. when your father lent him that money, and his public reputation is clean. If Duncan had asked around, he wouldn't have necessarily heard anything negative, not unless he dug really deep. And that note in his journal, about doing a favor for an old friend, might also explain it."

"You mean he might not have investigated Walsh until something made him uneasy after he'd already lent the money?"

"Could be. He never asked Nick about Walsh, but that was very much in keeping with how he handled his private loans." Adam paused, then went on. "Except in my case, when he was aware Nick had known me for years. But he might have used a P.I. unconnected with the bank—like that John Elliot we saw named in his notes—to investigate if he became uneasy."

Adam shrugged. "But we won't know that unless and until we hear from Elliot. Assuming he knows anything."

"So all we know is that Dad loaned Walsh money at the request of an old friend."

"Yes."

"Who? What friend?"

"I have no idea. Have you?"

Rachel thought about it, but none of the names flitting through her head made sense. "Dad had lots of old friends. Here, in D.C.— all around the world. It's a long list, Adam."

"I was afraid of that."

Slowly, Rachel said, "But no matter who it was who recommended the loan, you believe that Jordan Walsh is responsible for Dad's death."

"Yes."

"And . . . the attempts against me?"

"It seems likely. We haven't been able to find another answer, Rachel."

"I don't understand that. I didn't even know about Walsh until I found Dad's journal. And even then, how could I be a threat to him? You can't take a notebook to court and demand repayment of a debt."

"I know. We—haven't been able to come up with an answer for that either. All we can be reasonably sure of is that somehow you pose a threat to someone. Walsh seems most likely, but we don't know for sure. But he turned up in Richmond just after you came home. And things started happening."

Rachel was silent for a moment, then said, "How have you and Nick been investigating this?"

"Cautiously. I had to return to California shortly after the funeral, and with the work involved in settling Duncan's estate, Nick pretty much had his hands full. But in the course of that, he went through all the bank's records, which told us that whatever dealings Duncan had had with Walsh had either been in the very early stages, or were very private. From my experience with him, we knew he made private loans and investments." Adam paused. "What we didn't have was access to Duncan's private records."

Rachel drew a breath. "I see."

"Rachel—"

"That was your job, I take it. To cozy up to me and get access to Dad's papers."

"That's not the way it was."

"Oh, no? Are you saying it wasn't your . . . assignment to tell me about your private loan from Dad and so encourage me to go through all his papers probably sooner than I otherwise would have? That it wasn't your job to talk to me, and help me, and just possibly find the evidence you wanted?"

"Rachel—"

"Wasn't it?"

"You make it sound very cold-blooded."

That was answer enough.

She nodded slowly. "It is cold-blooded." Astonishingly to her, she was able to keep her voice calm, even reflective. "But I guess I can't be too upset about it, huh? After all, you and Nick were just trying to . . . avenge my father's death."

"And protect you."

"It started with Dad."

"I owe him a great deal, Rachel. So does Nick."

"And you didn't owe me anything. I understand that."

Her voice must not have been as calm as she'd thought, because he flinched.

"Rachel, please. I never wanted to hurt you. And I never lied to you. What happened between us—"

"Nothing happened between us, Adam."

A muscle in his jaw tightened. "You know better than that."

"No, I don't." A little laugh escaped her. "In a way, Graham was right. It was all a con. So I'd trust you, and confide in you. But the goal was always Dad's papers."

"Rachel—"

She got to her feet and moved toward the door. "I think I'll go home now."

Adam was there beside her suddenly, gripping her arm and forcing her to face him. "No. You have to listen to me."

"Listen? To what, Adam? More half-truths? I don't want to hear any more of them."

He was staring down at her, a little pale. "All right, then," he said roughly. "Don't listen." His arms went around her, holding her tight against him, and his mouth covered hers.

Rachel would have said she was too hurt and angry to respond to him with desire. She would have said this man still had too many secrets he wasn't willing to share with her. She would have said she could not become the lover of a man she had known less than two weeks.

She would have been wrong.

The naked hunger she had seen before in his eyes was alive in him now, a fever she could feel burning in his entire body. He kissed her as though he were utterly certain he would never again have the chance to do so, and held her as if he expected someone to try to snatch her away from him.

That intense, overwhelming need was not only strangely moving, it was also explosive. And Rachel had no defense against it.

Her body gave itself over to him, molding itself to him, and her arms slid up around his neck with an eagerness she was beyond trying to hide. All that mattered to her was that she give him what he needed.

What she needed.

Adam groaned against her mouth and held her even tighter for a moment. Then he eased back just a little, far enough to mutter, "Tell me you're ready for me, Rachel. Tell me you want me."

"I want you." She pushed his shirt down off his shoulders and pressed her mouth against his chest.

"Are you sure?" His voice was ragged.

"I'm sure."

He had no choice except to believe her; it was what he wanted, needed, to hear.

"Rachel . . ."

In the quiet of the hotel room and the darkness before dawn, nothing seemed to exist except the two of them. Nothing else mattered.

They were more like longtime lovers than strangers, with no awkwardness or hesitation. Each seemed attuned to the other, as though they had done this together many times. Every touch of the hands and brush of the lips was slow, deliberate, the restraint between them only intensifying the building passion until it was like a wild storm trapped beneath glass.

And the glass shattered.

. . .

Rachel pushed herself up on an elbow and looked down at Adam. "Just so you know, I'm still mad at you."

"Yeah, I had a feeling you were."

"You should have told me, Adam."

"I know. And I probably would have, days ago, but I'd given my word to Nick. He didn't think we should involve anyone else in this, or voice our suspicions until we had proof. Not even to you."

"God, he's secretive."

"He is that."

"Didn't he think I was concerned in the matter?"

"Of course. But neither one of us wanted to upset you when all we had were suspicions and speculation."

"And when somebody started trying to kill me?"

Adam reached up and brushed back a strand of her hair, his fingers lingering to stroke her cheek. "I wanted to tell you, Rachel. All along. Please believe that."

She nodded, telling herself it was all right to believe him because the alternative was too painful. "But, Adam, don't keep things from me for my own good, all right? I need to know what's going on."

"I agree. And I promise I won't keep anything else from you for your own good." His hand slid into her hair, and he pulled her down far enough for him to kiss her.

Rachel had the dim realization that he had somehow hedged on that promise, and it bothered her. But she pushed worry aside for the moment, unwilling to disturb the fragile peace between them. It had been a long time since she had felt physically close to someone, and she needed that, needed to feel wanted. She relaxed against him for a moment, then lifted her head and said, "I wasn't finished talking."

"Weren't you?" He shifted them slightly until he was raised above her, then pushed the sheet down so that he could see her. "I was."

She felt just the slightest bit self-conscious when he looked at her with a fixed intensity and absorption as tangible as a touch. "Do you realize what time it is? The sun's coming up."

His mouth trailed over the slope of one breast. "Is it? I hadn't noticed."

Rachel caught her breath as he toyed gently with her nipple. She could feel that incredible heat welling up, building again inside her, spreading outward from his mouth on her like molten ripples in a pool. Her fingers slid into his hair, and she held his head to her breast, astonished anew by what he could make her feel.

"Hadn't noticed what?" she murmured, willing to pay whatever price was demanded of her for this.

The sun was well up, bright light slanting through the narrow opening of the drapes, when Rachel stirred again. "I should probably call home. I didn't leave Fiona a note or anything."

"Tell her you probably won't be home for lunch."

"Won't I?"

"Not if I can persuade you to stay here with me. Room service isn't bad at all."

She had to climb across him to use the phone on the night-stand, and all during her brief conversation with Fiona, he distracted her by tracing the line of her spine with first a finger and then his lips.

"Where are you getting the energy?" she demanded when the call was finished and his exploration continued.

"I have no idea. Your skin is like silk."

Rachel felt her own energy rebuilding, and did a little exploring of her own.

She found more scars.

"Don't," Adam said unsteadily when quick tears welled up in her eyes. "I'm okay, Rachel. Now I'm okay."

Nevertheless, she tried to make it up to him, to offer him all the comfort and sweet passion at her command. Whatever brutality he had suffered at the hands of those cruel men, she wanted him to be very sure that there would be memories for him now of beauty and pleasure.

By the time they finally forced themselves from bed for a shower and room service, there was something in Adam's face Rachel had never seen before, a kind of contentment and peace. It was almost as if he had found something for which he'd been searching a very long time, something he had given up all hope of finding. He looked at her constantly, touched her often. Even his voice was different, lower and softer, like rough velvet.

Rachel didn't know what it meant, and it unnerved her more than a little, but she didn't question. For now it was enough to just be with him, to believe that whatever else he wanted of her, desire was real.

"It won't do any good to keep avoiding the subject," she told him finally as they finished with the brunch they'd ordered.

"What subject is that? We've been talking almost nonstop. I figured we'd covered everything."

"You know better."

Reluctantly, he nodded. "Okay, maybe I do. The world intrudes, doesn't it?"

Rachel pushed her chair back from the little table in the corner but didn't get up. "It has to. At least until we can stop whoever killed Mom and Dad."

Restless, Adam said, "You never talk about her."

"We weren't close, I'm afraid. It was nothing major, just very different personalities. Adam, you can't keep putting it off."

"Okay, you're right. So let's talk about it."

"What's being done to get evidence against Walsh?"

He grimaced. "Right to the point. And the answer is— it's a little complicated. Nick has let it be known, through various . . . connections he has in the city, that he might be willing to make a substantial investment if guaranteed a high rate of return."

"Meaning a risky venture. An illegal one?"

"That's the idea. And Walsh is nibbling at the bait."

"Does he think he's dealing with Nick personally, or the bank?"

"The bank. Nick's running a huge bluff at the moment, claiming he can control most of the bank's assets." Adam shrugged. "The original plan was based on our assumption that you intended to sell your interests to Nick. That way, he could have controlled what money he needed to without having to explain himself to the board."

"If he'd told me—"

"I know. I brought that up a couple of times. But he was determined not to involve you. He hasn't said, but I have a hunch he's backing his bluff with at least some of his own money."

"So . . . if Walsh takes the bait, he'll come to Nick with some kind of phony investment, but what he'll really have planned is—what?"

"Another money-laundering scheme, we think. Turning dirty money to clean is a very important cog in the mob's wheel."

Rachel frowned. "Okay. But how does that help Nick find evidence that Walsh rigged the plane to crash? Or that he's the one trying to kill me?"

"If Nick can win Walsh's trust, there's a chance he can get inside the operation and find the evidence we need. He's done this sort of thing before, and he's good at it."

Rachel was still frowning. "But doesn't something like that tend to take months, even years—assuming it works at all?"

"Sometimes."

"And it's dangerous."

"Very," Adam replied steadily.

She drew a breath. "And our only other option?"

"Hope we find something more among Duncan's papers." Adam shook his head. "If we knew why you're still a threat to Walsh, we'd have more of the answers. But that part just doesn't make any sense."

"And you're convinced it's Walsh who's tried to kill me?"

"Rachel, I had a friend with the police here get me a look at the evidence the fire marshal found after that store exploded. It was a state-of-the-art sparking device on a timer that triggered the explosion. And it came from the same hand that built the device on your father's plane."

"You're sure?"

"I know electronics. I'm sure."

Rachel didn't doubt him. And his certainty made her feel cold. "Then we have to go back to the house. We have to finish going through Dad's papers."

"Yes." He reached across the table between them, and when she put her hand in his, he held it strongly. "And you have to be careful, Rachel. Very careful."

"Not only me. Adam, you've been getting in his way. What if he decides that he can't get to me until he gets you first?"

"Don't worry about me. I'm always careful."

"Really? Dad thought you put yourself into dangerous situations deliberately. And you admitted yourself that you hadn't always chosen the safe path."

"I will this time." His fingers tightened around hers. "I have a lot to live for."

Rachel wished she could believe Adam would be cautious. But she had a feeling it was not in his nature to stand back and let things happen. She let the subject drop for the time being as they left the hotel and drove back to her house in Adam's rented car.

"That's one more leased car I'll have to have them pick up," Rachel noted wryly about her own abandoned car.

"Because you parked it outside the hotel in plain view. These people build bombs, Rachel. I don't want you getting into any car you're not absolutely sure has been in a secure place."

"I know, I know. I should have just taken a taxi."

"Maybe you should make that a habit until this is over."

It made sense. It also made Rachel feel trapped.

"I hate this."

"I know. I'm sorry." He paused while they got out of his car in her driveway, then added steadily, "Maybe you should go away somewhere."

Rachel looked at him. "Is that what you want me to do?"

He hesitated, then swore. "No. I'm not sure we could keep you safe somewhere else, even with real iron bars. The only way to stop this is to stop Walsh."

"My thoughts exactly."

He smiled. "You wouldn't have gone anyway."

"No. I don't think it would solve anything." She took his arm. "Come on. Let's go look for some answers."

Peace reigned inside the house; after so many days of furniture being shifted from attic and basement, Darby and her crew were working in her store today. And Cameron was out in the garden, painting.

"Thank God," Rachel said when Fiona informed her of this. "He's hardly touched his paints since Mom and Dad were killed. If he's painting, things are definitely looking up."

Fiona, who gave no sign at all that she knew Rachel had left the house in the middle of the night to go to a man's hotel room, sniffed and said, "Maybe he'll be going back to San Francisco now."

Rachel smiled at her. "This is his home too, Fiona."

The housekeeper sniffed again. "If you say so, Miss Rachel."

"We'll be in Dad's study."

"Shall I bring coffee?"

"A little later."

Fiona nodded, sent Adam a look he couldn't interpret to save his life, and left them.

"Is she making a wax doll in my image?" he wanted to know as they went into the study.

"I doubt it."

"You *doubt* it?"

At her father's desk, Rachel turned and smiled at him. "I very much doubt it."

Adam went to her and surrounded her face with his hands. He kissed her, taking his time. Then, huskily, he said, "Do you have any idea what it does to me when you smile at me like that?"

Rachel blinked. "No. Like what?"

Instead of answering, he kissed her again. Or maybe that was an answer.

When Rachel was finally able to catch her breath, she'd forgotten what they were talking about. "Didn't we come in here to do something?" she asked idly.

Reluctantly, Adam removed her arms from his neck and guided her gently back to sit in the desk chair. "Yes. Look for evidence."

"Right. Right." She looked at the desk for a moment, then shook her head bemusedly. "You have the strangest effect on me."

He touched her cheek with caressing fingers. "Likewise."

She caught his hand and held it firmly. "Adam, if you keep doing things like that, I won't be able to concentrate."

He sighed. "Likewise."

"Look—why don't I go upstairs and get started on the secretary in Dad's bedroom while you finish up in here?"

"I guess that would be best. But I don't have to like it."

Rachel didn't like it either, but she left him and went upstairs to her father's bedroom.

She'd scarcely been in the room since coming home, and for a moment, as she stood in the doorway, Rachel could hardly bear it.

It even smelled like him.

Then she squared her shoulders and spoke aloud. "Okay, Dad. I need to know all your secrets. And I need to know them quick."

She moved toward the secretary by the window.

F I F T E E N

By Thursday afternoon, Mercy had spent so many hours staring at her computer screen that she had a throbbing headache. Her search had to be meticulous; it was incredibly time-consuming. Duncan had stored a great deal of information in his various files; the problem was there was no rhyme or reason to his private system.

He had also installed virtually every appointment-keeping and information-organizing software program on the market, and with his love of high-tech toys, he'd used them all—indiscriminately. And since he tended to go back and make changes or just add notations to old files, not even the dates last worked on were any help.

So Mercy had been reduced to simply wading through years and years worth of files.

Duncan clearly had no use for the delete command.

When she wasn't frowning over apparently useless information such as accounts long since dead and notes of appointments ten years in the past, Mercy managed to do her usual work at the bank. Not that there was much left for her to do.

Until the last week or so, Nicholas had supplemented her final chores for Duncan with some for him, obviously hoping she'd find herself working for him in a smooth transition—and give up her objections to that. But recently, especially in the last few days, he had taken to spending much of his time closeted in his office, either on the phone or else doing work he didn't explain to anyone in the bank. And when he wasn't in his office, he wasn't in the bank, period.

He wasn't using Mercy as his assistant.

In fact, he was barely speaking to her.

That wouldn't have bothered Mercy so much, except for one thing. While he had, in the past, become so involved in a project that he had shut himself in his office and worked long hours, he had still made sure they spent three or four nights a week together.

But he hadn't been to her place, or invited her to his, in days— and showed no signs of planning to.

As she shut down the files she'd been searching through on Thursday afternoon and rubbed her stiff neck, Mercy figured she had a couple of choices. She could wait Nick out, holding strictly to the careful guidelines they had established for their no-relationship relationship, asking no questions and making no demands, pretending it didn't matter to her if he didn't feel like getting laid at the moment.

Or she could break a couple of their rules and force the issue.

The first option was safer. That way, she wouldn't look like a lovesick fool if this was Nick's way of easing out of the relationship. The second option was a lot riskier, especially if he had merely withdrawn from her temporarily because she'd gotten too close the last time they were together. If she pushed now, he could decide he wanted out for good.

But one thing Mercy knew was that she did not like being in limbo. So she left her office and went to his.

And he wasn't there.

"Nothing worse than getting all worked up for a confrontation that doesn't happen," she muttered to herself.

"Looking for me?" Nicholas came into the office behind her.

She jumped. "Jeez. Don't creep up on people like that."

His brows rose, but Nicholas merely shut the door behind them and went to his desk. "Sorry. I thought I was just walking into my office." He was terribly polite.

This was not going the way Mercy had planned.

She went to his visitor's chair, but put her hands on the back of it rather than sitting down. "I noticed Jordan Walsh came to see you this morning," she said. Which was not at all what she'd planned to say, dammit.

"He had an appointment, yes."

"The bank isn't going to do business with him, surely? Nick, I've been hearing things about him in the past few months. People in the financial community are beginning to talk, and what they're saying is that he can't be trusted at best—

and is a criminal at worst." She just couldn't seem to say what she'd come in to say.

"Listening to gossip, Mercy?"

"It's more than gossip."

Nicholas shrugged. "Sometimes the bank backs risky investments. And risky people."

"Not Jordan Walsh's kind of risky."

"I know what I'm doing."

"Do you?" Mercy looked at his expressionless face and enigmatic eyes, and felt so frustrated she could have screamed. "And it's none of my business."

"And," Nick said with that terrible politeness, "it's none of your business."

Mercy drew a breath and nodded. "Okay. I'm through for the day." *In more ways than one.* "I guess you aren't interested in dinner."

"I have a few more calls to make."

"Fine." She managed a smile, and knew it looked as false as it felt. "See you, Nick." And walked out of his office.

He stared after her for a moment, not moving until he heard a sharp sound and realized that the pencil in his hand had snapped raggedly in half. Then, hardly aware of speaking aloud, he muttered, "Christ, what's wrong with me . . ."

"Nothing." Rachel shook her head and looked at Adam, who had joined her upstairs about an hour before. It was almost impossible to concentrate when she looked at him, but she tried her best. "Plenty of notes and old letters, but nothing to help us."

"Then we depend on Nick," Adam said.

Rachel slowly returned a stack of unused stationery to one of the drawers, frowning. "Adam, it doesn't make sense."

"Which part?" he asked wryly.

"Dad. Except for his private records, his estate was in meticulous order."

"So his private records should be as well?"

"Well . . . yes. He knew I'd have to deal with all this stuff. He knew I'd be the one to go through his desk downstairs and this one, and that I'd find the notebooks and the journal. There should be more paperwork."

"Okay. Where would it be?"

"That's the problem. I don't know. The safes here in the house have all been checked. The safety deposit boxes at the bank. And now both the desks Dad used. There isn't anyplace else, not that I know of."

"If you're right about the records, there must be."

Rachel shook her head, then frowned again. "Maybe we're looking for the wrong thing."

"Papers?"

"Yes. Maybe we should be looking for a key. Maybe to a safe deposit box other than those at the bank."

Adam looked around the bedroom, which was filled with massive mahogany furniture—and a great many drawers. "A key. Great."

"And not just in here." Rachel sighed. "This is a big house."

"But would Duncan have made you look for it? I mean, shouldn't anything you needed to know be readily available, or at least easily found?"

"I would have thought so. All his business records were."

Adam saw her rub the back of her neck wearily, and came to

pull her up from the chair. "Enough. Let's go walk in the garden for a little while before it gets dark, and then I'm going back to town and leaving you to get some rest."

Rachel slid her arms up around his neck and leaned into him, feeling her body respond instantly to the closeness of his. When she was near him like this, all she was aware of was how much closer she wanted to be. "Suddenly, I'm not tired at all," she told him.

Adam wrapped his arms around her and held her for a moment, and that enveloping embrace moved her oddly. Once again, just as in the hours before dawn, she had the feeling that he thought she was going to be taken away from him.

"Adam?"

He eased back just far enough to look down at her, his eyes intense. Then he kissed her, one hand sliding up her back to the nape of her neck.

Rachel lost herself in him. She forgot about questions and puzzles and doubts, and threats to her life. She forgot about everything but the way he made her feel.

Adam made a rough sound and muttered, "You are not making it easy for me to leave."

Rachel looked up at him. "You could stay."

He touched her cheek lightly. "If I do, you won't get any rest. And I know damned well I won't."

"We might not sleep much," she agreed, "but there's a lot to be said for pillow talk."

He smiled, but it looked a little strained. "Definitely not making it easy for me. Rachel, you still have a sprained wrist and several bruises—"

"I think you counted them last night. Didn't you count them?"

Adam cleared his throat. "You might not feel it right now, but after that car almost ran us down, your body needs a chance to recover."

"I feel fine."

He rested his forehead against hers and sighed. "Why are you making me be the grown-up?"

Rachel couldn't help laughing, but her question was more than a little serious when she asked, "Am I being shameless?"

He kissed her once, hard. "You're being wonderful. I want to take you to bed right now and stay there for at least a week—never doubt that."

"But . . ."

"But you've been through a hell of a lot in the last few weeks. And it isn't over. We can't know the worst isn't yet to come."

It was Rachel's turn to sigh. "Well, if you're going to be practical about it . . ." Still, she knew he was right. Too many restless, dream-filled nights had come before last night's almost entirely sleepless and active night. She was exhausted, and she was willing to bet he was as well.

"I'll come back tomorrow, Rachel. Bright and early."

Repeating something he had said earlier in the day, she said, "I guess that would be best. But I don't have to like it."

The walk in the garden was peaceful, the leave-taking a while later something else entirely, and Rachel was left with a long evening stretching ahead and way too many emotions and worries running through her mind.

Adam found Simon parked just down the block, where he had a clear view of the front gate of the Grant estate, and Nick's scruffy private investigator gave him a somewhat jaundiced look when Adam pulled up beside him.

"Make me obvious, why don't you?" he said.

Adam ignored the complaint. "Anything?"

"Nah, not since you and the lady got here. Incoming, that is. Cameron Grant left a while ago."

Adam nodded. "I want you to watch this place, and I mean carefully. Rachel shouldn't be leaving, but if she does, stick close."

"Like white on rice."

"You have a partner, right?"

"Yeah. He's always on watch here, while I follow the lady whenever she leaves. Right now he's watching the river side of the property. Nobody goes in without one of us seeing 'em."

"And relief?"

"Two shifts, twelve hours on and twelve off. One follows the lady, the other one stays here, always. The other two are good, don't worry about that. Nick pays for the best."

"None of you kept us from nearly being blown up that day," Adam retorted. "Or being almost run down by a car."

Simon looked both sheepish and defiant. "I was supposed to follow and look out for dangers, yes—but how could I know that store was rigged to blow? I didn't have time to check it out before you two went in. As for the car, the fucking thing came out of nowhere. I didn't have time to do anything, I swear. Besides—you were there. Nick said you had great reflexes, and he was right. The lady hardly got a scratch."

Adam gave him a look, then said calmly, "If the lady gets even that much on your watch, my friend, you'll answer to me. And I won't just dock your pay."

Simon returned the stare and nodded slowly. "Nick also said

you were a lot tougher than you look, and since you look tough enough, I should keep it in mind. Okay, I got you. We'll keep a close eye on the lady."

"And if you see anything suspicious—anything, no matter how vague—call me at once. You have my pager number?"

"Yeah. And your number at the hotel. I'll call."

"Be sure you do. Very sure."

"You'll be in for supper?" Fiona came into the foyer to ask Rachel.

"Yes. Where's Cam?"

"Said he had a date. I didn't ask how much he was paying her."

Rachel laughed. "For heaven's sake, Fiona. He knows plenty of people here in Richmond, and that includes a few ladies who enjoy his company. I'm glad he's getting out."

Fiona sniffed. "At least he isn't underfoot, going through cabinets and drawers until a body'd think he was looking for secret treasure."

"Well, considering some of the things we've found in the furniture so far, you can hardly say he's wasting his time."

"I suppose. I'll just be glad when all this is done and past, and we've the house to ourselves again, Miss Rachel."

"It won't be much longer, Fiona."

The housekeeper sniffed again. "It's already been too long. You should get some rest tonight—assuming everybody'll leave you alone long enough, that is."

Rachel smiled. "I'm fine."

"I know." Fiona paused, then added in a different tone, "Or at least you will be. Now."

Rachel was too startled to respond until the housekeeper had turned back toward the kitchen, but then managed to say, "Fiona? It isn't because he looks like Tom."

Fiona paused for just a moment and looked at Rachel. "I don't know that it matters much whether or not that's the reason, Miss Rachel. You're alive again after ten years of just . . . walking through life. As much as he loved life, Mr. Tom would surely say that was a wonderful thing."

"And Adam?"

"If he loves you, he'll agree."

Rachel didn't respond to that, but as the housekeeper retreated to the kitchen and left her alone again, she couldn't help but think about a couple of things that made that statement sound hollow. Adam hadn't mentioned love. And he had more than once made it clear that he did not consider his resemblance to Tom a good thing.

Except, of course, that it had gotten him more easily and quickly into her house, her life. Her trust. Adam might not like the resemblance, but he had been ruthless enough to use it for his own ends.

Rachel couldn't help wondering if he was still doing that.

And what did she really feel? In a way, Tom's death had encased both her heart and her sexuality in ice, and that ice had remained through all the years of study and work. She had been so young when she lost him and all her dreams of them together; her very youth had encouraged her to cling to those dreams, to prefer them to the reality of going on without Tom.

For a long time, she had felt disloyal to Tom even in dating casually, and by the time those feelings had naturally and inevitably faded somewhat, work had been her focus and her outlet.

By that point, she had thought it easier just to maintain the status quo, especially while she'd been living and working in New York. Work had demanded all her time and energy, she hadn't had to face and deal with the ghosts in her life, and so she had been able to keep herself in an emotional limbo. Until she had come home.

But now she was home. And whether Adam was responsible or not, the ice had cracked, even shattered. The barrier between her and her own feelings had been removed. Everything she felt was stronger, sharper, and seemed to originate from someplace deeper inside her, a place untapped and even untouched for most of her life.

Her anger at Adam had come from there. So did her doubts and her passion.

So did her love.

For so much of her life she had believed that what she had felt for Tom had been the deepest, most powerful feeling she would ever know. Her commitment to him had been absolute, without hesitation or question, and the agony of his death had nearly destroyed her.

But recovery from a devastating loss was not all that had happened to her in ten years. There was also the transition from child to woman. And the development of her creative urges and abilities. And her independence.

The girl who had loved Thomas Sheridan for so long and so absolutely no longer existed.

What she felt now, for Adam, was so much more than she had ever expected to feel for anyone in her life. Far from simple adoration, it was a complex jumble of excitement and fear, growing love and paralyzing doubts, dreams and anxieties, passion and uncertainty, trust—and distrust.

And her physical response to him was so strong that it seemed to push everything else aside. Her body felt different, curiously alive and sensitized. An unfamiliar hunger lurked just below the surface and ambushed her unexpectedly whenever she looked at him or touched him. The mere sound of his voice made everything inside her go still in listening, and his slow smile made her want to smile in return.

But that was her. Her feelings.

Except for his undeniable desire for her, she really had no idea what Adam thought or felt. He was still too good at hiding from her anything he did not want her to know.

She knew he had secrets left to tell, that there were still details in his past and quite possibly his present that he wasn't ready to share with her. That he might never be willing to really talk to her about what he had endured in that brutal prison.

She also knew that if she had seen the scars on his back without the warning of her dream, she probably would have pressed him to talk to her about it, which would have been a mistake. As it was, her dream had shown her a barbarity so clear and detailed that she had not been able to bear even the idea of learning more. Not now, at least. Probably not for a long time.

You have to know where he's been, Rachel. You have to understand.

For the first time, the full import of her dream hit Rachel.

His scars. How could she have known about his scars, dreamed about them?

Oh, she might have guessed that Adam had been mistreated in

that prison, but the bloodied welts she had seen crisscrossing his back in the dream—and still saw, too vividly, when she let herself—closely matched the pale but visible scars he bore in reality.

Maybe even perfectly matched.

You have to know where he's been, Rachel. You have to understand.

It had been Tom's voice she had heard, subtly different from Adam's.

"I'm just tired, that's all," she said, her own voice startling her in the silence of the house. "Imagining things."

Tom's voice in her dreams. A note from him. A yellow rose on her nightstand. A gift delayed by a decade and a death.

"I don't believe in ghosts," Rachel heard herself say, firmly this time. But even as she did, a faint chill made gooseflesh rise on her arms as she recalled that terrible awakening ten years ago, and Tom's anguished appearance at the foot of her bed.

She had not dreamed that.

"Miss Rachel?"

Fiona's voice startled her, and Rachel was thankful to be pulled from her unsettling thoughts. "Yes?"

The housekeeper didn't seem particularly surprised to find Rachel still standing in the foyer, then Rachel realized that only a few moments had passed since their earlier conversation.

"I forgot to tell you before. Miss Lloyd left a note for you on the table by the basement door. A list of pieces your uncle has asked for."

Rachel nodded. "Thanks, Fiona. I'll take a look at it." She hesitated, then added, "Has Darby finished going through the stored furniture?"

"Not quite. There's still a part of the basement left. She's moved out what you wanted sold and what's been taken to be repaired, and tagged what's been gone over and added to the inventory. The rest she said she'd get to next week."

"I think I'll go down to the basement for a little while. I haven't been down there in years." Anything to get her mind off other things.

"Be careful on the stairs," Fiona warned automatically, as she always did.

"Yes, I will." Left alone again, Rachel headed for the basement, her thoughts taking a welcome new turn.

Her uncle Cameron had always been the artistic brother, uninterested in business; he hadn't wanted to be bothered by practical things, so he had a business manager who took care of his various investments. As far as Rachel could remember, her father and uncle had never even talked about business of any kind, and as for Cameron recommending that his brother lend someone five million dollars—the idea was absurd.

And that aside, he couldn't possibly be the "old friend" to whom Duncan had referred in his journal; the brothers had gotten along well enough, but neither would have called the other an old friend.

An old bastard, maybe, but not an old friend.

Cam's list was on a table beside the basement door, and Rachel scanned it quickly. A few items, none of which interested her particularly except to wonder idly where on earth Cam intended to put everything.

Leaving the list on the table, she opened the basement door and flipped on the lights as she started down the steps. The musty smell of basements everywhere wafted up to meet her, and for a moment she stopped on the steps, horribly reminded of the dream and Adam's prison.

She had to stand there, holding tightly to the railing, and tell herself several times that it had only been a dream, that this was not a prison she was descending into, not a place where people were trapped and tortured. It was just a basement, a space dug out of the earth to provide storage for a family.

Slowly, she continued down the stairs, and by the time she reached the bottom, her panic had faded. Bright fluorescent lights illuminated even the corners of the huge space, and underneath their cool glare there was nothing that resembled a prison, just the refuse of generations, furniture and boxes full of things ultimately cast off as broken, out of fashion, or simply no longer wanted.

From the steps she could see a more methodical, spaced arrangement of the things nearest her, and knew it was Darby's work. Farther away, toward the north side, it looked much more chaotic to her, with chairs piled atop tables, wardrobes pushed up against chests, and little room in which to move among the pieces.

Rachel walked away from the stairs, along an aisle with tagged furniture on either side, toward the north end of the basement. She looked at a few things in passing, noting that each had been beautifully polished and/or cleaned, and marveled at how much Darby had accomplished.

By the time she reached the north end, she had become absorbed in looking at what there was to see. She'd known there was a lot down there, but she was surprised at how many beautiful pieces a careful inventory had unearthed.

No wonder Darby was so thrilled.

Rachel couldn't move very far into the section that had not yet been inventoried. She could see boxes and trunks, yet couldn't get to them because of all the heavy pieces of furniture in the way. And the furniture was turned this way and that, some facing outward, some inward, and some even lying on their sides or backs.

The only way to get to most of the pieces was to do as Darby had done: Move one thing at a time.

"I wouldn't even know what I was looking for," Rachel muttered.

"Rachel? What the hell are you doing down here?"

Cameron was standing near the bottom of the stairs, staring across the room at her.

SIXTEEN

This, Mercy told herself, was a mistake. A big mistake.

She stared at the door for a full minute, gathering her nerve, drew a deep breath, and knocked. Mistake or not, she refused to spend yet another evening pacing in her apartment and asking herself whether she should force the issue or wait.

She really hated waiting.

Nicholas opened the door, holding a glass in one hand, and for a moment just looked at her.

"I need to talk to you, Nick."

He nodded slowly and opened the door wider, gesturing for her to come in. "I've been expecting you," he said.

That surprised Mercy somewhat, especially given the tense

scene at the bank only a few hours before. She came into his apartment, eyeing him uncertainly as he closed the door. He looked, she thought, as if he had had a very, very bad day. Coat and tie discarded, white shirt untucked and half unbuttoned, the sleeves rolled up loosely. His hair looked as if he'd run his fingers through it more than once, and there was something almost . . . numbed about his face.

"Maybe this isn't such a good time," she said slowly.

Nicholas crossed his sparse living room to the corner wet bar and splashed more whiskey into his glass. "For some discussions, there's no such thing as a good time," he said coolly. "Drink, Mercy?"

"No thanks." She hesitated. "How many does that make for you?"

"I have no idea. It's a new bottle." Which was now half empty. He turned back to her and lifted the glass in a mocking toast. "Don't worry. I'm not driving anywhere tonight."

In all the years Mercy had known him, she had never seen him even finish a drink of whiskey, much less consume several. It was scaring her to see him like this; for all his coolness and seeming detachment, he was curiously out of control. "Nick, this isn't like you."

"Maybe you don't know me as well as you think you do."

She shook her head. "What is it? What's wrong?"

"Just say what you came here to say, all right? Not that you have to."

"What do you mean by that?" Mercy didn't have a clue what he was talking about.

He shrugged, swallowed half his drink, and went to sprawl in a big armchair by the cold fireplace. "I mean, it isn't like I'm going to be surprised. I've been expecting it."

"Expecting what?"

He lifted his glass in another mocking toast and said matter-of-factly, "Expecting you to tell me it's over."

It was definitely not what she had expected.

After the first moment of surprise, Mercy dropped her shoulder bag on the sofa, shrugged out of her jacket, and moved across the room to sit down on the big hassock in front of his chair. In the same matter-of-fact tone she said, "How long have you been expecting it?"

"Oh . . . from the beginning." He was staring at his drink rather than at her. "Since the day after our first night together, I suppose."

"Why?"

"You want a list? Because I'm an ugly bastard and you're a beautiful woman who can have any man she wants. Because I'm prickly as hell, with a foul temper and worse moods, and I'm no picnic even on my best days. Because there's eleven years between us in age and a few lifetimes in experience. Because even the best lover in the world can't make a woman's heart respond to him the way her body will."

Nicholas shrugged and finished his drink in one swallow. "I tried, God knows. Tried not to crowd you, not to ask too much of you. But I knew it was only a matter of time. The other night . . . I knew everything had changed. After that, I couldn't hide the way I felt from you. Couldn't be casual anymore. What I felt wasn't something you wanted. So . . ." He looked at her at last, his pale eyes wearing a hard sheen. "So I was expecting you."

Mercy drew a shaky breath. "Well, as a matter of fact, that wasn't what I came here to say."

"No?"

"No. I came here to ask if—if I was right in believing that *you* wanted it to be over."

He leaned his head back against the chair, heavy lids dropping to veil his eyes. "And now you know. The answer is no." His voice was still cool and matter-of-fact.

Mercy wasn't about to leave it there. "Then why do you keep pushing me away? Shutting me out?"

"Have I been doing that?"

"You know damned well you have."

"If you're talking about bank business—"

"This isn't about the bank. This is about us. You know everything about me, don't you, Nick? All my favorite things, the way I feel about politics and religion. Where I shop, and who my doctor is, and where I get my car fixed. You know where I come from, who I am."

"So?"

"So I don't have a clue who you are. I told you that the other night. And you let me see a little bit. And the next day you were miles away again. So far out of my reach I couldn't even touch you. So I figured you just didn't want me even that close ever again."

"It isn't a question of what I want." For the first time, his voice roughened. "It's a question of what I can survive."

"I don't understand."

"I know you don't." His smile was twisted. "Let's put it this way. When it *is* over between us, I will survive losing you. I'll even survive losing the pieces of myself you'll take with you, the pieces you . . . own despite everything I've tried to do to keep myself intact. But I couldn't survive much more than that."

Mercy was having a difficult time believing this. Her heart was thudding and her hands were cold, and she was very, very afraid she might be hearing only what she wanted to hear. So she drew a deep breath and asked the one question that mattered to her.

"Do you love me, Nick?"

He closed his eyes, his face very still except for the muscle that moved suddenly in his jaw.

And the glass in his hand shattered under the force of his grip.

"My God, Nick—"

When she pried his fingers open, she found only one cut, and though it bled profusely, it didn't seem dangerously deep. With her efficient nature kicking into gear, she wrapped his hand in a clean dish towel, then found gauze, bandages, and antiseptic in his medicine cabinet. Sitting on the edge of the hassock with his hand across her lap, she carefully cleaned the wound and bandaged his hand.

Through it all, Nicholas sat silent, his gaze fixed on her. He seemed to feel no pain, obediently flexing his fingers when she asked him to but not moving otherwise.

Mercy cleared up most of the broken glass by simply gathering it into the dish towel, which she laid aside on the bare coffee table with the bandages and antiseptic. She could feel his eyes on her, but hardly knew what to say to him. Finally, she found an ounce of lightness somewhere and said, "You didn't have to slice your hand open to avoid the question, Nick. A simple no would have been enough."

"Of course I love you, Mercy." His voice was very quiet. "I've always loved you."

She looked at him then, and felt her heart catch at the utter desolation in his face. "Nick—"

"I hadn't planned to stay so long in Richmond, you know. Before you came to work for the bank, I was out of the country more often than in. But then you came. I took one look at you when Duncan introduced you as his new assistant, and I knew I'd be staying for good. Whether you ever wanted me or not, I couldn't walk away from you."

Mercy slipped to her knees between the hassock and the chair, her body leaning into his, almost between his thighs as she reached up to touch his face. "Nick . . ."

"I don't want your pity, goddammit," he said thickly. "Don't do that to me."

"It isn't pity." She slid her fingers into his hair and pulled his head toward her. "You stupid man. I love you."

His breath rasped and his fingers bit into her waist for a moment. "Mercy, don't say that unless—"

"Unless I mean it? Do you want me to show you my diary entry from nearly five years ago? *Started work at the bank today. I like my boss. But when I shook hands with his partner . . . God, it happened so fast. How can it happen so fast? How can I love a man I don't even know?*" Her lips feathered across his cheek toward his mouth. "I love you, Nick."

His arms went around her and held her with a strength just this side of painful, and his mouth slanted across hers wildly. For the first time, he held back nothing of himself or his need for her, and Mercy was almost crying when he gathered her up and carried her to his bed.

·   ·   ·

After the first surprised moment, Rachel moved back across the basement toward the stairs and her uncle. "I thought you'd gone out," she said.

"I went off without my sketch pad, and Kathie wants a sketch," he said more or less automatically.

"I don't have it," Rachel said lightly, assuming he referred to his date that night.

He frowned. "I know that. The basement door was open. I wondered who was down here. Are you looking for something, Rachel?"

"No. I wanted to see how much progress Darby had made." She paused, then heard herself ask, "What are you looking for, Cam?"

"Me? I told you. Just came back to get my sketch pad."

Rachel got to the bottom of the stairs and stood there, looking up at him gravely. "That isn't what I meant. What are you looking for in the furniture, Cam?"

"I don't know what you're talking about."

Cam turned and went back up the stairs.

Rachel followed. She found him in the living room, which was his favorite place in the house. He had poured himself a scotch, and was standing by the cold fireplace, gazing up at the painting of his brother that hung above it.

The painting was his own work.

"We didn't like each other very much," Cam said when she came in. "You knew that?"

"I knew you were very different."

"That's one way of putting it. Another is that we were encouraged to compete in a way that wasn't healthy for either of us."

"Brothers often are."

"Yes." His mouth twisted. "But our father—your grandfather—was a master of the game. He started when we were young, and he never let up. I was pushed into sports because Duncan excelled at them, and never mind that I wasn't athletic. Duncan was tortured with art and music lessons despite the fact that he loathed them."

Rachel came farther into the room and sat on the arm of a chair, watching him. "I had no idea. Dad never spoke of anything like that—and I never knew Grandfather."

"No, he died not long after you were born."

Rachel nodded, and waited.

"He was one of those people who thrive on conflict. Everything had to be a struggle, a battle of wills. He made our mother miserable, browbeat the servants, alienated the rest of the family. Life with him was . . . hard.

"Duncan and I were pushed all the time. And our father blew hot and cold with both of us, promising things he never delivered, threatening punishments. Full of praise one day and scathing criticism the next. It was like living in a mine field, never knowing when the next step would cost an arm or a leg, or some other piece of yourself."

"It sounds horrible."

"It was." He leaned a shoulder against the mantel and gazed at her steadily. "And it only got worse as we grew up. We both had to fight for our identity, to struggle against his domination. Leaving home for college gave us our first taste of independence. First Duncan, then me. But we had to come back here because he commanded it. And neither of us was strong enough to win that battle."

"Cam, why are you telling me this?" Rachel felt uncomfortable, keenly aware that she was learning things her own father had not chosen to tell her in his lifetime.

"So you'll understand."

"Understand what?"

Cameron hesitated, then drew a deep breath. "From the time we were old enough to understand, our father talked about how he meant to leave his fortune when he died. That was the carrot he held out in front of us, and the stick he beat us with. When one of us was in his good graces, he was promised the entire fortune, everything—the other was taunted that he'd be left out in the cold. It went on for years. And he even went so far as to have two different wills drawn up. One promised everything to Duncan, the other promised everything to me."

"That isn't how he left his estate," Rachel said slowly.

Cameron's smile was brief. "Oh, but it is."

"You have Grant property. Real estate, stocks. They came from your father."

"No. They came from Duncan."

Rachel understood immediately. "Grandfather went with the will naming Dad—and Dad deeded you part of the estate."

"Half. He said he'd be damned if he'd live under our father's rule a moment longer, that those wishes and intentions meant nothing to him." Cameron shrugged. "So I got half the money, which I at least had the sense to invest, and Duncan got the other half—and built it into a major fortune."

"So Grandfather lost."

"Did he? He made my brother and me virtual strangers, Rachel. Each of us reminded the other of our father and his torments. So, not long after our father died, I moved to the West Coast. In the nearly thirty years since, I've come home only for brief visits. Until last year, when Duncan invited me to stay here while my place was being renovated."

"Did you two get any closer before he died?"

"No. But at least the old ghosts were quieter after so many years. There was a kind of peace between us. And I'm glad of that."

Rachel nodded. "I'm not sure if I should thank you for telling me all this, but I'm glad you did." She paused, then added, "I still don't understand, though, what it is you're looking for in the furniture."

Readily now, Cameron said, "One of the things our father always said, one of his promised rewards, was a large piece of property overseas. An island, in fact. He swore he owned it, that he had the deed. But when he died, it was never found."

"You're looking for the deed to an island?"

"Rachel, my father was a devious old bastard, and he loved playing games. He told us once that he'd hidden the deed here in the house. That was when we were boys, and Duncan and I both searched for it. We never found it. Maybe it never existed. But it occurred to me that it would have been just like him to hide something important in a piece of discarded furniture."

"I see."

Cameron smiled at her. "It probably isn't here. Probably never existed. But, just once, I'd like to win one of my father's games. The promise of that keeps me looking."

"Thank you for telling me, Cam."

"I'm just sorry I didn't confide in you before." He shrugged. "But you've been busy, with a lot on your mind. Naturally, if I do find the deed, you'll be the first to know. I'd like to keep looking."

"Of course."

His expression lightened. "Thanks, Rachel. Now I think I'll go get my sketch pad and then meet Kathie for dinner. I'll probably see you tomorrow."

"Good night, Cam."

"Good night, honey."

Rachel sat there on the arm of the chair for a long time after Cameron left. She heard him go upstairs, then come down again a couple of minutes later. Heard the front door close, and his car start up outside. Heard him drive away.

She wondered why he had lied to her.

There were holes in his story, several of them. For one thing, he'd had thirty years to search the house; why was it only now important to him to get his hands on a possibly nonexistent deed? Granted, furniture was just now being moved out of the house, but Cameron had to know already how thorough Darby was, and that a deed to an island would have been useless to Darby even if she was disposed to steal it—which she wasn't.

No, the deed was probably nonexistent.

So what was Cameron really looking for?

"Do you really keep a diary?"

Mercy pushed herself up a bit so she could smile down at him. "It's more of a journal. But, yes. I'll show it to you if you like. It was the only place I could safely make a fool of myself over you."

He toyed with a strand of her dark hair. "I never guessed. Never even imagined you could feel anything for me."

"I couldn't let you know. Mysterious, enigmatic Nick, who

never seemed to give me a second look—until the night he offered me a ride and we ended up stark naked on the rug in front of my fireplace. Was that planned, by the way?"

Nicholas smiled slightly. "That, love, was the most incredibly lucky night of my life. I kissed you because I had to, figuring I'd get my face slapped. But when you responded . . ."

"You thought I might be agreeable to a nice, undemanding affair?"

"I thought it was the most I could hope for."

Mercy shook her head. "And I thought it was the most you wanted from me. Just a warm body in your bed now and then. You were always so damned careful to make sure neither of us owed the other a thing."

"I didn't want you to feel any pressure."

"And didn't want to risk yourself?"

"That too."

She leaned down and kissed him, but pushed herself away when he showed definite signs of losing interest in talk. "Wait a minute."

"Why?"

"Because we aren't finished talking."

Nicholas looked at her warily. "No?"

"No. We have to reach an understanding here."

"I thought we just had."

She firmly pushed his hand away when it began roaming over her hip. "Nick, I'm serious. I walked a high wire for nearly a year trying to figure out what you wanted of me. So now I want you to tell me."

He slid a hand into her hair and pulled her down so he could kiss her. Against her mouth, he said huskily, "I want you with me for the rest of my life. I want to go to sleep with you and wake up with you—and maybe even make babies with you."

More than satisfied with the answer, Mercy smiled and murmured, "What excellent ideas. So when do we go for blood tests?"

"Are we getting married?"

"Well, I won't have babies out of wedlock. Not the way I was raised. So if you want babies, you'll have to marry me."

Nicholas surrounded her face with his hands and gazed at her for a long time. Whatever he was looking for, he found, because he smiled slowly, his eyes alight. And his ugly face wasn't ugly at all.

"I love you, Mercy."

"I love you too."

He pulled her over on top of him. "Enough to see this face across the breakfast table for the next thirty or forty years?"

"Oh, easily." She kissed his chin. "I love this face."

His arms tightened around her. "You're a remarkable woman."

"That's good. I found myself a remarkable man." She folded her hands on his hard chest and rested her chin on them. "And speaking of how remarkable you are . . ."

He groaned, but he was also smiling. "Let me guess. That singular curiosity of yours is back at work, and you want to know once again what I'm up to."

"You love me," she said. "You must trust me."

"It's not a matter of trust, Mercy."

"Then what is it a matter of?"

He hesitated, then spoke slowly. "Experience. Habit. In some situations, the fewer people who know what's going on, the safer it is for all concerned."

"Then you're into something dangerous. I thought you were."

Again, Nicholas hesitated. "It's . . . no place I haven't been before."

"Somehow, that doesn't surprise me much." She lifted her head and looked at him gravely. "What was it—military? Or something a lot more secretive?"

"The latter. I was recruited when I was barely out of my teens, and the adventure appealed to me. Also the education. I showed an aptitude for finance, so they trained me to understand that. I was used as an investigator more than anything else, an information broker."

"But not always."

"No. There were dangerous situations. Times when I had to use a gun as well as my brain. International finance is a marketplace worth hundreds of billions of dollars, so the stakes are always high."

"Did you work for the CIA?"

"Close, but no. The people I worked for didn't list their address and number in the phone book."

"Worked for. Past tense?"

He nodded. "For years now. But I still have some connections, informants, resources."

"Which you're using now. To do what, Nick? What are you and Adam Delafield up to?"

This time Nicholas barely hesitated. He told her about Duncan's plane crash and what Adam believed had caused it. He told her whom they suspected and why, and what they planned.

It was a story that took time to tell, and when most of Mercy's questions had been answered, they were sitting up in bed drinking wine and eating cheese and crackers, with Mercy wearing his shirt and Nicholas wearing nothing.

"Well, I can see why you've been preoccupied," she said finally.

"I have had a few things on my mind."

"Nick, you're taking an awful risk. From what I've been hearing lately, Jordan Walsh is pure poison. And according to the grapevine, people who do business with him have a nasty habit of turning up dead."

"I know."

"Isn't there some other way?"

"Doesn't appear to be. As yet, the only connection we've found between Duncan and Walsh is that loan and the notes he made in his journal, and neither tells us much."

"No idea who this 'old friend' is?"

"None. Duncan had a lot of friends. A lot of old friends. You saw them at the funeral, men and women from all over the country, the world, most of them clearly devastated by his death. We had to count them all as possibles, and it's a long list. We're checking them out one by one. But so far there isn't a sign of a connection to Walsh."

Mercy brooded for a moment, then said, "Along other lines, I suppose it would be useless to ask you if Adam is working for the same people you used to work for?"

"That isn't my story." Nicholas smiled. "But let's just say that legitimate American businessmen who are smarter than most and can handle themselves in tight situations are a definite asset."

"Mmm. How honest has he been with Rachel?"

"I don't know."

Mercy eyed him.

"I swear. All I can tell you is that Adam is utterly committed to finding out who killed Duncan and his wife, and even more determined to make sure nothing happens to Rachel."

"Because of the loan Duncan made him?"

"He owes his success to Duncan, and he's a man who pays his debts. Even more, Duncan believed in him. At that point in his life the belief and trust were worth more than gold." He had briefly touched on what happened to Adam, the betrayal and prison, simply as an explanation of why Duncan had offered the loan.

"And is that why he's romancing Rachel? Because he owed Duncan?"

Nicholas smiled at her belligerent question. "No, I think the romancing is all on his own account."

Mercy stared at him. "Do you trust him, Nick?"

"Yes."

"It's odd that he looks so much like Tom."

"He didn't arrange it that way, if that's what you're asking me. No surgery, not even hair dye. He simply looks enough like your brother to be his double." Nick shrugged. "I've encountered stranger things in my life, that's all I can tell you."

"He won't hurt her, will he?"

"I don't think so. Certainly not deliberately. Mercy, I don't know all of Adam's secrets, but I know one thing. In some way I don't understand and he's never explained, he is somehow connected to Rachel. And has been for a long time, I think."

"What do you mean?"

"I'm not sure. She's always been his focus. Finding out who killed Duncan and his wife is justice and repayment of a debt, but Adam's here for much more than that. In some way he's here for Rachel. Came here for her even before we knew she'd be in danger."

"But he never met her until a couple of weeks ago."

"As far as I know."

Mercy shook her head. "This whole thing is so—I don't know. Bizarre. Almost unbelievable. That somebody brought down that plane to kill Duncan, and now is trying to kill Rachel. Why?"

"If we knew that, we'd have all the pieces of the puzzle."

"Nick, I want to help."

"No."

"Nick—"

"I don't want you involved."

"Look, I wasn't proposing to pick up a gun and go hunting, but I *was* Duncan's assistant for five years. I owe him too. And I know there's something I can do to help."

"Mercy, what we've set in motion has found its own momentum now, and I want you to stay out of it. There's nothing you can do anyway. Please—I don't want to have to worry about you."

She opened her mouth to tell him about her computer search, then changed her mind. Chances were, she wouldn't find anything anyway.

"Mercy?"

"All right. I'll stay at the bank and mind my own business. If you promise not to keep me in the dark from now on."

"I promise."

"Good. Now, do you want to put this tray on the floor? It's getting in my way."

SEVENTEEN

The long stone corridor stretched before her, but Rachel had no intention of going that way. Not this time. Not again.

She couldn't bear the thought of seeing Adam like that again.

She turned around and walked steadily, relieved when the stone walls gave way to smooth, painted Sheetrock, and the candle sconces became electrical fixtures.

"Secrets. Everybody's got secrets."

Rachel stopped, listening. The whisper had seemed to come from no particular direction—and all directions.

"Who's there?"

"Look for secrets, Rachel."

"Tom?"

"Secret things in secret places."

Frustrated, she said, "Why won't you tell me where to look? What to look for?"

"You already know."

"No, I don't. I—"

"You know. You only have to remember."

"Help me!"

"I can't."

"Tom, please!"

She saw him then as he stepped out of the shadows just ahead of her. It was Tom and yet . . . not.

"This is a house of secrets, Rachel. Don't you know that yet?"

She took a step toward him. "Whose secrets?"

He shook his head, and the faint light glinted off the polished surface of his face. His mask. "I can't hurt you."

She frowned, baffled. "Knowing who the secrets belong to will hurt me?"

"Yes."

"It's someone I trust?"

He was silent.

"Someone I love?"

"Remember about secret places, Rachel. Remember."

He backed away, out of the light.

Rachel started forward quickly. "Tom? Wait!"

But hard as she tried, she couldn't catch up to him. He was always just ahead, within sight and out of reach.

Then she realized that the Sheetrock walls had given way to stone ones again, and her steps slowed. "No. Not here. I don't want to be here."

"You have to."

"I've already looked. You made me look. I don't want to look ever again."

The door was just ahead. But there were no sounds coming from inside it, not this time. And there was no lock this time.

"Open the door, Rachel."

"What will I see?"

"What you must. Open the door."

The voice came, suddenly, from inside that room.

Slowly, she reached out for the handle and opened the door.

At first, all she saw was darkness. But then light glowed from a small central point, getting brighter until she could see him. There were no torturers now. Just him, standing in the center of the chilly room.

"Tom?"

"No. Yes."

"I don't understand."

He reached up and took off his Tom face, revealing an Adam face beneath it that was cracked and stained. An Adam mask.

And Adam's voice said, "Which one of us do you want, Rachel?"

"I . . . want you."

"Who am I?"

"Adam."

"Am I?"

"Don't do this to me! Don't play these games!"

"Games? Rachel, I would never play games with you."

What she saw wavered suddenly, like heat shimmering off pavement on a summer's day, and she heard Adam's urgent voice coming from outside the room.

"Don't listen to him, Rachel. It isn't me. Don't you understand? He wants you back."

She backed away from the open door. "What? Who?"

"Thomas Sheridan. He wants you back."

"But he's dead."

"Yes, Rachel. He's dead."

The man inside the room came toward her, arms outstretched. "Rachel. My Rachel. Come to me, darling—"

Worms squirmed from the eyeholes of his Adam mask, and blood dripped from the mouth.

Rachel turned, crying out, and ran.

Behind her, the footsteps were loud and close.

Adam jerked upright in bed, the sounds of her screams ringing in his ears, and stared around the hotel room that was bright with early morning light. Bright, and empty of any threat.

A dream. Just another dream.

"Jesus Christ," he muttered.

Rachel huddled against the headboard of her bed, hugging her drawn-up knees as she waited for the shakes to stop, for her breathing to return to normal. It took a long time.

A very long time.

When Adam showed up early that morning, he found Rachel in the sunroom with coffee and an untouched breakfast on the table. He paused in the doorway, watching her, unannounced since Fiona had merely told him where Rachel was.

She looked tired, he thought. More than that, really. Her face was too drawn and pale, her eyes too dark. Almost haunted.

It certainly was not the inexpressive face she had worn when he had first talked to her in this house. Her face had been masklike, the animated beauty she had been known for as a girl buried so that the only hints of its existence had been her slow smiles. She had appeared to feel nothing deeply. At some point in the past couple of weeks, however, Rachel had most certainly begun to feel again.

Adam wanted to believe he was responsible for that change. He just wished the face he saw when he looked in his own mirror had not been one shared by a dead man. And he wished he could take Rachel far away from all this.

As he watched Rachel, she looked down at her left wrist, flexing and turning it absently. She was no longer wearing the elastic bandage, but obviously still felt the sprain, if only a little.

Adam drew a breath and came into the room. "Good morning."

"Adam." She came out of her chair and into his arms as if it were the most natural thing on earth.

He held her tightly for a long while, then bent his head and kissed her. He couldn't hide his desire, and she was so responsive, it stole his breath and made his heart ache. There was, he thought, something almost desperate in the way she clung to him.

He framed her face in his hands and looked down at her gravely. "Are you okay?"

"Bad night." She smiled. "But I'm all right now."

"Did you get enough rest?"

"I got enough sleep," she answered, the distinction wry. "Here—have some coffee."

Adam joined her at the table and accepted the cup she fixed for him. "Thanks. Was it . . . dreams?"

"Nightmares." Rachel shrugged. "Wandering a house with endless corridors and getting . . . unpleasant surprises. I seem to return there every night. Natural, I suppose. There have been so many changes in my life in the last few months, it's no wonder my subconscious is going nuts trying to sort everything out."

He looked at her a moment, and decided not to dwell on the subject. He didn't want to burden her with his own nightmares, or force her to relive hers just because he had the crazy idea they were both dreaming the same dreams.

A really crazy idea.

Instead, he said, "Any new ideas about where your father might have left a key for you to find?"

"Not really." She frowned suddenly, and added almost under her breath, "Secret places."

Adam felt a little chill. "Secret places?"

She shook her head. "Something from my nightmare. Secret things in secret places."

"Do you know what that means?"

"No—except that I found out a few secrets last night." She told him about the conversation with Cameron, finishing by saying, "He's looking for something, and since he lied about it, I guess it's secret."

"You said there was virtually no chance Cameron could have been the one to ask your father to lend Walsh the money. Do you still believe that?"

Rachel nodded. "I don't think his search has anything to do with the loan to Walsh—or any other. No, Cam is looking for something else. I just don't know what."

"Secret things in secret places."

"That must be why that showed up in my dreams. It was on my mind."

"So you don't believe it has anything to do with what we're looking for?"

"I don't know, Adam. That's probably one more thing my subconscious is trying to work out. So—maybe. I was also . . . told in my dream that I know the answer and I just have to remember." She smiled faintly. "So far I haven't remembered anything useful." She didn't want to go into more detail about the dreams, and most especially did not want to mention Tom's name. Not to Adam.

"Then try not to think about it." He smiled at her. "That's the kind of thing that never comes when you're trying."

"I know. It sneaks up on you later and blindsides you."

"Let's hope not." He paused, then said, "I talked to Nick a while ago. We may have gotten a break on Walsh."

"What kind of break?"

"One of Nick's contacts swears he knows someone who works for Walsh and wants out. Supposedly, this man is one of those Walsh has used to construct various explosives—like the ones that brought down Duncan's plane."

"That sounds very convenient," Rachel said.

Adam grimaced. "Yeah. Walsh may be on to us. But we have to follow the trail, Rachel. We don't have a choice."

"You think this man—if he really exists—might be the one who—"

"Built the explosive that brought down Duncan's plane? Maybe. Though something tells me that would be too easy." He shook his head. "The best we're hoping for is that he knows something that might help us."

"Is it as much of a long shot as it sounds?"

"Pretty much. But if there's anything to it, we'll find out soon enough. Nick and I are scheduled to meet with him in a couple of hours."

"I guess I'm supposed to stay inside the castle, huh?"

He reached across the table and took her hand. "It won't be much longer, I promise. One way or another, we're going to finish this."

"Don't take any reckless chances, Adam. As prisons go, this is a lot better than most."

"I'll be careful." He hesitated, then said, "Just so you know, we've had a couple of men watching this house—and you if you leave."

She blinked. "You mean, when I went to your hotel in the middle of the night—"

"You had an escort." He smiled. "But very discreet. The one who follows you tends to hang back if I'm with you, which is why he wasn't close enough to do anything to help when that store exploded and the car tried to run us down. But he and his partner are watching the house from the front and the river. They'll see if anyone tries to sneak in."

"Almost as good as a moat." She returned his smile, hers a bit rueful. "It makes me feel a little creepy, though. Being watched."

"I thought you'd probably feel that way. It's why I didn't tell you before now. But it's necessary, Rachel. So far, none of the attempts against you have come here, but we're not sure where your car was when it was sabotaged, assuming it was. And even though this is a walled estate, the front gate stands wide open and there's easy access from the river. So we have to keep an eye on the place."

"I'm not arguing. I just want it to be over, Adam."

"I know." He squeezed her hand, then released it reluctantly. "I have to go. Nick and I have some things to go over, and we have to check out the meeting site in advance."

"Will you come back and tell me what happened?"

"Of course I will. But it may take all day, depending on whether Nick's informant is right and this guy really does want to talk."

"I'm not going anywhere," Rachel said.

The whole day stretched before her, and Rachel was more than a little restless. She didn't want to work on the plans for the boutique, and she couldn't think of where her father might have left a key for her to find. She didn't like the idea of Adam and Nick doing dangerous things outside the walls of her prison while she sat inside like some medieval maiden awaiting rescue.

With her ghosts.

She told Fiona not to bother about lunch for her since this was the housekeeper's habitual day to go to the market, and went upstairs in search of some way to occupy her time and her thoughts until Adam was safely back with her again.

Without planning to, she found herself in her mother's room, which was across the hall from her father's. This room, too, aroused memories, and Rachel was surprised by how strong they were.

The lavender scent her mother had always used.

The needlepoint pillows she had spent endless hours doing.

The costume jewelry she had loved.

The delicate gilded furniture that had suited her petite beauty and seeming fragility.

For the first time, whether because her emotions were so near the surface now or because she simply had a better understanding now of how complex people and relationships could be, Rachel was able to mourn the loss of her mother. She was able to grieve for all their differences and misunderstandings, for the distance that had grown between them from the time Rachel was a teenager. For all her regrets.

Needing to feel close to the woman she now felt she had hardly known in life, Rachel sat at her mother's dressing table and looked at all the pretty things, touched them.

She even tried on the long string of pearls her mother had often worn, and smiled wryly at herself in the mirror because pearls didn't suit her.

Finally, she began to tentatively go through her mother's things, deciding what to keep and what to pack up or give away. The clothing, which she didn't bother sorting at the moment, was easy. Most would go to a thrift shop, where others could get some use out of it, and the more formal things could be put aside for charity auctions or some such thing.

After making that decision, she then went to her mother's elegant little desk and began going through the drawers.

Somebody else had done the same thing.

She wasn't sure how she knew, but there was no doubt in her mind that since her mother's death, these drawers had been opened, their contents rifled through.

Rachel murmured, "Dad's desks were locked, and I had the keys. But Mom never bothered to lock hers."

There had been a great many strangers in the house at various times since her parents' deaths, but Rachel couldn't think of any reason why her mother's personal things would have been inspected. There was, she thought, little of interest in these drawers, and certainly nothing of any intrinsic value. Stationery not yet used. A few letters, none of which looked important. An appointment diary that held only social engagements noted with detachment. The usual drawer lint composed of paper clips and rubber bands and stamps and pens that no longer worked.

Nothing else.

Frowning, Rachel got up and went to check a few more places, finding the same rifled disorder in her mother's nightstands and tall chest of drawers. There was no question they had been searched.

For a moment, she stood in the center of her mother's bedroom, looking around. All right. Someone, for whatever reason, had searched through her mother's things. Cameron was her first thought, but it didn't make sense that he might have expected to find anything of value among her mother's personal things.

She went into her mother's dressing room/closet, to the island of drawers in the center of the room. She looked through each, carefully going through sweaters and casual shirts and frilly, scented sleepwear and underwear. None of this appeared to have been searched.

But there was also nothing to find.

Nor was there anything unusual in the built-in drawers for jewelry, or the storage areas for shoes and hats.

But in the specially designed case that held all her mother's collection of antique lace handkerchiefs, Rachel did find something unexpected.

A false bottom.

And underneath it, a bundle of letters tied up with faded blue ribbon.

Rachel carried the letters back into her mother's bedroom and sat down with them at the desk. Even before she untied the ribbon and looked at the first letter, she felt a bit queasy.

She didn't recognize the handwriting, but the scrawled signature was all too clear.

Secret things in secret places.

The first letter, dated only a few months after her own birth, began with devastating simplicity.

My darling Irene . . .

"I don't like the setup," Adam said.

"Do you think I do?" Nicholas shrugged. "But he was only willing to meet us on his terms. And that means here."

Adam looked around at the warehouse, which had been unused and deserted for a good many years. Even with the warm spring day outside, inside this place was chilly and dark and dismal.

Not to mention dangerous.

"We're sitting ducks. Look at those catwalks up there. Anybody could take potshots at us."

"There's nobody up there. I checked."

"Are you kidding? You could hide a dinosaur in this place."

"You're jumpy today."

"Damned right I am. My life is beginning to look really good, and I'll be extremely unhappy if something bad happens to mess that up."

Nicholas, who was leaning idly back against a huge but empty wooden crate in the shadows, said calmly, "Then stay out of the light."

"You have no nerves at all, do you?"

"None to speak of."

Both men kept their voices low, and despite the contentious tone of the conversation, it was obvious they were entirely comfortable with the tension of the situation. It was no place both of them hadn't been before.

But Adam was restless, and it showed. "I'm still bothered by the fact that we don't know who else has been following Rachel and me."

"Assuming Max was telling the truth."

"I think he was. I think he saw Simon for sure. We were out only during Simon's shift, so he had to be one. But the other one . . . Big, blond, casually dressed, yet somehow polished, smooth. Not a cop but maybe a spook?"

"In Max's opinion."

Impatiently, Adam said, "The point is that there's a player out there we don't have identified." Then he frowned. "Or is he somebody you just haven't told me about?"

Nicholas folded his arms across his chest. "You are jumpy. I'm not keeping anything back, Adam. You know what I know."

Adam looked at him a moment, then nodded. "Okay. Sorry."

"It could be one of Walsh's men, you know. Keeping an eye on Rachel, maybe looking for an opportunity to get at her."

"Maybe. But Walsh would almost certainly use a man he knew was loyal to him, a wiseguy. And if there's anything Max would recognize, it'd be a wiseguy."

"In that case," Nicholas said, "we'd better hope we get this settled before whoever it is has a chance to surprise us."

"Yeah."

They both heard it at the same time, the faint sound of an engine outside the warehouse.

Adam said, "You're sure your guy won't object to me being along?"

"I'm sure. Sammy owes me so much, he couldn't object if I brought the district attorney to a meet with him."

They stood there in silence, waiting, and a couple of minutes later one of the front doors creaked open and a thin, worried-looking man about Nick's age slipped into the warehouse. He came immediately to where they were waiting, his eyes darting around with profound nervousness.

"Hello, Sammy," Nicholas said.

"Nick." He looked warily at Adam. "Who's this?"

"A friend. You can trust him. Where's the one you were supposed to bring?"

"I think he might've got whacked, Nick." Sammy's voice was matter-of-fact, but underneath the calm was crawling sheer terror.

Nicholas didn't change position or alter the calm tone of his voice. "What makes you think so, Sammy?"

" 'Cause I went to pick him up like we'd planned, only he wasn't there. He lives about halfway between here and Arlington, in a real quiet neighborhood, respectable as hell. But when I cruised by his place, it was—well, there were cops all over. And the coroner's wagon." Sammy swallowed hard.

"Had he told anyone else he meant to inform against Walsh?" Adam asked sharply.

"I don't know what he told anybody else, just what he told me. Said he was scared to get out, scareder staying in, and that he knew way too much about Walsh's operations, especially here in Richmond. He figured he didn't have a chance of staying alive on his own, and maybe Nick could protect him like I said. I been talking to him, Nick, like I told you I was. Tryin' to convince him you had the juice to protect him no matter who was after his ass. He was jumping out of his skin, said he'd done something really stupid and Walsh would hunt him down on account of the evidence—"

"Evidence?" Nick's voice was also sharp.

Sammy nodded. "Said he'd stumbled across a computer disk when he was doing a job for Walsh a few weeks ago, and the idiot took it."

"With what on it?"

"Records. A shitload of records, he said. For bribes and payoffs, bank account numbers. All the big jobs. Hits ordered and carried out. Lists of bought judges and cops—even some government people. His whole Richmond operation, and it dates back further than anybody knew. Walsh has been pulling strings in this town for years, Nick."

"He never showed his face in Richmond until a few months ago," Nick said.

"Yeah. But, man, was he here in spirit."

"Jesus Christ on a pony," Adam muttered.

Sammy nodded as if wholeheartedly agreeing. "Yeah. That stuff gets made public, and a lot of big shots besides Walsh are going down."

Nicholas said, "Do you believe he actually had evidence of this?"

"He showed me a disk, Nick, that's all I know. He said—"
Sammy broke off, looking uncertain.

"What?"

"Well, when we talked last night, he said if anything was to
happen to him before he could talk to you, I was to take you to a
certain place, and maybe that disk would be there."

Nicholas scowled at him. "Sammy—"

"I swear, Nick. I don't have a way in to the place, which is why
I couldn't get the disk myself even if I wanted to do that. But he
said you could get it. He said you could get it easy. He picked the
place special when I first told him about you a couple of weeks
ago."

"Sammy, if you're lying to me—"

"Nick, I swear to God it's the truth. Don't I owe you my life?
Didn't I swear I'd repay you someday? I said I'd be there when you
called in the favor, and I'm here, Nick. You can trust me."

"I hope so, Sammy. I really hope so."

"I don't like this," Adam said. "It smells like a trap."

Sammy was offended. "No way."

"You might not know about it, Sammy," Nicholas pointed out.
"He could be using you."

Sammy looked uncertain a moment, then shook his head. "No.
I believe him, Nick. He was on the up-and-up."

"Okay," Nicholas said. "Where is this place, Sammy?"

Before the other two could stop him, Sammy had darted back
toward the front door. "Come on. He said I was to take you there,
not just tell you where it is."

"Sammy—"

But the worried little man didn't hesitate. He yanked open the door. For just a moment, he was silhouetted, the light from outside pouring through the open door.

Then a shot.

Adam and Nick reached the door as a squeal of tires outside declared the successful departure of the shooter. Sammy lay in a rapidly spreading pool of blood, and grim experience told both the other men he wouldn't last long.

"Goddammit," Adam said bitterly as they knelt beside Sammy.

"Nick . . ." Sammy reached up and grasped the lapel of Nick's jacket with bloodied fingers. "Listen—"

Nicholas bent low, his ear no more than an inch from Sammy's labored whisper.

Then Sammy's hand dropped away, a rattling sigh left his mouth, and his sightless eyes gazed into eternity.

"Well?" Adam watched as Nicholas straightened. "Did you get it?"

Nicholas looked at him with an expression that defied description, and said slowly, "Yeah. I got it."

EIGHTEEN

I t took Rachel some time to read all the letters. She didn't want to read them. They hurt more than she would have thought possible. But she forced herself to because she wanted no more secrets in this house.

Why didn't you burn them, Mom?

Love letters. Love letters from her uncle to her mother. And from what had been written, it was clear they'd had an affair during the summer he had been home from college, just scant months after Rachel's birth. It didn't seem to have lasted long, only a couple of months, but it was obviously intense while it was going on.

The only relief Rachel got from reading the letters was in knowing that the affair had begun *after* her birth and not before. That was clear in what Cameron wrote; though he claimed to have been in love with Irene for years, he had not dared to speak until that summer.

No reason for either his silence before or his change of mind that summer was offered.

It was also clear from the letters that Cameron had been the supplicant, wildly begging Irene Grant to leave her husband and infant daughter, promising that he could give her a better life. She had been unhappy, married to a man who had not, apparently, needed her as she'd wanted him to.

Rachel, remembering her pretty, serene mother, also recalled arguments during her childhood when Irene had wanted Duncan to get involved in the society events she had so enjoyed—and he had despised. Rachel had not thought much about the arguments, because they had seemed low-key, with her father's refusals and her mother's frustration expressed calmly, almost more like debates than arguments. Neither had seemed particularly upset either during or afterward, and there had always been other escorts available to Rachel's mother, friends or otherwise "safe" men who could escort a married woman without causing talk.

Rachel wondered now if there had been lovers as well.

Which was a hell of a thing to wonder about your mother.

Her parents had had separate bedrooms as long as she could remember, and though she had memories of affection between them, especially during her sporadic visits home in the last ten years, she could not remember anything even remotely romantic.

Was that it? Had Irene craved the sort of romance that the plain-speaking, practical Scotsman she'd married was incapable of giving her?

Two brothers, one blunt and unromantic, the other artistic and somewhat dramatic—and handsome, in his younger years.

Two brothers, raised by a father who had pitted them against each other, pushed them to compete on every level, rewarding success and ridiculing them when they failed, setting them up to feel that what one had the other had to better.

Two brothers. And a woman who might have loved them both.

"I wish you'd kept a diary, Mom." Then again, Rachel thought as she slowly retied the blue ribbon around the letters, maybe she didn't wish that at all. It was profoundly disconcerting for her to face this window into her parents' troubled relationship, and even more so to learn that her mother had very nearly run off with her uncle.

Because it looked as though that had nearly happened.

That Irene Grant had not left her husband appeared to be, at least according to Cameron's bitter words, almost solely due to her love of social position. Duncan, as the elder son and likely heir to his father, had far greater potential than Cameron, the younger son and a struggling artist to boot.

She had apparently ended the affair shortly after her father-in-law had died, and did not change her mind when her husband deeded half his inheritance to his brother.

With only Cameron's letters to tell the story, Rachel had no idea how accurate his assessment of the situation was. He had been clearly bitter and unhappy, hugely resentful of his brother, and had accepted Irene's decision with the declaration that he would never love anyone else.

Rachel didn't know what she felt about this. She had no idea if her father had known of the affair. She had no real idea of what her mother's emotions and motivations had been.

And it had been nearly thirty years ago.

But Rachel did wonder, now, if her mother's serenity had been natural to her personality before the affair with Cameron. Or had that tranquility, like her daughter's twenty years later, stemmed from an agonizing loss she had been unable to completely recover from?

There was, of course, no way for Rachel to know now. But wondering made her feel the loss of her mother more bitterly than she ever had before, because it seemed possible that they'd had far more in common than Rachel had ever guessed.

"I thought there'd be time," Rachel murmured to herself, gazing down at the evidence of her mother's secret soul. "I thought I'd come home one day, when it didn't hurt anymore, and we'd have time to fix all the broken things between us and be close."

But there hadn't been enough time, that plane crash stealing forever any chance Rachel might have had to repair the damaged relationships with her parents. While she had remained in New York, working long hours so she didn't have to think or feel, keeping herself in limbo because that had been less painful, they had been snatched from her life, her future.

Rachel faced that for the first time.

She had thought loss was the most painful thing of all, but now she knew there was something more painful. Regret.

When she finally got hold of herself once again, Rachel discovered that she was lying across her mother's bed, the letters thrown aside. Instinctively, she reached under the pillows for the lavender-scented handkerchief that had always been there, and not finding it made a fresh wave of grief sweep over her with a force she couldn't fight.

It was a long time before Rachel finally pulled herself off the bed. She went into her mother's bathroom and splashed cold water on her face, avoiding any glance in the mirror. She undoubtedly looked awful, though she certainly felt better. Drained, but more at peace somehow.

She returned to her mother's desk and gazed down at the letters for some time, thinking, before she finally made her decision. This was not her story. It had not affected her life while her parents had been alive, and it did not seriously change her feelings, in any negative way, for either of them now that they were gone.

It wasn't her business, all things considered. And the only surviving member of that triangle deserved his privacy.

Cameron's urgent search, undoubtedly for these letters, was clear evidence of his feelings on the matter; she had no doubt he would have destroyed them—or kept her from knowing about them, had he discovered them himself.

Rachel's first impulse was to leave them on his pillow to find when he returned from the trip he had taken today into D.C. to check out various galleries. But when she thought of both of them being painfully aware of her knowledge of the affair, it was simply not something she wanted to have to deal with.

She would never be close to Cameron, but she did not want old secrets and regrets to shadow her relationship with her uncle. There were some things a niece just didn't need to know.

With that decision made, Rachel picked up the phone and called Darby.

"Hey, pal," she said when Darby answered. "I need a favor."

"You've got it," Darby replied without hesitation.

If Nicholas had not wielded considerable influence over numerous officials within the Richmond police force because of his background and connections in law enforcement, and commanded enormous respect among its various politicians because of all the successful business ventures he had backed, he and Adam would have no doubt been forced to spend the entire day with the police answering questions about Sammy's murder. Even so, it still required a couple of hours for them to tell their story—the one they had decided to tell, at any rate—and be granted leave to be on their way.

As long as they didn't leave the city, of course.

"It's a good thing you routinely use informants to gather information for the bank," Adam commented as they finally left the warehouse and the crowd of police officers and technicians behind. "How long do you think it'll be before somebody starts to get very curious about exactly what information you wanted that would have gotten Sammy killed?"

"A few days, if we're lucky." Nicholas shrugged. "Not that it'll matter if we get our hands on that disk and it holds even a fraction of what Sammy claimed it does. We'll just go public holding a hand full of aces, and all will be forgiven."

"If we get our hands on that disk."

"You always tell me to think positive. Now it's your turn."

Adam looked at him curiously. "You really think the disk is where Sammy told you it would be. Why?"

"Because," Nicholas said, "the irony is just wonderful. And I've always believed the universe had a wicked sense of humor."

Adam was puzzled, especially since Nick had not yet told him where the disk was supposed to be. But, moments later, when the big black car turned into the parking lot beside the bank, puzzlement turned to surprise.

"You're kidding," Adam said.

"Like I said." Nick turned off the engine and smiled. "The irony is wonderful."

Rachel was just closing the basement door behind her when Fiona appeared.

"Miss Rachel, I'm going to the market now. Is there anything special you want me to get?"

"Nothing I can think of, thanks, Fiona."

The housekeeper frowned at her, but did not comment directly about swollen eyelids. "There's cold chicken and salad in the refrigerator. You need to eat, Miss Rachel."

"I will—if I get hungry." She smiled. "Don't worry about me, Fiona. I'll be fine."

Fiona sniffed. "If you say so. I'll be back in a couple of hours."

"Take your time."

Alone once again, Rachel slowly went back upstairs. She turned toward her father's room, intending to try once more to figure out where he might have hidden a key for her to find. But she stopped dead in the middle of the hallway just past her own room, staring.

A yellow rose lay on the rug at her feet.

She bent slowly and picked up the flower, turning it in her fingers as she straightened. She had glanced in her room as she passed, and the rose had been in the vase on her nightstand, as always. Now this one . . .

"If this is some kind of joke," she murmured in a shaky voice, "I'm not amused."

She hadn't expected an answer, but a glimpse of movement made her look quickly at the far end of the hallway. The door that led up to the smallest of the three attics was there. And it was slowly opening.

If she had behaved rationally, Rachel realized a long time later, she would have turned around and gotten out of there, especially when the distant doorway remained empty. Instead, she found herself walking slowly toward it, the rose still gripped between her fingers, her heart thudding.

Just a stray breeze, probably. Darby or one of her guys had undoubtedly left the door ajar, and some stray breeze had blown it open.

That was all.

Rachel stopped in the doorway, gazing at the stairs leading upward. Then she took a step back. Ridiculous. This was ridiculous—

"Rachel . . ."

It was only a whisper of sound, so faint she could almost convince herself she had not heard it at all. Almost. Except that the hair on the back of her neck was stirring, and she knew this was not her imagination.

Drawing a deep breath, she flipped up the switch on the wall at the foot of the stairs, then slowly climbed upward. At the top of the lighted stairs, she paused, looking slowly around. This space, like the other attics and the basement, was stuffed with furniture and other cast-off items, and since nothing had yet been tagged or sorted, it was clear Darby had not yet begun her work here.

But Rachel's realization of that was distant and occupied little of her attention. She knew what she was supposed to be looking at. It was a storage chest that had, for most of her life, been in her bedroom. On one of her brief visits home after Tom's death, her mother had explained that she had moved the chest to the attic. To spare Rachel, because in it she had kept all the mementos and notes and silly little gifts from Tom.

Rachel had not been able to bring herself to sort through any of the things, not then, and not in all the years since.

Now the lid was raised invitingly, the bare lightbulb hanging directly above it seeming to spotlight the open chest, and Rachel knew without a doubt that she was being asked—commanded—to look inside.

"No." Her voice sounded to her unnaturally loud in the close silence of the attic.

"Rachel . . ." Almost inaudible, like a breath of wind.

"*No.*" She felt her eyes sting with tears, blurring her vision, and she had to swallow hard before she could go on. "I'm sorry. But you're . . . you're gone, Tom. You've been gone a long time. And I love somebody else now."

She opened her fingers and let the rose fall to the floor.

There was a moment when the lights seemed to flicker, or something else seemed to happen, and when Rachel looked down, blinking the tears away, there was no rose. When she looked at the chest, it was closed, the layer of dust atop it undisturbed.

She stood there for a long time, listening, but heard nothing. She turned around and went back down the stairs, turning off the lights at the bottom and closing the attic door carefully.

She walked on, pausing only when she reached the door of her bedroom, and looked inside. There was no yellow rose on her nightstand, no bud vase. And when she went to open her jewelry box, there was no gold identification bracelet inside. She was afraid to look in her desk drawer, but when she did, the note from Tom was there.

On white notepaper, the kind he had used ten years ago.

Rachel sat down on her bed and murmured, "I must be a lot more tired than I thought I was."

Or perhaps she had just needed concrete things to make her face and deal with her feelings about Tom. It seemed as good an answer as any, and infinitely preferable to the notion that she was losing her mind.

After a while, Rachel got up and went downstairs. A glance at a clock surprised her; only a few minutes had passed since Fiona had left the house. Shaking her head, Rachel went into the study and looked around slowly.

Maiden in a locked castle she might be, but only she had known her father well enough to have any hope of figuring out where he might have left a key for her to find. And without that key, they might well never have all the answers they needed. She concentrated on that.

Secret things in secret places.

However secret his private loans had been, Duncan Grant would not have left even that part of his estate untended. He would have made certain that everything had been set up in such a way that when Rachel eventually and inevitably discovered what he had been doing, she would not only be unharmed financially, but would have the option of safely continuing what her father had begun so many years before.

That meant detailed records, tax information, and a clear explanation of his system.

And given his secrecy on the matter, he would have left that information where it would not be casually discovered after his death, but where Rachel *specifically* would know where to look for it once she found the notebooks and journal.

Of course, he had certainly not counted on his daughter being so distracted by attempts on her own life and the fact that she had fallen in love, so what might have seemed obvious to him eluded her now.

"Where?" Rachel muttered, looking around absently. "Where does X mark the spot? Come on, Dad, I need your help. Where did you leave it? Where would you hide a key?"

A key.

Secret things in secret places.

Her mother's handkerchiefs had hidden secret letters.

A woman would hide her secrets among treasured things put safely away; where would a man hide his secrets?

More important, where would he hide them if he expected his daughter to know where to look?

"You already know."

"No, I don't. I—"

"You know. You only have to remember."

The dream conversation came back to her vividly, and Rachel frowned as she considered it. Her subconscious nagging at her again? *Was* there something she needed to remember?

Her father.

Secrets.

Secret things in secret places.

Secret things in secret places.

"Of course. My God—why didn't I remember it before now?"

"It's our secret, Rachel. Just yours and mine."

As a small child, she had often played in her father's study, and she had been endlessly fascinated with the desk he had designed and had custom-built years before. She had loved the gleaming wood, the deep drawers, the leather desk set he had always used.

And the secret.

Rachel had to sit down on the floor in order to get far enough underneath the desk, and it took her several moments to remember which place in the kneehole to look, but eventually she found it. A small section of wood with no seams showing, so cunningly crafted it would have taken an inch-by-inch measurement—if not a total dismemberment of the desk—to determine hidden space.

Carefully, Rachel's fingertip probed, and she felt the tiny indentation. And pressed firmly.

Obediently, the secret compartment popped open. And her fingers closed over a small box hidden inside.

Adam looked over Nick's shoulder as he worked at the computer on his desk. "I still can't believe this Alan Fuller just walked into your bank a couple of weeks ago and calmly rented a safe deposit box." He shook his head. "We might well have had all the answers we needed right under our noses for two weeks."

"It was a smart thing to do," Nicholas noted absently as he began to access the information on the disk. "As long as either he or Sammy got word to me, getting the disk was easy for me, even without the renter's key. In the meantime, Walsh didn't have a clue where it was—and he's been in and out of here at least twice recently."

"I'm wondering if Walsh had Fuller's place searched before or after he was killed. If he did, and if he got his hands on the key, he'll be turning up here or sending somebody else quick."

Nicholas nodded. "If we get anything at all off this disk, we'll need to move fast."

Grim, Adam said, "Let's just hope whatever we get is worth

two lives. If we don't get him for anything else, I want to burn Walsh for Fuller and Sammy."

"You and me both." Nick's skilled fingers moved lightly over the keys. "Ah."

After a moment, Adam said, "I'll be damned."

"So he was an explosives expert, just as he claimed," Nicholas noted as he read the information on the screen. "But also a computer genius. It looks like Walsh was just a bit careless with access."

"People who don't understand computers often are," Adam observed, also reading. "Look at that—Sammy was right. Lists of paid-off judges and cops, with dates and amounts. Bribes and kickbacks. Everything necessary to bust Walsh's entire operation here in Richmond."

"The D.A. is going to love us," Nick said.

"What about Duncan's death? Is there some record of that explosion?"

Nick frowned as he read. "Nothing so far. Let me go back a few more months. . . ."

In her office, Mercy worked at her own computer.

She knew Nick and Adam had gone out and that they'd returned, and she'd been unable to answer Leigh's so-casual question when the office manager had come in to ask her why Nick had made a sudden and unexpected trip downstairs to the lock boxes.

She had, of course, wondered herself, but made herself do as she'd promised Nick. She stayed in her office and asked no questions.

And worked at her computer.

It was an hour or so after Nick and Adam had returned that she suddenly frowned and leaned toward her screen. Well, now, that was odd.

That was very odd.

The box was small and made of intricately carved wood. It had been a gift from Rachel to her father several years before. Another way Duncan had ensured she would search for what was hidden; eventually, she would have wondered what had happened to the box, because her father had loved it.

"Oh, Dad . . ."

Rachel climbed back up and into her father's chair, and put the box on top of the desk to open it. Inside, as she had expected, was a small key, obviously to a safe deposit box. And a note.

Rachel—

By now you undoubtedly know what you'll find when you use this key. Everything you'll need is there. If you choose to continue this work, I know you'll do well, and many people will benefit. But make your life your own. I love you, sweetheart.

Dad

The key to the safe deposit box was neatly labeled with the name of the bank.

Rachel shook her head over it, but she was smiling. She had no idea if her intuitions and judgments about people would prove as accurate as her father's had been, but she was willing to put them to the test.

Then her smile faded, and she looked at the key in her hand, wondering if among that information lay the connection that she and Adam—and Nick—had been searching for. The connection between Jordan Walsh and someone Duncan had known and trusted.

She wanted to leave now, to rush out to the bank and find out exactly what information awaited her in the box. But she also wanted Adam to be with her. Whether or not his meeting had been successful, he might be at the bank with Nick—

The phone rang.

Hoping it was Adam, Rachel hurried to pick up the receiver. "Hello?"

"May I speak to Rachel Grant, please?"

Rachel didn't recognize the voice. "This is she."

"Miss Grant, this is John Elliot. I got a message to call this number and speak to either you or an Adam Delafield."

For a moment, Rachel was totally blank.

"I'm a private investigator," he added.

"Oh. Oh, of course. I'm sorry, Mr. Elliot, things have been a bit hectic, and I'd forgotten. . . . The reason we called was that we wanted to ask you a question about some work you might have done for my father."

"Duncan Grant?"

"Yes. Among his papers, we found a note indicating that he might have asked you to investigate someone shortly before he was killed."

"As a matter of fact, Miss Grant, he did. But he was killed just days later, and we never finalized the arrangement."

"I see. Was it Jordan Walsh he asked you to check out?"

Immediately, Elliot said, "No, ma'am, it wasn't. He just said he was looking at a potential business problem, and wanted me to do a little digging, very quietly."

"Did he give you a name?"

"No, ma'am. He said there were a couple of things he wanted to check on himself first, and that he'd be in touch as soon as he did that. I can't be sure, of course, but from the way he talked, I got the idea it was somebody he'd trusted up till then, somebody close to him."

"I see. And that's all you can tell me?"

"I'm afraid so, Miss Grant. As I said, the arrangement was never finalized."

Not very helpful, but there was nothing Rachel could do about that.

"Thank you anyway, Mr. Elliot, for calling. I'll pass on the information to Mr. Delafield."

"I'm sorry I couldn't be more help, Miss Grant."

"So am I. Good-bye, Mr. Elliot."

"Miss Grant."

Rachel hung up the phone slowly.

And then a voice came from the doorway.

"Hello, Rachel."

Mercy opened the door of Nick's office without knocking and marched in. She saw both men look up in surprise from the computer they'd been intent on, and spoke before either of them could.

"I know you boys like the cloak-and-dagger stuff, but let's cut to the chase. Do you know about Graham Becket?"

N I N E T E E N

achel stared across the study at Graham. She felt very
cold, and not only because he had a gun.

A gun pointed squarely at her.

"Graham? What's going on?"

"Haven't you figured it out yet, Rachel? I thought surely you—
or your lover—would have found what you were looking for by
now." His voice was the one that had been so familiar to her for so
many years, quiet and pleasant.

Involuntarily, Rachel glanced down at the box on the desk.

Graham was quick. "Ah, so you have found something. A little
note condemning me, perhaps? Or something more damning,
maybe information Duncan managed to gather on someone else?"

"No."

"I don't believe you, Rachel. You never were a very good liar." He came farther into the room, that gun still aimed at her. "Move away from the desk. But not too far away."

She obeyed, but heard herself offer an idiotic protest. "That's just about some information Dad left for me. About more loans he made. Like the one to Adam."

Graham looked at the note briefly, then pocketed it and the key. "Yes, I'm sure he kept meticulous records somewhere. I always suspected it. But there wasn't much of a risk of anyone finding them until you came home and started going through everything. I could have found them myself, but you had to be the one to sort his private papers. And since he'd locked up his desks and, as I recall, left the keys for you in one of the safes, I couldn't slip in here and get it done before you came back to Richmond."

"I must be very slow," she said, hearing the reluctance in her own voice. "It was you. You were the one who recommended Dad lend Jordan Walsh all that money."

His eyes flickered. "So you already know about the loan."

"We found a notebook." She hesitated. "Adam has it. So whatever you're planning won't work. He knows. And Nick knows."

"Maybe. But they don't have proof, or they would already have moved on it." He patted his pocket with his free hand. "I'll make very sure they never have proof."

"And what about me?" She swallowed. "Another exploding building? Another car playing hit-and-run?"

Graham frowned. "I had nothing to do with either of those things."

"I don't believe you, Graham."

"I can't help what you believe, Rachel."

"You tried to have me killed."

His frown remained. "The cut brake line was meant only to scare you, to send you back to New York."

"And the rest?"

"I told you. I didn't have anything to do with the rest."

"Then it was your boss. Jordan Walsh." And that certainly seemed to touch a nerve.

"Walsh is not my boss," Graham said shortly. "But he's a powerful man, Rachel, a man you don't say no to. You must see that."

"And he told you to kill me?"

A nerve throbbed beside Graham's mouth, but the gun never wavered. "He told me to deal with the problem. His people couldn't seem to—I'm sorry, Rachel. This isn't the way I wanted it to end. If it hadn't been for Delafield—"

"What does Adam have to do with it?"

A little sound escaped Graham, a sound that was a laugh but held no amusement. "Not a goddamned thing, Rachel."

She drew a breath. "Graham, I don't understand this. How would it harm you—or Walsh, for that matter—for that loan to come to light? Or for me to know you asked Dad to make it to Walsh?"

"The loan wasn't the problem. With Duncan gone and that loan made on a handshake, there was no way the money could ever be collected. But I made a mistake in giving in to Walsh and recommending he go to Duncan in the first place. The money was for a legitimate business, you know, a nice, respectable front Walsh could have used in years to come. It all would have worked out if only Duncan hadn't seen Walsh here in Richmond, somewhere he shouldn't have been. He got suspicious."

"Until then, he'd accepted your recommendation of Walsh."

"Of course. I was an old and valued friend as well as his attorney. And Walsh had such a good cover story, you see. About all the good he was going to be able to do with that money. But then he blew it. He put Duncan on guard, made him start wondering."

Slowly, trying to understand, Rachel said, "And any investigation of Walsh would have turned up information that you had also been involved in illegal activities."

"It was a concern. Duncan could have ruined me with that information. And it would have focused way too much light on Walsh's activities here in Richmond."

Rachel felt queasy. "Your reputation as a fine, upstanding attorney meant more to you than other people's lives. More than the life of a man who'd called you friend for fifteen years."

"I'm glad I never had to make that decision," Graham said, almost thoughtful.

Rachel stared at him. "You sabotaged Dad's plane."

"As a matter of fact, I didn't. I wouldn't know the first thing about how to bring a plane down. No, that was a fortuitous accident."

"The plane was brought down, Graham. It was made to crash."

For the first time, he looked uncertain, but the expression quickly passed. "Well, perhaps Walsh acted without telling me. In any case, we were safe after that. Until you came home. I really am sorry, Rachel. You should have stayed in New York."

Getting a little tired of his meaningless apologies, Rachel said steadily, "Well, I didn't do that, Graham. So what are you going to do with me now? A bullet would look a bit suspicious, don't you think? Especially with Adam and Nick working to get Walsh."

Graham shook his head. "Rachel, how could you even imagine that I could kill you like that?"

She wasn't reassured. "No?"

"No. We're just going to take a little walk, that's all."

"Where?"

"The river." He smiled. "It's such a pity you never learned to swim."

It was the most chilling thing she'd ever heard in her life.

Rachel knew without a doubt that Graham could—and would—push her into the river. A river that had sometimes refused to give up its dead.

"Let's go," he said, gesturing toward the door.

A little desperately, she said, "Don't you think that my death coming so soon after Mom and Dad's will make people wonder?"

"Not really. Their deaths were tragic, but that crash was ruled an accident. Everyone knows it was an accident. You, on the other hand, have been terribly despondent about the new burdens that have fallen onto your fragile shoulders. I mean, everyone knows you never really recovered from Thomas Sheridan's death, and now you've lost your parents in a senseless accident—another plane crash. The estate so complex, all the details overwhelming. And the double of your dead lover showing up on top of everything. Well, who could be surprised that it all just got to be too much? Especially after I spread the word about how depressed you've been, how you cried in my office and talked about suicide. It's such a pity I didn't take you seriously."

"What about Adam?"

"Oh, he might try rattling a few cages, making some noise. But he won't have any proof. If he gets too bothersome, Walsh will take care of him."

"You bastard."

"Start walking, Rachel."

"If you think I'm going to just tamely walk to the river with that gun in my back—"

"Rachel, understand something. I've gone too far to turn back now. If I have to, I'll knock you over the head and carry you to the river. It's your choice. On your feet or slung over my shoulder. But make up your mind. I intend to be long gone by the time Fiona returns from the market."

Habits, Rachel thought, could sometimes be used as weapons. He had known Fiona's regular market day and had waited, knowing it was his best chance of catching Rachel alone in the house.

Panic was a mild word to describe what she felt, but even with that fear and horror running through her mind, she remembered something. She wasn't entirely alone.

There were guardian dragons outside the gates. One watching in front—and one watching from the river.

The only question was, could either of them help her before Graham managed to kill her.

"Let's go, Rachel." He smiled. "And do try to remember that I can pull this trigger before you could throw anything at me—and certainly before you could run away. I don't think a bullet hole would matter too much after you'd been in the river awhile."

She had an awful feeling he was right.

"I hate to sound like a bad TV movie, but you'll never get away with this." She moved toward the door.

"Oh, I think I will. No, don't bother looking back at me. Just keep heading for the back of the house, Rachel."

Help didn't come from the river.

Rachel was near the foot of the stairs, moving as slowly as she dared, when the front door suddenly burst open and a total stranger came flying in. Almost literally flying. He landed on the rug, outstretched hands holding a businesslike automatic, and his command was shouted.

"Move, Rachel!"

Things happened very fast after that. Rachel darted toward the stairs, which was the only direction she could move in. Graham whirled toward the newcomer, his gun leveling.

"Drop it, Becket!"

Two shots sounded so close together that they seemed one.

Rachel looked back over her shoulder and saw Graham stagger back against the wall at the foot of the stairs, scarlet blooming on the upper arm of his jacket. But it wasn't his gun hand that hung useless.

And the man on the rug was still, his gun in limp fingers.

Rachel didn't hesitate; she ran up the stairs as fast as she could. She knew this house better than Graham ever could, and if she could just get upstairs with a few seconds' grace, there was a good chance she could elude him—at least for a while.

"Rachel!"

She reached the top just as another shot rang out, and wood chips flew from the banister beside her.

"Stop, Rachel! The next one goes in your back."

She didn't make a conscious decision to stop; she was willing to take her chances and keep running. But suddenly she felt as if she moved through water. There was resistance in the very air, an odd impression of something tangible slowing her forward momentum until she stopped moving.

She turned to watch Graham come the rest of the way up the stairs toward her. Again, she felt that curious sensation, and it compelled her to begin backing away, step by slow step.

She felt strangely calm.

"Don't make me shoot you, Rachel." He reached the top of the stairs and paused. "We're going back down, and we're walking to the river."

"You're bleeding, Graham," she observed with a detachment that astonished her. "And that other man is hurt as well. What do you mean to do about him?"

"A watchdog Nick or Delafield hired to stand guard, I suppose? He's dead meat. I'll throw him in the river. Let's go, Rachel."

She was waiting for something. And she didn't know what.

"Rachel—" He took a step toward her.

Footsteps pounded on the walk outside.

From the open front door, Adam yelled, "Becket!"

Graham started to turn.

For just an instant, Rachel thought her eyes were playing tricks on her. They had to be. Because out of a shadowy area near the top of the stairs, Adam appeared, and moved toward Graham.

And then she realized it wasn't Adam.

There was no way of knowing what Graham felt behind him. Maybe he felt powerful, furious hands or maybe, like Rachel, he merely felt the sensation of an irresistible force compelling him onward. All Rachel knew for sure was that utter and complete terror showed briefly on his face before he pitched forward and fell.

Rachel closed her eyes as the horrible sounds of Graham's heavy body crashing down the stairs seemed to fill the house.

When the sounds finally stopped, she opened her eyes slowly, looking at the top of the stairs.

There was nothing there.

"Rachel!" Adam came up the stairs two at a time, his face pale and eyes almost wild. He had a gun, which he hastily stuck inside his belt at the small of his back as he reached her, so that he could put his hands on her shoulders. "Are you all right? Did he hurt you?"

"No. No, I'm . . . fine." She looked up at him. "Did you see? Did you see him?"

"Yes," Adam said. "I saw him." And then he pulled her into his arms.

As it turned out, Graham had been wrong about Simon being dead meat. He wasn't happy, and he was in a great deal of pain, but he was very much alive when the paramedics wheeled him out.

That made Rachel feel better. She didn't know how she would have been able to bear it if a man had died trying to protect her.

As for the man who intended to kill her, he was not as lucky as Simon. Then again, maybe he was lucky. The fall broke Graham's neck.

Which, Adam said viciously, would save the state a bundle and had probably made those in hell happy to see a new face.

Rachel didn't know how she felt about any of this yet. She was numb about part of it, about Graham's massive betrayal and the incredible violence that had occurred here today. Yet there was a definite relief in the knowledge that it was over now, that finally her life could return to normal.

And with that relief she found her mind dwelling instead on what she had seen at the top of the stairs.

Tom?

It was absurd, of course. Like the rose and the notepaper, the odd trip to the attic and the gift Tom had never given her, it had only been her imagination. Some trick of the light . . .

Except that Adam had seen him too.

Rachel couldn't help remembering waking up on that early morning a decade before to see Tom standing at the foot of her bed. And she knew, she was absolutely certain in her own mind, that she had not dreamed that.

He had come to her once in a moment of anguished farewell.

Had he come to her again today, knowing somehow that she was in danger and needed him?

Adam had seen him. And Nick might have seen him, since he'd been right behind Adam as they rushed into the house.

They had all seen . . . a dead man.

Rachel definitely didn't know how she felt about that. On top of the emotions she had worked through, her feelings about Adam and Tom, her imagination working overtime, and the nightmares filled with tangled symbolism that had haunted her nights, to believe that Tom had actually come back to help her . . .

For the first time, she had to wonder if it had been more than the voice of her own subconscious in those dreams and nightmares, if Tom had actually used that means to reach out to her, to try to help her, and warn her.

And question her feelings about Adam.

That was unnerving, to think that the first love of her life might be observing from some betweenworld, frowning over her choice of lovers.

"I'm imagining things," she muttered to herself. "Still imagining things. That's just not the way it works."

Or was it? Did the dead watch over the living?

"Here, Rachel—Fiona sent this in." Mercy carried a tray into the study, where Rachel was curled up on the couch, wrapped in an afghan Adam had put around her.

"She shouldn't have bothered. She's as shaken up as I've ever seen her," Rachel commented, a little surprised by her own steady voice.

"Well, she needs to be busy." Mercy put the tray on the coffee table and sat down beside Rachel. She fixed her friend a cup of tea and handed it over. "And you need this."

Rachel sipped, then smiled. "Hot and sweet. You know, I've been drinking an awful lot of this stuff in the last couple of weeks."

Mercy eyed her thoughtfully. "Is that incipient hysteria or real, honest-to-God humor?"

"The latter."

"Glad to hear it. Graham Becket isn't worth a tear or a wasted regret."

Rachel frowned. "The guys are out in the foyer still talking to the police, aren't they?"

"Oh, yeah. Graham dropped the lockbox key when he fell, but the cops are more than half convinced they ought to keep it as evidence anyway. If I were going to bet, I'd bet on Nick and Adam getting it back." Mercy fixed a cup of tea for herself.

Rachel said, "Well, while they're out there doing that, would you mind telling me how you guys showed up at just the right moment?"

"That's simple enough. Me." Mercy, who had waited in the car until the shouting was over, grinned at her friend.

"Thank you. What did you do?"

"I found a note in Duncan's personal computer files at the bank."

Rachel blinked. "I didn't know he had any."

Mercy rolled her eyes. "Did he ever. I'd have turned them over to you eventually as part of settling his estate and clearing his things out of the bank, but when I realized Nick and Adam were up to something, it occurred to me that the only common denominator was Duncan. So I started going through the files on his computer. I thought I might recognize something odd more quickly than the rest of you." She paused. "Of course, I also wanted to teach Nick a thing or two."

"Along the lines of—anything you can do I can do better?"

"Something like that." Mercy grinned again. "They were both really focused on the cloak-and-dagger aspects—which, to be fair, turned out to be where almost all the answers were. But I found one tiny little key among Duncan's files."

"What was it?"

"It was a note Duncan had made just a few weeks before his death. He'd been looking at some kind of storage property near the river, and he saw Graham come out of a seedy building—with Jordan Walsh. Something about what he saw bothered Duncan, even though he knew they knew each other. But the point was what his note told me. Nick had finally confessed about what was going on, what he and Adam were up to, and he told me who they suspected. He'd also told me they hadn't found a sign of a connection between Walsh and any of Duncan's friends. So I burst into Nick's office and asked them if they knew about Graham."

Fascinated, Rachel said, "And then?"

"When he realized that neither of the watchdogs they had guarding you had any reason at all to suspect Graham, and had in fact already let him come and go freely here, Adam went the whitest shade of pale I've ever seen and dove for the phone. In the meantime, Nick was pulling a couple of guns out of a drawer—guns in the bank! Can you believe that?—and the next thing you knew we were all in Nick's car, breaking every speed law to get here."

"My God."

Mercy chuckled. "We picked up two squad cars along the way, which turned out to be handy."

Rachel took a healthy swallow of her tea, then said, "The cloak-and-dagger aspect. So that meeting today gave them some answers?"

"Pretty much all of them, from what Nick told me on the way over here. Lots of lovely damning information about Walsh and his operations here in Richmond, all nice and neat on a computer disk. Unfortunately, though, the witness they thought they had turned out to be dead."

Rachel sighed. "With Graham gone, the witness gone—how much of this will ever come to light in court?"

"Nick thinks most of it." Mercy shrugged. "Your testimony is enough probable cause to start digging into Graham's records—and what do you want to bet that, being an anal lawyer, he kept good ones? I bet he'll hurt Walsh more than that other witness ever could. And then all those computer files the witness made copies of will give the prosecutors plenty of other places to dig. They'll get him, Rachel."

"I hope so."

"They will. And in case you're wondering, they'll make it way too hot for him to even *think* about coming after you."

Rachel smiled. "It crossed my mind that I might be stuck here in the castle for a good long while."

"Not if Adam has anything to say about it. I gather he plans to take you away somewhere for a while. Maybe on a honeymoon?"

"He hasn't said. Or asked, for that matter." Rachel eyed her friend thoughtfully, smiling a little. "How about you and Nick?"

Mercy widened her eyes innocently. "What about us?"

"Ah. I thought so."

"Rats. What gave me away?"

"Oh, just the way you talk about him."

"I gotta watch that," Mercy muttered, then grinned. "I've got a bet with Nick that Leigh will faint dead away when I walk into the bank with a wedding ring."

"It's that serious, huh?"

"I chased the man ferociously until he caught me."

Rachel smiled at her friend. "I'm glad. He unnerved me for the longest time, but I have plenty of reason to be grateful to Nick."

"He's a remarkable man." Mercy shook her head. "Secretive as hell, though. I'm going to have to cure him of that."

"I have complete faith in you."

"Thank you. So do I, as a matter of fact."

Rachel laughed. "That poor man doesn't have a chance, does he?"

Walking into the study just then, Nicholas said with perfect calm, "If you're referring to me, the answer is no."

Mercy gave him an innocent look than laughed. "What makes you think we're talking about you?"

"Just a hunch." He put a casual hand on her shoulder, then

looked past her at Rachel. "Not much longer now. The cops have agreed that your statement can wait for a day or two."

"Wow," Mercy murmured. "I for one am impressed."

"Adam was . . . insistent," Nicholas said. "In any case, they're clearing out now. I know it's been a hell of a day, but you should have some peace and quiet shortly. You can put all this behind you."

Rachel hesitated, then said, "When you and Adam came in, did you see what happened to Graham?"

"Yes."

She looked at him, unsure how to phrase the question.

Nicholas smiled slightly. "There have been times in my life when I know someone helped me. There was just no other way to explain it. Maybe we all have guardian angels. Whether they exist, or are who we think they are, doesn't really matter, does it? In times of crisis, we somehow find a way to survive. It's all that's important, in the end. Survival."

"And asking no questions?"

"Sometimes, that's for the best. We don't need to know all the answers, Rachel."

Mercy looked between them curiously. "Say, what?"

Nicholas glanced down at her, still smiling. "I'll tell you later."

"You bet you will."

Rachel drew a deep breath, then smiled at him. "Did I say thank you?"

"No need. We'll have a lot to talk about, but that can wait." He paused, then added seriously, "And you can feel safe in this house again, Rachel. We have men stationed outside, and this time they're both close and very aware of who the enemy is."

"Thank you."

"You'll have your life back soon," he promised her. "Walsh is about to find himself caught in a meat grinder. He'll be too worried about his own hide to come after you again."

Rachel nodded, then looked past him as Adam came into the room.

"They're gone," he announced.

"And so are we." Nicholas took Mercy's hand and drew her to her feet. "We'll go back to the bank and copy that disk, then personally deliver a copy to the D.A. Might as well get things rolling."

"Watch your back," Adam warned. "We don't know we weren't seen at the meet with Sammy."

"We'll be fine."

Mercy said to Rachel, "I'll call you tomorrow," then went out hand in hand with Nick.

"How about that?" Adam said absently.

"They'll be good together," Rachel predicted.

"I imagine so. She seems lively enough. Gave Nick hell on the way over here once he told her—" He broke off.

Calmly, Rachel said, "Once he told her about that meeting you two had today? It went badly, didn't it? Mercy said something about a witness being dead."

Adam sat down on the couch beside her. "Nick's informant was shot. Killed. But he lived long enough to tell us about the disk."

Rachel was afraid to try counting up the lives lost because Graham Becket hadn't wanted to tarnish his sterling reputation. So she pushed that aside for the moment. "Did the police let us keep the key?" she asked.

"It's in my pocket," Adam told her. "So we can go check out that safe deposit box tomorrow, if you feel up to it."

She didn't know how she would feel tomorrow, but nodded. Another question was bothering her. "Adam, when you guys burst into the house, you had a gun."

"I still have, as a matter of fact." Adam shrugged. "You're safe here, Rachel, I promise, but I mean to be very careful nevertheless. At least until Walsh is too busy to give us a second thought."

Rachel leaned forward to put her empty cup on the coffee table, then sat back and smiled slightly as she looked at him. "Since when is an electrical engineer and designer comfortable with guns?"

Adam drew a breath. "Well, I told you about meeting Nick in Rome."

"Yes."

"After that, I sort of helped him out now and then."

"But you were a college student."

"Most recruits are in college or fresh out. I wasn't that young, Rachel. Besides, they used me mostly as a courier, and there wasn't much risk involved in those assignments. A lot of foreign travel in the summers and during my breaks, but I enjoyed that."

"What about after South America? Was Dad right? Did you put yourself in dangerous situations after that?"

"Maybe." He shook his head. "At that point in my life, maybe I needed to risk to feel free. I don't know."

"And now? You still work for them, don't you?"

Readily, he said, "Until this year, until Duncan was killed, I took an assignment every few months. It was travel outside the country, a break from my work that always seemed to reenergize me. I had a solid cover as a legitimate American businessman, and I was useful. It was still mostly courier work."

"But not always."

"No. Not always."

Slowly, she said, "I know I should be grateful, in a way. Your training and experience obviously left you with good instincts and quick reflexes, and I'd be dead if not for you."

Adam shook his head, but said, "However?"

"However, if these past weeks have taught me anything, it's that sometimes life can be dangerous enough even when we don't go out looking for trouble."

He reached over and took her hand. "I know. Rachel, I'm out of that business now, and I don't mean to go back."

She looked a little troubled. "What if it's something you need?"

"All I need," he said, "is right here with me now."

Rachel managed a smile. "What about that company out in California?"

"I'm thinking . . . we need an East Coast office. And Richmond is a great place for a business. You'll sell one-of-a-kind designs in clothes, and I'll sell electronic gadgets."

Before Rachel could respond to that, Fiona appeared in the doorway and announced belligerently, "I've got supper ready and you two need to eat. Miss Rachel, you haven't had a bite since breakfast, and I don't doubt Mr. Adam hasn't either. So I don't want to hear any arguing."

She vanished from the doorway.

Adam looked at Rachel with raised brows. "Mr. Adam?"

"The ultimate sign of approval," she explained. "You're in."

He grinned, then got to his feet and grasped her hands to pull her gently up and out of the afghan cocoon. "Fiona approves of me. How about that? I thought I was going to have to buy her diamonds or something."

"Diamonds wouldn't have worked. So I'm glad you didn't waste your money."

He chuckled, then put an arm around her as they began heading for the dining room. They had to pass through the foyer, and though no evidence remained of what had happened there, Rachel knew he felt her tense a bit.

"You'll stay with me tonight?" she said.

His arm tightened around her. "I was hoping you'd ask."

TWENTY

They retired to bed not long after supper, early enough that Cameron had not come in yet, and they decided to leave it until the morning to tell him what had occurred. Both Rachel and Adam were weary, and both fell asleep long before midnight.

"Rachel. Come, Rachel."

She was instantly awake, and even as she lifted her head from Adam's shoulder and looked down at his sleeping face, Rachel realized that what she had heard had not been spoken in the room, but inside her own mind.

Her first impulse was to close her eyes and go back to sleep. But something was nagging at her, the vague sense of something left undone, unfinished. The voice in her mind, she thought, was only her subconscious prompting her once again.

She slipped out of bed, careful not to wake Adam, and found the nightgown and robe she'd discarded—or Adam had—the night before. She put them on and paused only to run her fingers through her hair, then left the bedroom, closing the door quietly behind her.

She had no idea where it was her subconscious wanted her to go, but when she glanced toward the far end of the hall, she was not surprised to see that the door to the attic was open once more.

She went down the hall. It didn't seem strange to her to be leaving the haven of a warm bed and Adam to respond to the proddings of her subconscious—which was, perhaps, the oddest thing of all. She turned on the attic lights and went up the stairs. The storage chest was open.

This time, Rachel barely hesitated. She knelt before the chest and began lifting things out one at a time. Most were the usual mementos girls kept, like theater stubs and dried flowers and love letters. Ribbons from gifts. Tom's football jersey from college. A half-finished box of Valentine's Day candy. A book of poetry he had given her.

They cost her no more than pleasant pangs of memory, which told Rachel more clearly than anything else had that she had finally left Tom in the past, where he belonged.

She took them out of the chest and looked at them, and put them aside, and when the chest was empty, she slowly put everything back.

When she picked up the book of poetry, an envelope fell out.

At first, Rachel thought it was just one of the love letters that had gotten separated from the others, but when she opened the envelope, she found something else entirely.

"I knew it was here somewhere."

She looked quickly toward the top of the stairs to find Cameron standing there. He was fully dressed, as he always was when he left his room in the morning, and he looked very tired. Almost absently, he added, "I saw the attic door open and the light on when I came out of my room, so I came to see . . . I never thought to look up here."

"This is a check written from you to Tom," Rachel said slowly. "For ten thousand dollars. And it's dated the day of his last trip."

"Yes. I gave it to him just a few minutes before he went to you to say good-bye. Remember? I was here that weekend on one of my visits. I gave him the check, but he left straight from here, didn't have a chance to deposit the money or take it home. He never carried anything but cash on trips, and when the check never turned up and you never said anything, I figured there was a chance he'd left it here somewhere."

"This is what you've been looking for? Why?"

Cameron drew a breath. "Because I didn't want you to find it. I didn't want you to know it was . . . my fault Tom was killed."

"What?"

"He had a cargo run only as far as Mexico, Rachel. I hired him to fly from there down to South America. We'd done it before, but—"

"Cam, I don't understand. Why did you hire Tom to fly to South America?"

"I had a man down there who bought emeralds for me. Raw emeralds. But it was so damned hard to get them back here without, well, without going through customs."

Even a week ago, Rachel would have been shocked to hear that. But now she felt only a little surprise, and a small wrench of disappointment. "Tom did that? He brought gems into the country for you?"

Cameron nodded, avoiding her steady gaze. "The money didn't mean anything to him, of course. He enjoyed the thrill of it. More and more with every trip, in fact. I guess the fast cars and fast planes weren't exciting enough after a while."

Remembering how Tom had been the last time she had seen him alive, Rachel could well believe that. He had been the picture of a man looking forward to enjoyment, eager to leave her despite their approaching wedding date, promising blithely and carelessly to return. And now she had a good idea of how to explain his sometimes secretive smiles as well as her own instinctive feelings that he'd been doing something dangerous.

She wondered how many others besides her uncle had found Thomas Sheridan ready and willing to bend or break a few laws just for the thrill of it.

"I'm sorry, Rachel."

Rachel returned the check to the envelope and held it out to him, smiling a little sadly. "Don't worry about it, Cam. You aren't to blame for what happened to Tom."

He stepped forward to take the envelope, his expression lightening with a relief obvious in his voice. "I stopped buying the gems after that. And if I had it to do over again—"

"Yes. I imagine Tom might make a different choice too." But would he, given the chance? Rachel wasn't sure. And that was the saddest realization of all.

Cam retreated to the stairs, but paused at the top to look back at her. "Fiona was still up when I got in last night. She told me what happened here yesterday. About Graham. I don't know what to say, Rachel."

She managed a smile. "We'll talk about it later, Cam."

"Of course." He hesitated, then went on down the stairs.

Rachel knelt there a few moments longer, her hands folded in her lap and her thoughts years away. Then she finished putting all the mementos back in the chest and closed the lid on them.

The clock on the nightstand said only eight A.M. when she slipped back into bed beside Adam. He was still sleeping deeply, but made a satisfied little sound and gathered her close even so, and she relaxed in his arms with a wonderfully content sense of homecoming.

Nothing nagged at her now. There was no sense of something left undone, and her subconscious—or whatever the voice in her head had been—was silent now.

She decided that she would retrieve Cameron's letters from the untagged secretary in the basement, which Darby had promised to make sure he was given the opportunity to search first—and burn them. It would be less painful all around, Rachel thought. And it felt like the right decision. She made a mental note to tell Darby the plans had changed, and that was her last clear thought. Without even realizing she was going to, Rachel fell asleep.

She woke a couple of hours later, alone in the bed, and was almost immediately aware of the faint sounds of Adam in the shower. She stretched languidly for a moment, smiling, then got out of bed and found her robe, which had somehow gotten itself pushed off the bed and to the floor. Their clothes from the day before also were scattered, and she grinned to herself as she moved around the room picking up her things and his, and laying them neatly on the foot of the bed.

When she heard something metallic fall from his pants pocket, she thought it was the safe deposit box key. But something gold glinted up at her from the carpet.

Rachel laid the pants aside and bent down to see what had fallen.

A locket.

She picked it up in suddenly nerveless fingers, and slowly straightened, staring at it as it lay in her palm. It was easy to see, on one side of the locket, the initials TS. And when she turned it over . . .

The initials RG.

Rachel found her way to a chair without even realizing she was moving, and sat there, dry-mouthed, thoughts whirling.

But it couldn't be.

The locket had vanished with Tom, he'd always worn it, never took it off even to shower or sleep. He'd had it around his neck when she had last seen him, when he had come to tell her about the unexpected trip and to say good-bye to her.

How could Adam have it?

This couldn't be the same locket. The initials were the same, but that could be a coincidence, surely. Had to be.

Unless . . .

With trembling fingers, she carefully opened the locket. On one side, a St. Christopher medal.

Her picture on the other.

"Oh, my God," Rachel whispered.

"You kept me alive," Adam said.

She looked up to where he stood in the doorway of the bathroom, a towel wrapped around his lean waist and a look of terrible foreboding on his face, and what he'd said made no sense to her.

"How did you get this?" she asked.

Adam came into the room far enough to reach the chair across from hers. He did not sit down, but gripped the back of it with both hands. His knuckles showed white through taut skin, but his voice was even, calm. "Thomas Sheridan gave it to me."

Rachel shook her head. "No. No, he wouldn't have. He couldn't have."

"He did, Rachel."

"When? Where? How—how did you know him?" She drew a shaky breath. "And why in God's name didn't you tell me before now?"

He answered the last question first. "I didn't know how to tell you."

"What? Adam—"

"Rachel, I didn't know how to tell you. I still don't."

Her whirling thoughts settled, and she said slowly, "Start at the beginning. How did you know him?"

"We met . . . in South America." The words were careful, measured. "In the prison."

"I . . . don't understand. You said you were in that prison months after Tom's plane went down."

"Yes. He wasn't killed in the crash, Rachel. His plane was shot down, and he survived."

"No."

"Yes. They thought he was running guns in, weapons to help fuel what was obviously going to be a coup. The cargo line he flew for had done that sort of thing before, so it was under suspicion."

Rachel wanted to say that Tom wouldn't have done that, but she was reasonably sure he would have.

"He wasn't even carrying any cargo, according to what he told me. But they didn't know that, or chose not to believe it. They shot him down. But he didn't die."

"He was still alive months later? When you were put in that awful place?"

Adam nodded. "Barely. He'd been injured in the crash, and they—well, the guards of the old regime were no better than those who dealt with me."

Rachel bit her bottom lip, afraid to probe for details.

He hesitated, then said steadily, "I was put into a cell next to his. Given Tom's condition, his appearance, I didn't realize how alike we were myself, not then. There was a loose stone in the wall between us. Not big, barely room enough to see each other, to talk without attracting the attention of the guards. So we did.

"I think he knew he was dying. I've wondered since if he held on just long enough to do what he had to do."

Rachel swallowed hard. "What?"

"Tell someone he could trust about you. My face wasn't as—damaged—as his, so he knew I could have been his twin, even though I didn't. It must have reassured him somehow. Then again, in his condition, he probably would have talked to anybody who spoke English. He gave me the locket and made me promise that if I ever got out of that place, I'd find you and return the locket to you. Make sure you were all right. He wanted you to know that he loved you. That he was sorry he couldn't keep his promise."

Quick tears burned her eyes, and Rachel looked down at the locket in her hands. "He never could keep his promises," she murmured. She looked back at him. "You should have told me, Adam. Why didn't you tell me?"

"Why?" Adam held out a hand almost beseechingly. "Do you think I wanted to tell you that Thomas Sheridan didn't die quick and painless in a plane crash, as you'd always thought? That he lived on for months? That he suffered? That his last days were pure hell?"

Rachel flinched.

Adam nodded jerkily, his mouth twisting. "Oh, yeah, that was really something I wanted to tell you. Just like I really wanted to tell you that your name was the last word on his lips, Rachel. Of course, it was a scream, but I heard it clearly enough."

"Don't," she choked out.

He swore under his breath, hesitated, then went over to the bed and gathered his clothes, dressing quickly, his movements automatic. Maybe he did it just to give them both a minute or two to collect themselves. Or maybe such naked words demanded the frail protection of clothing, Rachel thought dimly.

Dressed now, Adam moved back toward her, sitting down in the chair across from hers. His face was very pale, his shoulders were hunched, as though to ward off a blow. His voice was suddenly very quiet and calm. "We didn't really have much time to talk. He was in bad shape then, and fading fast. Whatever he was waiting for, after we started talking, he didn't last long. A few weeks. He was delirious at the end."

Rachel tried and failed to get a terrible image out of her head. "Oh, my God," she whispered.

It was Adam's turn to flinch. But he didn't look at her. Instead, he clasped his hands before him and stared at them. Still in that calm voice, he went on. "I was mostly alone after that, in that cell day after day and night after night, except the few times the guards had a merciful impulse and let me get some fresh air outside in a walled courtyard. There wasn't much to do except count the days. And stare at that locket."

He drew a breath. "I knew your face better than I knew my own. Years before we met. When I said you kept me alive, I wasn't kidding. You did. You were my lodestar. You represented all that was beautiful in the world outside that jail. I'd stare at your picture by the hour, open and close the locket, polish the gold."

"Adam—"

He didn't let her interrupt, just kept talking in that calm voice as if too much had been stored up inside him for too long.

"I fell in love with you before I ever heard the sound of your voice. And with every month that passed, that love grew stronger." A rough laugh escaped him. "Oh, I know what you're thinking. It was just a picture of you, without personality, so how could I believe I loved you?"

"How could you?"

"It's nothing I can explain, but that locket was a real, tangible connection to you, Rachel. I felt it. Maybe because you'd given it to Tom in love, or maybe because he'd been so damned determined that his last message reach you. I don't know. All I do know is that when I went to sleep at night, you were in my dreams. And in my dreams I heard your voice, and felt your worries and sorrows, and knew you. I left that prison and spent time with you. Almost every night."

Slowly, Rachel said, "I was dreaming about Tom a lot in those first years."

Adam nodded. "But sometimes, in your dreams, he was just out of reach, wasn't he? Not easy to see. You spoke to him, and sometimes he answered you, but sometimes he was just there, watching. Because sometimes he was me, Rachel."

"People don't dream the same dreams," she protested.

"We did, the whole time I was in that prison. And we've been dreaming the same dreams the last couple of weeks. Do you want me to describe the house with all the rooms and hallways? The masked men? The way Tom and I kept wearing masks of each other? And that stone-walled room where they hung me up and beat me?"

Rachel was silent.

Adam went on, his voice calm again, almost detached. "The locket was a connection to you. I don't know how I was able to keep the guards from finding it, but I did, just as Tom had. And somehow, it made all the months, and finally all the years, bearable. I just kept telling myself that I had to survive, I had to beat the bastards and live long enough to get out, because I had to find you, just as I'd promised I would. And not only for Tom's sake, but for mine as well.

"When that dictator was finally overthrown, and the first decent regime in decades took over, they opened the cell doors and told us we could go home. Even so, since I was an American, it took several weeks for me to get home."

He paused. "Then, of course, I had to face reality. As badly as I wanted to go and see you, there was no way I could, not then. I was in fairly bad shape and looked like hell, aside from being dead broke. And then there was the story I had to tell you."

Adam looked at her finally, his eyes very dark and still. "I didn't want to. It seemed to me that it wasn't something you needed to know. Thomas Sheridan was dead. Period. How he died didn't really matter. I figured you'd gone on with your life, and there was no need to distress you by hearing such terrible things from a stranger."

He shook his head. "That's what I told myself. But I barely waited long enough to settle with the company before I started looking for you. I knew where to start, of course, and it didn't take me long to find out you'd gone to New York. That you were okay, happy, I assumed. I could hardly approach you in any sense, I knew that. Especially since I'd found a picture of Thomas Sheridan by then, and knew just how like him I appeared. But I couldn't quite let go either. So I came here to Richmond. Saw this house, found out all I could about your family."

"You didn't know Nick was Dad's partner?"

Adam hesitated. "He wasn't Duncan's partner then. Rachel, it was my suggestion that Nick approach Duncan about joining the bank."

She stared at him. "Why?"

"Several reasons. I had contacted Nick almost as soon as I got out of prison, and I knew he was looking to set up in some kind of financial business, that he wanted to settle down for a while. I knew he'd be damned good at it, and that he'd be able to lighten some of your father's burdens."

"I never thought of him as burdened," Rachel murmured.

"It wasn't more than he could handle, Rachel, I just got the feeling from what I'd found out about him that taking on a junior partner might give him more time to do some of the things he seemed interested in. And I wanted someone near your family, in a position to let me know if anything happened. If anything changed."

"I see. Then later, when you called looking for Nick, it was a ruse?"

"That wasn't quite the way it happened. I'm sorry, Rachel, for lying about that. But without explaining about the locket and why I was in Richmond, it was the only way I could think to account for how I happened to get that loan from your father. In reality, I

approached him openly, approached the bank, I mean. I told
Duncan it was because I knew Nick, and Nick was out of Richmond at the time. The rest happened just as I said. Duncan listened to me, and offered the private loan."

"He must have been shocked that you looked so much like
Tom."

"Surprised, yes. I don't think much shocked him, though."
Adam shrugged. "In any case, I went back to California and got to
work. I came out here once or twice a year, as I told you. And kept
in touch more often with Nick."

Rachel drew a breath and kept her voice steady. "Then Mom
and Dad were killed."

He nodded. "And I found the bits of that timer, realized there
was more to it than a tragic plane crash. I saw you at the funeral,
but I stayed back, out of sight. I thought the way I looked might be
one blow more than you could take just then. Nick and I had
already decided to find out what was going on. I knew it was only a
matter of time until we met. But you'd told him you were going
back to New York until the estate was nearly settled, and I wasn't
about to introduce myself to you when you were burying your
parents."

Rachel said, "After I came back to Richmond, just before my
car's brakes gave way, I saw you watching me."

"Yes. I'm sorry I frightened you."

"Why didn't you approach me then?"

Adam's gaze dropped to his hands once again. "Nick had said
he'd introduce us, and we'd already realized we could get access to
Duncan's private papers only through you, but I wasn't ready to
face you. By then I knew what everybody said, that you'd buried

your heart with Tom, that you were still mourning him even after so many years."

"Is that what you thought when we did finally meet? That I was still mourning him?"

"I knew how you'd looked at me in the moments after the crash, and in the hospital, when you thought I was Tom." His gaze returned to her face, dark and grave. "Yes, I thought you were still mourning him. And I knew that my looking so much like him would only complicate that."

"I *was* still mourning him," Rachel said. She paused, seeing his face tighten and those eyes grow even bleaker. Then she said, "It had become almost a habit, I think. Something I hadn't questioned until you showed up. Then I had to face it, because you were here and I was feeling things for you. I was so confused at first."

"I know."

She looked at the locket still lying open in her hand, and slowly closed it. "And this . . . I'm glad it helped you. I'm grateful to anything that helped you survive that place. And I'm glad you told me about Tom. But he's gone, Adam. He's been gone a long time."

"Is he? We both saw him yesterday, Rachel. We both saw what he did for you. And I was told that several times a man was spotted following us, watching. A big blond man, athletic, polished. He kept to the shadows, and walked as if he wouldn't make a sound. There's no way of knowing, of course, but it's a possibility I can't eliminate."

Steadily, she said, "Nick said maybe we all have guardian angels. And maybe they look the way we expect them to look. I don't have any other answer, Adam. All I know is that Tom is dead—and we're alive."

"You loved him."

"Yes, I loved him. I was a nineteen-year-old girl with my life ahead of me, and I thought that life was with him. But ten years changes a lot of things. It changes people. It changed me. I'm not that girl anymore, Adam. Just like you're not the young man who flew to South America to do a job. We both got through what we had to, and it changed us."

"I know."

"Do you?" Still holding the locket, Rachel left her chair and knelt beside his. She put the locket in his hand. "This belongs to you. It was yours much longer than it ever was Tom's—or mine."

He looked at the locket for a moment, then at her. "I promised—"

"You promised you'd bring it back to me. You did. And you delivered Tom's message."

He nodded, silent.

"I think we should change the initials on one side. I don't think Tom would mind."

"Rachel—"

"I love you, Adam. Don't you know that?"

He caught his breath. "I hoped."

Rachel linked her fingers together behind his neck and smiled slowly. "In case you're wondering, you are not a substitute for Tom. And I am not in any way confused about my feelings, not anymore. I love you with everything inside of me. I want to spend the rest of my life with you."

His arms went around her, tightly. "Rachel . . ."

Unnoticed by either of them, the locket slipped from his fingers.

And glinted gold in the carpet.

EPILOGUE

A year later

achel was surprised to be there.

She was at the garden gate, the one that opened onto the path that led through the woods and to the river.

The gate was open.

She passed through it and followed the path toward the woods, conscious of an odd sense within her. There was a tinge of sadness, but, more than that, there was a kind of joy.

When she entered the woods, she paused on the path, looking ahead to a very bright light.

"Hi."

Rachel turned her head to see Adam beside her. He reached out and took her hand, and the twining of their fingers made her smile.

"Hi. Why are we here?"

He nodded toward the bright light ahead. "One last visit, I think."

She looked ahead, and saw a man standing with the light behind him. She knew who he was, even though he wore no mask this time.

And this time, Tom didn't speak. But he was smiling, and his face was at peace. He spread his hands wide in a gesture taking in the both of them.

Then he turned and walked away into the light.

Rachel opened her eyes slowly, and for a moment just lay there thinking about the brief dream. She raised her head and looked down at Adam, not surprised to find him awake.

And she didn't even have to ask.

"That hasn't happened in a while," she said.

"No. I guess he thought we needed an ending." Adam smiled.

Rachel smiled and reached to touch his face, the gold of her wedding band glinting in the morning light. "Or he did."

Adam's arms went around her. "I prefer beginnings."

"So do I," Rachel said. "Oh, so do I . . ."